SURREALITY

Ben Trube

Copyright © 2015 Ben Trube

All rights reserved. This book or any portion thereof may not be reproduced or used in any manner whatsoever without the express written permission of the author except for the use of brief quotations in a book review.

For more information contact:

bentrubewriter@gmail.com

This is a work of fiction. Names, characters, businesses, places, events and incidents are either the products of the author's imagination or used in a fictitious manner. Any resemblance to actual persons, living or dead, or actual events is purely coincidental.

Printed by CreateSpace

Available on Amazon.com and other online stores

ISBN: 1519453191

ISBN-13: 978-1519453198

DEDICATION

*In memory of our beagle Simon,
who always knew when I needed a dog in my lap.*

CONTENTS

ACKNOWLEDGEMENTS	i
CHAPTER ONE	1
CHAPTER TWO	6
CHAPTER THREE	20
CHAPTER FOUR	29
CHAPTER FIVE	42
CHAPTER SIX	55
CHAPTER SEVEN	69
CHAPTER EIGHT	81
CHAPTER NINE	88
CHAPTER TEN	102
CHAPTER ELEVEN	113
CHAPTER TWELVE	132
CHAPTER THIRTEEN	145
CHAPTER FOURTEEN	158
CHAPTER FIFTEEN	170
CHAPTER SIXTEEN	183
CHAPTER SEVENTEEN	201
CHAPTER EIGHTEEN	210
CHAPTER NINETEEN	222
CHAPTER TWENTY	233
CHAPTER TWENTY-ONE	246
CHAPTER TWENTY-TWO	254
CHAPTER TWENTY-THREE	263

ACKNOWLEDGEMENTS

It's taken seven years, and nearly as many computers, to see this book to completion. I was revising an early draft on beggar's night many years back when our cat Dax decided to make her home with us, and I wrote the finishing touches with our new beagle, Murphy, curled in my lap. This book was written in friend's homes, in favorite restaurants since closed, on vacations, weddings, and on my front porch. There are countless people who helped in ways large and small to make this book a reality.

Thanks to my Mom, who kindled my love of mystery and suggested I read The Caves of Steel by Isaac Asimov, which showed me how science fiction and detective stories can be blended together.

Thanks to my Dad, for weekly hangouts, and for long discussions of plot intricacies and my writing bumps along the way.

Thanks to my editors, Brian and my wife Hannah, for their suggestions, challenges, and all the ways they whipped my words into shape. You both kept me honest and helped me to see past my blind spots.

Thanks to Jessica, our cover model, and a good friend who has always provided invaluable support.

Thanks to all my alpha and beta readers. You all provided encouragement and feedback to help me tell a better story.

And special thanks to my wife Hannah for suggesting the story be moved to Columbus, for all the nights she supported me going out to write, and for my new basement office. This book wouldn't have made it past the first draft without you.

SURREALITY

CHAPTER ONE

The island was empty. There was the idea of grass, a cool breeze, and an azure sky above, but all were clouded in mist. The island was half a mile on its longest side, a quarter on its shortest, irregular in shape, and surrounded by an endless ocean. A few hundred feet from its shore was a dense fog, though a bridge suggested a connection to some unseen land beyond.

At the center of this island a man appeared, followed by two women, a penguin, and a podium. As they took shape so did new sounds: the rush of waves and the faint breath of the wind.

These four were soon joined by hundreds. As more eyes perceived the environment, it took solid shape and new objects appeared out of thin air; a red rope separated the crowd from the podium. With hundreds of new inhabitants the island was a cacophony of voices.

The presence of new people pushed away the fog, revealing a bustling metropolis beyond the bridge that stretched for miles in every direction. Though the city was impressive, it wasn't the reason any of them were there. Invitations had been privately messaged to a number of prominent reporters and tech industry bloggers, but there were also businessmen, politicians, and even a few B-list celebrities. In addition to the penguin, there was also a small menagerie of other creatures.

The only thing they knew for certain was who had sent the invitation: Franklin D. Haines. Haines was one of the original designers of the world they now inhabited.

The penguin gestured rudely as someone pushed in front of him, and the crowd which had barely been waiting five minutes was growing restless. Reporters whipped out notepads, tape recorders, and cameras. These digital representations of analog devices in fact fed Twitter feeds, live blogs, Instagram photos, and countless other social media. Untold millions watched the event via these feeds, making #hainespremiere a trending topic in a matter of minutes.

Out of the millions watching, maybe a dozen noticed a brief flicker in one of the camera feeds, but all dismissed it as buffering. The flicker was picked up on several other cameras, gradually leading toward the podium, but by that time everyone's gaze was elsewhere.

A single cherry blossom traced a meandering path to the ground directly in front of the spectators. More blossoms fell, a few at first, but they soon grew to hundreds, then thousands. Some fell immediately to the ground, while others swirled and circled around the spectators. The sky, which had been a serene blue, was now a whirlwind of pink and white.

The petals turned faster and faster until they began to fuse together, cherry pinks turning to azure, crimson, and gold. Shimmering columns of leaves became marble, and gently weaving filaments fused into mahogany. Walls began to grow around them, impossibly high and paper thin, yet strong and unwavering.

High above, a vaulted ceiling began to take shape, while below a gentle carpet formed under their feet. As things grew less transparent, the true form of what the blossoms had built could be seen. The design was a synthesis of modern engineering and 1930s sensibilities, an art deco masterpiece stretched to dizzying heights.

In a matter of minutes, the quiet island had been subsumed by a three-story lobby. High above the crowd hung a crystal chandelier casting light in every direction. Two curving staircases led to a mezzanine above, behind which a long hallway stretched for dozens of rooms. The attention of the crowd, however, was focused on the bustling grand room in front of them, still behind the velvet rope, but clearly visible through open paneled doors. Waitresses ferried drinks to the players sitting at blackjack tables, where dealers who wore small bolo ties threw cards to busted hands.

"Welcome to the casino Arcadia, the jewel of Surreality," a voice boomed from above.

Franklin Haines was tall. He wore a steel-gray Armani suit, pressed white shirt, and striking brick-red tie. His hair showed no signs of gray, his eyes betrayed no signs of age, and his face wore a smile more perfect than a Norman Rockwell painting.

"This is the beginning of a new era in Surreality. Just a few short years ago, our user base was a few dozen college students at an Ohio State dorm. Now we're an international center for commerce, research, and entertainment. Anything our users can dream, we can build.

"This casino is just one example of that ingenuity. We have unique entertainment you can't find anywhere else. You can play high-stakes poker against the greatest sharks of the game, or try your hand at the roulette wheel opposite the gangsters who built Vegas. This isn't just a casino; it's any casino you want it to be."

Haines's characteristic theatrics were on full display. As if on cue, a dozen dancers appeared on the stairs on either side of Haines, wearing enough feathers between them to cover a chicken. The women sashayed down into the eager crowd as Haines continued.

"And that's only the beginning. Starting today, the tools that made Arcadia a reality will be available for the public to use, so they can create their own businesses. Those of you who've been part of making Surreality what it is today know it's more than just a game, it's a second chance at life!"

The crowd, those who weren't too preoccupied with the dancers, began applauding. Haines smiled, drinking it all in as he had many times before in his life, always with the same relish. Imperceptibly, his smile began to tighten. As Haines's lips pressed tighter and tighter together, his face began to turn a bright shade of red.

The smile broke and his mouth opened wide violently, gasping for air but finding none. His nostrils flared, his ears reddened and began to buzz, and his legs collapsed under him. Haines grasped out with one desperate arm against the banister and another to his throat. Uselessly he tore at his tie and shirt.

With a loud crack, the wood of the banister snapped, and Franklin Haines fell forward into the crowd, who moments ago had been applauding. In fact, the whole incident happened in the space of seconds, so that when Haines's head hit the crimson carpet, his neck snapped instantaneously. A few stray claps still echoed in the otherwise quiet hall. Haines's face, his neck twisted almost 180 degrees, registered bewilderment more than terror.

The Net paused. In another few seconds, instant opinions and commentaries would form, videos would circulate, and Haines's speech would be remixed and auto-tuned. But in those seconds, the crowd stopped, as did the millions watching them, unsure whether this was another stunt or something else.

That's when the first crack appeared. It stretched from Haines's body to the impossibly high ceiling, glowing white-hot with blinding fury. The crack branched and spread, splitting the bonds the cherry blossoms had formed minutes earlier. The ceiling looked like shattered glass, and rained plaster and dust on the panicking crowd. The walls split apart into thick rocks which smashed pillars, collapsed the staircases, and pinned those in the crowd too slow to dodge them.

People ran for the doors amid the terrible cracking sound, which drowned out their screams as it grew louder and louder. The penguin flailed about, pushing through the crowd and beating his wings to try to speed up those in front of him. Some of the more levelheaded individuals simply logged out, but most ran with little regard for those around them.

The chandelier swung violently as more of the ceiling fell, eventually tearing out its mounts, landing in the middle of the teeming mass of people. Broken glass shot out in a wave, fire danced and began to catch, and dozens were quickly trapped under the chandelier's bulk. Most who were trapped vanished a few seconds later, but others lay helpless, watching the ensuing chaos from their involuntary but unique vantage point.

The ones who made it outside didn't linger long. Some turned as a final rumble marked the collapse of the remaining supports. Arcadia imploded, the debris compacting downward with only a faint wall of dust reaching out from the wreckage.

When the last pillar fell, no one was around to see it. The world had left to catalog their experiences in blogs, tweets, and memes. The roar of the waves and the soft breeze of the air reasserted themselves, and the sky shone down bluer than before.

Somewhere in a darkened room, Franklin Haines threw his keyboard angrily across his desk.

•

CHAPTER TWO

Detective Daniel Keenan exhaled as the revolver fell out of his limp hands. The barrel struck the wet pavement, giving off a small hiss of steam from the heat of six bullets traveling in rapid succession through the chamber. The gun hit the ground before the man those bullets had struck. The metallic clanging was followed by a dull thud.

Sinclair was dead; there was no doubt about it. His unseeing eyes never broke contact with Keenan as lifeless legs failed him. He was smiling. Seconds before, he'd been laughing. It was the laugh of jackal, of a wild animal, and he'd died like one.

Blood mixed with rain as Keenan stood there staring at that wild grin. A glint of metal betrayed the knife that had been his excuse to fire. He hadn't seen it. He hadn't needed to.

Keenan labored to breathe, fighting back waves of nausea. He turned out into the darkened empty street. His chest felt heavy, like someone was standing on his rib cage.

The rain licked his cheek, and then his nose.

• • •

Keenan groaned as his eyes opened to find his English bulldog, Garfunkel, licking his face and standing on his bladder.

"All right, I'm up! Get off me!" Keenan grumbled as he rolled onto his side. Garfunkel leaped off the couch where Keenan had fallen asleep and stood expectantly on the floor of the apartment.

Keenan looked groggily at the clock. Eleven a.m. "I already fed you this morning."

Though Garfunkel was always willing to accept whatever Keenan wanted to offer him, food was not his purpose in rousing his master. Three sharp knocks and the cheery voice of Tom Daily soon made the dog's purpose clear.

"Just a minute!" Keenan looked through the detritus that covered the coffee table and parts of the floor and decided tidying up would probably be futile. His clothes were in a similar state of dishevelment, which Keenan corrected by running his hands over the front of his shirt as he stumbled to the door.

The couch was in the middle of the one long room that was most of the first floor of Keenan's apartment. Living area, dining room, and kitchen flowed in an open plan, with no clear border for each. Tucked in a corner of the kitchen was the desk that was Keenan's home office. He'd been meaning to buy a laptop, if for no other reason than to be able to work in front of the TV, but for the moment the desk was dominated by a bulky white machine.

The apartment had vinyl wood flooring. To the left of the couch were the stairs that led up to Keenan's small deck, though in the shortening days of fall he had not gotten much use out of it except to clear away piles of leaves. Next to the staircase was a brick wall that the previous owner had evidently felt was the room's best feature, illuminating it like a work of art with recessed lighting that did little more than heat up Keenan's futon.

Keenan opened the door slowly.

"Rise and shine, Dan," Tom Daily said, thrusting a plastic bag into Keenan's hand. He walked into the living room, stepping around the debris and plopping down in a corner of the couch that moments ago had been supporting Keenan's head. As if on springs, Garfunkel leapt beside him, shoving his head under

Tom's hand. Daily began scratching behind Garfunkel's ears automatically. Garfunkel, in obvious pleasure, leaned with his full weight into Daily's lap before he could even take off his coat. Tom wasn't getting up for a while.

"We're awfully chipper this morning," Keenan said, shutting the door and shooting the dog an amused look. If he had been a better owner, he might have tried to make the dog get down, but Daily wasn't normal company. Tom knew the drill, and actually enjoyed the attention. His wife was not a dog person.

"All right, we'll call it morning if you insist, Dan. Haven't you had a cup of coffee yet?"

"Ran out a few days ago, and haven't been able to get to the store." This statement was backed up by the empty takeout containers on the kitchen counter. "Only decent place to get a cup of coffee in this area is the diner, and too many of the guys go there before work."

Daily nodded, neither man wanting to get into any of that right now.

"Hope you don't mind corned beef for breakfast," Daily said, changing the subject.

That explained the smells emanating from the bag Keenan still absently held in his hand. Opening it up, he saw two rolls of paper the size of hoagies, with cups of fries nestled on either side.

"What's this?"

"Another signpost on your search for the perfect Reuben." Keenan unwrapped the paper and discovered the contents did indeed contain all the ingredients of a Reuben, though one that had been fried on the outside.

"It's an Irish egg roll, an appetizer if you'd believe it. That's Thousand Island horseradish next to it."

"Where'd you get it?"

"The 'Dube," Daily answered, temporarily dislodging Garfunkel as he leaned forward to accept the roll Keenan was holding out to him.

The Blue Danube, a dive just a short walk north of OSU campus, had an eclectic cuisine, with everything from quesadillas to liver and onions, to their French menu, consisting of Dom Pérignon served with two grilled cheese sandwiches. On the ceiling was an ever-changing array of hand-painted tiles from the various students and locals who frequented the establishment.

Keenan slumped onto the other side of the couch. He dipped one-half of the thick sandwich into the cup of sauce and took a bite.

"Not bad. The horseradish is a nice touch," Keenan said, taking another big bite, "almost as good as coffee. No, you can't have any."

This last was to the dog, who had already accepted a donation of several chunks of corned beef from Daily, and was hoping for the same from his master.

"So, what's in the folder?" Keenan said, not taking his eyes off the sandwich.

The folder to which he was referring had been under Daily's non-sandwich-bearing arm, and was thick with paper.

"Dessert," Daily said, wiping his hands and casually taking a fry. "It's your next case."

Keenan continued eating without looking at Daily. "I'm on leave, Tom, remember?"

"Short-term."

"Yeah, until they fire me," Keenan said, crumpling his paper.

"They" was the Columbus Metro Police Department, which had mandated Keenan's leave a few months ago. The chief had made it sound like a recommendation, not an order, but Keenan knew better.

"The deputy chief asked for you specifically."

Keenan glanced briefly at the folder, then grunted, "A folder that thick has been across a dozen desks. I was hardly his first choice."

"Don't you even want to hear about it?" Daily asked. "A man was strangled in front of hundreds of witnesses and nobody saw his assailant."

Keenan munched on a fry, pretending not to be interested. "Did the ME find anything unusual?"

"He wasn't able to make a thorough examination of the body."

"Were all the coroners on vacation or something? Do you have any photos?"

Daily tapped the top of the folder. "In the file."

Keenan groaned and pulled the folder onto his lap. Opening to the first page, he saw the sprawled body of a man, his neck tilted at an unnatural angle, and lots of debris.

"Was this guy in an earthquake? What is all this stuff?"

"Building fell on him."

"I must have missed the news. This seems like the kind of—" Keenan examined the photograph again. Except it wasn't a photograph, but a screenshot.

"It's a nice try, Tom, but I'm not helping you beat your latest game. I don't know how you find the time for that stuff anyway."

Daily ignored Keenan's rebuff and continued, "Do you know who that man is?"

"I'm not sure who he is, or even who he looks like."

"That's Franklin Haines, one of the original co-founders of Surreality."

"What's Surreality?"

"Well . . . it is a game."

"This is sounding better and better, Tom."

"It's more than just a game; it's another world being played out online. You can buy a house, start a business, marry, have children, die, and be reborn, all in the space of a few afternoons."

Keenan nodded. "I think I played that one. Isn't it the one where the characters can only talk in grunts and mumbles?"

Daily shook his head. "This isn't just a game you play casually on your computer. It's an online community, with real money involved. A lot of it."

"What's this got to do with Haines?"

"Well, as I said, Haines was strangled in front of a crowd of people at the premiere of something called the casino Arcadia."

"In the game," Keenan said flatly.

Daily sighed. "Yes. But there's more to it. When his character 'died,' his Surreality account was erased, and all the funds associated with it are missing."

"Missing? Don't they have a backup or something?"

"Apparently whoever did the stealing transferred the money before erasing the account. There's no trace of it, or the transactions, on Surreality's servers. The money's just gone."

"How much money?"

"Eighty million dollars."

"Holy . . ." Keenan swore. "How can there be that much money in a silly computer game?"

"Most of it was investments, money tied up in this Arcadia venture. That's the debris you're seeing in the picture. The killer blew up the building too. Haines says Arcadia was poised to make something like seventy million in the first year."

"So Haines is alive and unharmed."

"Yeah, and steaming mad, especially since the investigation's been going nowhere. It'll take him weeks to get Arcadia up and running again, and he's already missed his shot with the press."

"Isn't he worried this might be a death threat?"

"If he is, he hasn't said it to me," Daily shrugged.

Keenan leaned back against the couch and exhaled. "Why do you need me for this, Tom? I don't know the first thing about games, and not much more about computers. Surely one of the interns stands a better chance at tracking this thief than I do."

Daily shook his head. "The tech guys had their shot and came up empty. Whoever did this was 'master class.' Their words. But I haven't met a criminal, hacker or otherwise, who can hide forever from good investigative skills."

"I didn't know you held my investigative skills in such high esteem."

"You?" Daily laughed. "I was talking about me. But I'm busy right now so I guess you'll have to do."

"What about my leave?"

"Over, probationally anyway. Deputy chief wants you to have a talk with the psychiatrist a few times over this whole Sinclair thing, so until then no side arm, at least out in the real world."

Keenan nodded. He hadn't picked up a gun in two months, and wasn't exactly looking to do so anytime soon.

Daily smiled and patted him on the back. "Head on down to the station and the guys in the lab'll get you set up with what you need: login credentials, Surreality installer, and all that. Oh, and one other thing . . ."

Daily reached into his coat and pulled out a couple of thin plastic packages and another small plastic box.

"I thought your computer could use a bit of a tune-up. Want me to install them?" Daily asked.

Keenan took the RAM and new graphics card and set them on top of the computer tower. "I've always wondered what it looked like in there. I could use the excuse to look."

• • •

Keenan slipped into the station as quietly as possible, using the back stairwell to avoid the bullpen. Still, as he opened the door to the third floor, he heard a familiar voice to his right.

"About time you came back."

Sonya Caliente stood up from behind her desk, closing the space between them and wrapping Keenan in a warm hug. After a few seconds she let him go and smoothed the front of her uniform.

"I wouldn't get used to it," Keenan said. "I'm not long for this world around here."

"The chief asked you to come back, didn't he?"

"Only because real detectives like you and Daily have better things to do than play video games all day."

"From what I hear they want you on this case because no one else can solve it."

"Daily tell you to say that?" Keenan asked.

Caliente shook her head. "Don't need him to."

"You're being unusually nice to me," Keenan observed.

Caliente shrugged. "So? Would you rather I bust your chops for not talking to your partner for the last two months?" Despite being six inches shorter than Keenan, this was not an idle threat.

"You could have called," Keenan said.

"I tried to, a couple of times. You never answered."

Daily, Caliente, and Keenan had all been in the same class at the academy, their career paths running mostly parallel the last eight years. Caliente had been Keenan's partner for a little over a year, and friend for a lot longer. She'd been pulled onto another case when Sinclair crossed Keenan's desk, and he'd been gone before she came back.

"Sorry. I just didn't feel like talking to anybody for a while."

Caliente put a hand on his shoulder. "That's all right, Dan."

Her green eyes met his for a few seconds, then she patted him on the arm. "It's good to have you back."

"Thanks, it feels good to be back."

Actually it didn't feel like anything of the kind. Keenan tended to feel edgy and out of place if he was out of the office for a week, and this had been two full months. This feeling was only reinforced when he walked into the lab and didn't recognize two of the people leaning over computers.

Whoever they were, they didn't seem very happy to be handing the case over to Keenan. He tried to tell himself it was just professional pride. Most lab junkies didn't like to admit when they'd been licked and tended to pour coffee and sleepless nights into a problem until it was fixed. Actually, that was the way Keenan acted most of the time too.

Their frustration was largely vented in the form of repeating the case at length to Keenan, including a lot of technical details he did not understand, though their final meaning was clear. They'd tried a bunch of elite hacker stuff to catch this guy, and had come up empty. The only thing of real use they provided was an installer CD for Surreality. They had originally tried to give it to him on a USB flash drive, but he'd made them burn the disc.

"So I can listen to it on the way home," he'd joked. In reality he wasn't sure where the USB ports even were on his computer.

. . .

On the way back home, Keenan stopped in the store and picked up vitally needed coffee and wet dog food for Garfunkel. He used to buy the dry dog food mix, but it looked a bit too much like his cereal, and it was cheaper to improve the dog's dinner. Keenan had discovered pretty early on that he would need to let Garfunkel out more than twice a day. He knew cats were pretty much born litter trained, but he figured he could do the same thing for a dog. It hadn't been easy, but now when Garfunkel greeted him at the door, Keenan knew it was because he was happy to see him, and not eager to relieve his bladder.

In fact, the dog had run right up to the door even before Keenan could get it open. Keenan kicked the door gently to get the dog's attention. "Easy boy, got to let me get the door open first."

Garfunkel's face was as happy and droopy as Keenan's was tired. He leaned down to scratch the dog behind the ear before pushing his way toward the kitchen. He scooped the liver-flavored mush into Garfunkel's bowl and left it beside the counter, then walked over to turn on his ancient computer.

Installing Surreality gave Keenan time to slip into his fleece bathrobe and brew eight cups of coffee, four of which went into the big green thermos beside his desk. As Keenan sipped his coffee, a flurry of small windows appeared and disappeared seemingly at random. He briefly wondered if the techs had installed some kind of virus to mess with him, but brushed it off.

Keenan drained half the thermos before the installer quieted and presented him with a login screen. He typed in the credentials the techs had given him and was prompted to choose an alias. He typed in his full name, but paused before hitting Next. No reason he couldn't have a little fun with this. After considering a number of possible combinations, he finally settled on Coleman Hayes, in part because the last name Hayes just seemed like a given for an OSU football fan.

Confidently hitting Enter, Keenan expected to find himself inside the world of Surreality. Instead, he was presented with another options screen to customize his character. He took a moment to appreciate the fact he hadn't had to make this many decisions when starting his real life. He looked the way his parents looked, and they'd chosen the name.

One thing he definitely knew for sure, he wasn't a hipster, which was the default option the screen presented him with. He scrolled through a couple of the ready-made body types, but finally started adjusting all the dials himself. He briefly considered modeling himself on Coach Hayes, but decided it wouldn't project quite the right image. His height he kept close to his own, 6'2", with a little less weight and a slightly fuller hairline. A better jaw too. To give his avatar a little character, he adjusted the nose until it looked it had been broken at least once.

The clothes came next. The free options didn't give him a whole lot of variety, but fortunately, the department had given him a little money to spend. The trench coat and fedora were a must, as were shiny black shoes, a charcoal suit, and a white shirt. He finished it off with a thin black tie he wouldn't have been able to pull off in real life. He turned his character, and smiled with satisfaction as the bottom of the coat swayed a little to the side before falling back into place.

A question popped up over his character's head as he closed the creation windows. "Where would you like to go?" He typed in the code Tom had given him for Keenan's Surreality office. The screen blurred, and a moment later he was standing in a small dark room. The floors were wood and creaked as his avatar swayed back and forth. A dusty green banker's lamp cast the only light in the room, though he could still make out the only other object on the desk, an exact replica of his gun.

"There are bullets in the drawer on the right," a voice called from offscreen. Startled, Keenan whirled around, and misjudged how far he'd have to move to get the speaker in the frame. He slowly panned back as she snapped on the light on her own desk. Sitting on the desk was a woman in her mid-twenties. Her blond hair was done up in a style reminiscent of the 1930s. Her eyes twinkled mischievously as she smiled at him.

"And you might be?" Keenan asked, typing his question and watching his avatar repeat it after he'd finished.

"Synthia. I'm your assistant. Tom asked for me and this place special. It was hell for the designers having to do a job this quickly, especially that gun." She put out a hand, and Keenan tried to shake it but missed, shaking the air instead.

"Not used to this, are you?"

"No, not really. I've never been much of a gamer."

"I can tell. You might want to pick up a headset or something for the next time you login. If you run into any action you might want your hands free."

Keenan was glad Synthia couldn't see the sheepish look he was probably wearing. "Thanks, I'll do that. Do you mind if I ask you a question?"

"Shoot."

"Are you real?"

"Of course I'm real. I'm as real as everything you see here," she laughed. "I'm not real in the sense you mean, as in a human controlling a puppet in here, but I am real. My full name is Synthetic Intelligence Algorithm, or Synthia for short. Pleased to meet you." She gave a little mock salute.

"So . . . you're a program?"

"Not my preferred term but essentially accurate, though that's a little like reducing your whole existence down to how you think. I have a body and interact with my environment just like you do. Yes, my thought patterns are determined by complex mathematical algorithms, but yours might be too. After all, you are a detective. Your thought process has to be ordered or you'd never solve a case, right?"

Keenan mulled this over. "I suppose that's true," he said. "So why did Tom ask for you?"

"He said you needed someone familiar with Surreality to be your guide to some of the stranger parts of life here. That, and something about you always needing a secretary."

"Tom told you that?"

"No dear, he talked to my designers. They incorporated all background data on the case and your personal history into my memory. If you wanna go over the case with me anyway, I'd be happy to hear it straight from you. I don't know if that's part of the whole detective process."

"That's fine, thanks," Keenan groaned, wishing he knew how to make his character do that. He wasn't sure about the whole idea of a computer partner, but he did need a guide.

"All right, toots, you're hired. The pay's lousy and the hours are long, but since you're a prog . . . algorithm, I guess you won't mind." He looked back to the gun. "What's with the gun, anyway? Decoration?"

"Standard issue," Synthia quipped. "All video games come with guns now."

She's fun, Keenan thought.

"Wouldn't surprise me, but what's it for?"

"Same as what a real gun's for, except this one ends virtual lives instead of real ones. The Surreality Committee gave you special permissions, for the duration of this case, to erase characters. It doesn't have to be a clean hit either. Just a graze from one of these bullets will send your thief back to the drawing board."

"That's not going to do me much good if I don't know who that person is in the real world," Keenan replied.

"Your man's not the only dangerous element here, particularly where you'll be going. Sometimes it just helps to get someone off your tail. And most people take their avatars almost as seriously as their lives. They might be willing to talk to you rather than risk losing hundreds of hours of work."

During this explanation, Keenan had discovered to his dismay that he had already emptied the thermos. Fortunately, reinforcements were close at hand. Though his speakers were on as loud as possible, he couldn't quite make out the last thing Synthia said.

"I'm sorry, what was that last bit again?"

Synthia shook her head. "Y'know, it's kinda rude to walk out in the middle of a conversation. You wouldn't do that to a pretty lady in the real world, would you?"

"For a program, you're touchy," Keenan smiled.

"Synthetic Intelligence Algorithm," Synthia said slowly.

"My mistake," Keenan said. He picked the gun up and put it in his jacket. "Guess I better learn how to use this thing."

"Yeah, before I do," Synthia said with an inscrutable expression.

CHAPTER THREE

All Keenan had to do was drag and drop to load the six-shot imaginary gun in his hand. "So where's the firing range?"

Synthia had begun filing her nails, an activity that seemed largely without purpose, but Keenan decided it was best not to comment. Without even looking up, Synthia answered, "Through that door on the left."

"Thanks," Keenan said.

As he put the box of ammunition in his other coat pocket, Synthia said, "The gun will automatically reload while you're in the simulator. Oh, and don't let them push you around."

Keenan looked at the screen, puzzled, which didn't do any good since his character did not change expression. He shrugged and opened the door. The scenery shifted, and he was standing on an open grassy plateau. It looked like something on the coast of Ireland, Keenan's ancestral home.

There was a brief flash, and when Keenan turned around, the door had disappeared.

"Synthia?" he called, but there was no answer.

Repeated attempts were no more successful. He wasn't sure if this was because Synthia couldn't hear him, or whether she just didn't feel like responding. He walked toward the edge of the plateau, which ended in a sheer drop of about sixty feet. Looking down he could see the ocean: foamy white waves crashing against the cliff face. He turned to look back up and discovered his movements had slowed. He called out again, but there was still no answer. As he stumbled back toward where the door had been, four large balloons appeared in his path.

The balloons were perfectly spherical with no attached strings, and were all different colors. Because of the lag, the balloons seemed to skip from one place to another rather than floating smoothly. Keenan guessed these were the targets and drew his gun. He shot at one and it burst with a loud pop, sending shards of rubber in his direction. The pieces of broken balloon hit him like bricks and knocked his character uncomfortably close to the edge of the cliff. He inched forward slowly. His movements were choppy as the computer struggled to keep up. Keenan fired at the second target, but the shot bounced off, and Keenan had to dodge the balloon as it whizzed by.

The balloon flew by him past the edge of the cliff, but instead of slowly floating down, it hovered. Despite the balloon's bulk, it was able to hover at the same altitude no matter how far away it was from the ground. He turned, about to run in the other direction, only to discover two more balloons coming at him from behind. He fired two rounds at the balloon on the right. His first shot glanced off the surface and spun harmlessly over the edge of the cliff. But the second shot hit dead center. Again the shards hit Keenan but also pushed the other balloon to the side. It was then that Keenan realized why the balloon had burst. Apparently in this game he only got credit for bulls-eyes.

Keenan took aim at the second balloon, but as he was about to fire, his world pitched downward and he was pushed to the ground. The screen went black. At first Keenan thought his computer had crashed, but when he looked closer, he was able to discern individual blades of grass. It was then that he realized the balloon was crushing him. He tried desperately for a few seconds to remember some of the other controls for movement when he remembered he could kick his legs. He thrust backward, which lifted the balloon off of his back.

Unfortunately for Keenan, his foot stuck in the balloon and he was soon flying high above the ground. The other balloon darted toward him and repeatedly tried to smash him against the one that was carrying him. Keenan again took aim and fired. Finding his mark, he shattered the balloon right before it hit. He kicked at the one that was holding him hostage, and he began to fall. As Keenan broke free, he fired at the center of the balloon. The bullet bounced harmlessly off the red rubber right before the screen went black.

• • •

Five seconds later he was back in his office. Synthia, who was doing her nails, looked up at him.

"Back already? Guess you lost, huh?"

"No. I actually took out three of them," Keenan said proudly.

Synthia laughed, "Not bad for a rookie, ace. Only trouble is the game has fifty levels. Listen," she continued, "Franklin Haines wants to meet with you at the scene of the crime as soon as you can get over there."

"I thought the dead didn't talk."

"This one does, and he's got plenty to say. Your lab techs didn't do much to impress him."

Keenan shrugged. "So what do I do, anyway, call a taxi?"

"Just walk out the front door. Type 'Arcadia' into the destination field, and the portal will take you there."

"That sounds simple enough." Keenan moved toward the door.

"One more thing," Synthia said as she began digging through her purse. A moment later she pulled out a pink cell phone with a hippie flower painted on the back. "This will allow you to keep in touch with me no matter where you are. My number is the first one programmed."

Keenan raised an eyebrow and accepted the phone reluctantly. He stuffed it deep into his trench coat before stepping through the door.

Outside was a blue void, a color Keenan found very discouraging. After a few seconds, the sides of the screen dissolved into wisps of gas, and Keenan could see that he was actually moving through a tunnel. Zooming out, he saw the tunnel he was moving through was one of thousands connected together in a rough lattice. The web of tunnels converged at various points into central nodes, which in turn split back out into new lattices. The nodes erupted with color like a plasma storm, with bursts of light moving from one tunnel to another at lightning speed.

As Keenan branched into one of the larger tunnels, he could see the flashes moving all around him. Some raced past him while others glided lazily through the tunnel. As he moved by one of the slower flashes of light, he could see that it was another avatar, a woman with long wavy brown hair wearing a flowing green dress. He tried to say hello, but she didn't seem to hear him as she flew past into a tunnel on the right.

The hippie phone rang, and Keenan dug it out of his inventory to find Synthia calling him. "Just thought you'd want to know what's going on. You're traveling through Surreality's transit system. The tunnels and nodes are a representation of the entire network. The designers thought it would be more interesting than a plain loading screen. The speed of the people you see is determined by their Internet connections and the performance of their computers."

"Why didn't that woman hear me?"

"You can't talk to anyone in the transit system unless you're going to the same place. Meet someone you liked already?"

Keenan ignored her. "I had no idea Surreality was this big. How much traffic is there?"

"Well, probably less than the designers would like you to think. Most people just create a character, try it once, and then forget about it. Still, there are at least a hundred thousand or so people in the network at any one time."

Keenan floated toward one of the central nodes. Inside he saw that some of the tunnels were red, contrasting the blue of the rest of the network. "What are those red tunnels?"

"Unsupported worlds," Synthia said. "Surreality's dark net, or at least the part of it the network is aware of."

"What's a dark net?" Keenan asked.

"It's a hidden area, like a club with a secret password. Some of the more careless players jump to these red zones from an area the Surreality servers can track, and their paths get mapped to one of these red tunnels. Still, there are probably tens of thousands of zones we don't know about."

"Why does the Surreality Committee allow hidden areas in the first place?"

"It's built into the original source code. Surreality used to be an open-source collaborative project before Haines made the software proprietary and switched to in-house developers. Cutting off those worlds now would mean destroying thousands of user-generated areas. The best the committee can do is try to track them down."

"Have you ever been to one of these red zones?"

"I'd void my EULA," Synthia replied jokingly. "By the way, if your investigation takes you that way, the committee can't guarantee your safety. Do you have good virus protection?"

Sure, an old computer, Keenan thought. Just then there was a flash as he entered the node and slipped through another portal. A moment later he was standing on a grassy island covered in rubble. The island looked a lot like the firing range, though thankfully without the cliffs. Instead there were long beaches and a wide grassy plain. He could make out a large bridge on the other side of the shore, connecting to a busy metropolis. The island seemed to be uninhabited, save for a small contingent of workers who were clearing away large chunks of debris a few hundred yards off. They were all dressed in blue jeans and white T-shirts, with yellow hard hats. All looked exactly alike and moved as a single force. Keenan watched as they cleared the rocks and wondered what they were really doing.

As he approached, one of the workers broke from the group and began walking toward Keenan. As he did, another identical worker flashed into existence and picked up the previous man's tools. The man looked Keenan up and down and frowned. "Just who are you supposed to be?"

"Detective Daniel Keenan, CMPD." Keenan flashed his digital badge. "Where's Mr. Haines, your boss?"

The man frowned again. Keenan really wished he could master that. "I'm Franklin Haines. This appearance is merely temporary until I'm able to restore my personal avatar."

"No backup?" Keenan asked.

Haines shook his head. "Wiped out with the rest of my assets. I've had my boys comb the servers, but every detail has been wiped clean. But you should already know all of this."

Keenan nodded. "It's in the report, but I'd like to ask some questions of my own if you don't mind."

"Of course, Detective, but keep it brief. We're behind schedule as it is, and I'll be losing half the evening with the benefit tomorrow."

"I'll do my best. What exactly are you doing here? I would've thought you'd be able to restore the casino from a backup. Or was that erased too?"

Haines shook his head again. "As you can see, this island is only a small part of a larger area, hosted across dozens of servers by as many companies. The destruction of Arcadia was just an artistic touch. This debris is the real trouble. The code for the rocks has been spliced into our code, and the code of just about everyone else in the city. But they all render here on the island, preventing us from rebuilding Arcadia until we can clear it away. It's taking our programmers time to isolate each stone and coordinate with the appropriate company to delete it. Some of them wouldn't mind if the Arcadia project was delayed indefinitely, and we've had to find other means of clearing the rubble."

"Like hacking into their servers?"

Haines's eyes narrowed. Even with this generic avatar he had better control of its expressions than Keenan. "I don't like your tone, Mr. Keenan. I'd remind you that this code is malicious, and was planted by someone who had no scruples about breaking into all of those companies."

"Sorry, that's none of my business." Keenan tried another tack. "Would any of these competitors be interested in seeing you dead?"

"Yes, but they would have killed me in real life."

Keenan chuckled. So Haines did have a sense of humor. "What about strangling your avatar and sending you on a swan dive off the top balcony?"

"Again, a very theatrical touch, but one designed to ruin my premiere, nothing more."

Keenan wasn't sure if he'd be so sanguine about watching an avatar of himself die, particularly while he was in it. Haines, on the other hand, didn't even seem to see it in those terms.

"All right, so who'd want to ruin your premiere?"

"There are a number who come to mind, though few who would have been able to capitalize on their desire. The premiere was by invitation only, with announcements going out a couple of days in advance."

"Anyone spring to mind?" Keenan probed.

"Well . . . there's my ex-partner, Robert Glassner."

"Glassner . . . didn't the two of you create Surreality together?"

"That's right, but Robert never saw the full potential of this place. He was always more of a dreamer than a businessman."

"Why would he want to attack you?"

"Robert thinks I edged him out of the company, steered Surreality toward profit rather than advancement of human potential."

"And did you?"

"It was the board's decision. I merely accepted the mantle they thrust upon me."

"Right," Keenan said coolly. "What does Glassner do now?"

"He's trying to build a second Library of Alexandria here in Surreality, a mecca of science, art, and philosophy."

"It doesn't sound like he'd be much competition."

"For Glassner, it's not about money, it's about his vision of Surreality. For him it's just another place to discuss ideas, to think about life. But it's so much more than that. We're living another life here, Mr. Keenan, grander than any we could hope for in the real world. Anything you can dream of, you can do, without consequences. You can recreate yourself. What's wrong with a little fantasy?"

Keenan's fantasies tended toward the mundane: an evening with his dog, perhaps both enjoying a good sandwich. He didn't really see how Surreality would make any of that better, but nodded in agreement anyway.

"Just one more thing before you go, Mr. Haines. You wouldn't have a backup of the scene of the crime before you started dismantling it?"

"I'm sorry, Detective, but as I told your lab techs, it isn't practical to keep a backup of everything happening in Surreality at all times. You've got a list of IP addresses who were at the premiere, but that's really all we can give you."

"I understand, Mr. Haines. It just doesn't feel right investigating a murder without a chance to see the body. Good day." With that, Keenan logged out, feeling a slight jolt as he realigned to the real world.

Garfunkel had gone to sleep by his feet, and Keenan was amazed to find it was pitch black outside. The dog's breath was hot and his snoring was loud. Keenan had been so absorbed in the world of Surreality that he hadn't noticed anything around him. He cast a quick look at the clock and was dismayed to find it was 1:30 in the morning.

Haines is quite the taskmaster, he thought idly as he slowly scooted back so as not to wake up the dog. Keenan doubted he was going to get many chances for rest himself over the next few days. He padded softly to the couch, falling asleep almost as soon as his head hit the leather cushion.

CHAPTER FOUR

Sleep did little to revive Keenan. He had long ago learned that the weight he now felt in his chest was not an impending heart attack, but just Garfunkel standing on him. The dog was full of energy and had no sympathy for Keenan as he groggily rolled over.

His head was still swirling from his latest dream. He'd been standing in the middle of the firing range, surrounded on all sides by the floating balloons. Only now they had teeth and were opening and closing their mouths like Pac-Man. He'd awoken right before one of them swallowed him whole, and he shivered briefly at the thought. Keenan's irrational fear was being eaten by animals, which was one of the reasons he made sure Garfunkel was well fed. Still, it was a better dream than the other one he'd been having.

Sitting up, he pulled jeans over his boxers and threw on an undershirt. He picked up Garfunkel's leash and harness from the table by the couch and proceeded to the arduous task of getting the dog to wear them. After a few minutes, Keenan swore as he realized he'd been trying to put the harness on backward. Garfunkel was no help, plopping the front of his body down onto the floor so that Keenan had to physically lift him up and thrust his legs through the holes.

"Damn it," Keenan swore again as he looked at the empty coffee maker, having forgotten to program the machine the night before. He briefly debated making a pot, but Garfunkel was already tugging him toward the door and barking eagerly.

The morning was cool and crisp. Across the street the Bodega was quiet, though by lunchtime it would be bustling with outdoor diners eating twelve-dollar sandwiches. The gastropub's happy hour and proximity to Short North Tattoo had always been a source of amusement to Keenan, except when he had to break up fights.

There were a few other people walking dogs on the street, though most weren't dogs by Keenan's standards. He might have been tempted to let Garfunkel chase them, but his dog was too busy tracking the smells of the previous night's revelry. Most weekdays weren't too bad, but from Thursday until Sunday there were pockets of thick noxious air, particularly near alleys and the doorways of cheap bars.

The conditions of the sidewalks varied from block to block. Some areas were being remodeled for upscale apartment housing, but go up or down a few blocks and the buildings were much older. The sidewalk tended to be cracked or uneven in these sections and Keenan had to look down at his feet or Garfunkel would trip him.

Every couple of blocks, black metal arches hung over the street. At night they were lit by dozens of tiny bulbs, though lately the city had not gotten around to replacing them when they blew. The arches were one of the defining features of the Short North, the other being the thriving art community. Once a month, Columbus's art and music enthusiasts filled the streets for the Gallery Hop. During those nights, the galleries along the strip threw open their doors, and many of the restaurants and bistros stayed open late. Keenan tended to find an excuse to be inside on those nights.

After walking down High Street for about a mile, the two turned right onto a brick road, walked another block, and then crossed the street to the northeast edge of Goodale Park.

Garfunkel perked up and began tugging at his harness. In the spring and summer, he would tear Keenan's grip loose as he chased after the Canadian geese and ducks that hung around the small pond and fountain on this side of the park. If the birds had been smarter they would've retreated to the water, since Garfunkel was not much of a swimmer. Apparently the sight of an English bulldog bearing down on you could cause you to take temporary leave of your senses.

Garfunkel began the customary rounds to his favorite trees as they walked down the paved path around the pond. The trees weren't dense, but they were tall, and they lined the narrow walkways. At times, the white gazebo to the south would house jazz quartets or small gatherings. But at the moment it had its usual morning occupant, an old grizzled man drinking from a barely concealed forty. He mumbled incoherently as Keenan passed.

The only sounds were those of the tall fountain in the pond and the distant rush of cars on High Street. When he had to be down at the station, there was little time for these weekday walks. One of the few pleasures of the extended leave was the opportunity for Keenan and Garfunkel to just walk around. He'd learned more about his neighborhood in the last two months than in four years of living there.

Garfunkel indicated with a short grunt that he was ready to head home. The park was a nice change of pace from the confines of the apartment, but both of them were chilly this morning and desperately in need of breakfast. On the weekends, Keenan tended to go to the Goody Boy diner, which was only a couple of blocks from his apartment. The food was greasy but satisfying. On weekdays, however, his options were few unless he wanted to stick around for brunch. He thought briefly about buying some fresh bread from Tasi, a small trendy café a couple of blocks east, but he'd never quite gotten the hang of the hipster crowd.

He tossed Garfunkel one of the dog biscuits he'd been carrying in his coat, and thought briefly about taking a bite himself, but remembered he didn't really like the meat-flavored ones. They headed back out to High Street and arrived home about half an hour later. The return trip always took a little longer as the sidewalk seemed to go uphill for miles. The grade was slight but detectable on feet that were still getting used to two-mile morning walks.

The answering machine light was blinking when Keenan opened the door. He carried a cell phone for work, though he'd left it on his bedside table this morning. The apartment had a landline, though even when he was home he tended to screen his calls. There was a brief message from Daily asking him how things were going and suggesting breakfast the following morning at Jack & Benny's, a regular haunt for the two of them just north of campus.

The second message was a bit unexpected.

"Are you going to get back to work at some point, Detective?" Synthia's voice rang from the machine. "I've been going over the files and I think there are a couple of names your boys might have missed. I thought cops didn't sleep when they were on a case."

Keenan pressed Erase with a sigh and looked down at Garfunkel. "And I thought Caliente was persistent. Remind me to thank Tom for requesting Synthia, maybe by having him buy me breakfast."

. . .

Keenan booted his computer, the new graphics card and RAM still sitting unopened on top of the tower. A moment later he was in his virtual office, an impatient Synthia staring at him with her arms crossed.

"Does the virtual girl have to do all the work around here?"

Keenan shrugged. "I had to walk my dog."

Synthia smiled. "You sound like a dog person. What's his name?"

"Garfunkel."

Synthia laughed. "That's cute. Well, I got another name for you. This one's a hacker for hire."

"How'd you find him?"

"Well, I may not have your lab tech's skill with backtracing IPs, but I never forget a face." She picked up a photograph from her desk and handed it to him.

For a moment Keenan thought his avatar frowned. "This is a penguin."

"He goes by 'Tuxedo.' A lot of people use nonhuman avatars here. It can give you a whole new way of looking at the world."

"But a penguin?"

"That penguin has contracted with dozens of Fortune 500 companies. On paper, everything's aboveboard, but Tux provides all sorts of services to his clients, including corporate espionage. Nothing happens in Surreality without Tux hearing about it, or causing it himself."

"It sounds like he'd make a better suspect than a witness."

"Maybe, but that's your department. All I know is, he was at the Arcadia premiere, and it looks like he didn't have an invitation."

"Where do I find him?"

"He hangs out at a nightclub called 'The Source.' It's a red zone, naturally."

"Naturally," Keenan replied. "What time does he come in?"

Synthia shook her head. "Not sure, but the bartender's a friend, or more accurately, an earlier prototype of mine. He said he'd let me know the next time the penguin comes to roost."

"That's chickens."

"Whatever."

Keenan smiled. He still wasn't sure exactly what to think of Synthia, but it was nice to know she had a sense of humor. "Good job. I'm going to talk to this Glassner fellow. You'll call me if you hear about Tux?"

"Dr. Glassner is already expecting you. He said he'd be working at the library all morning and that he'd be happy to speak with you whenever you wanted."

"Swell. By library I'm assuming Glassner means the one he's building in Surreality?"

Synthia nodded. "I looked it up. It's listed under 'Alexandria Project' in the directory."

"Simple enough. He's a doctor?"

"Yes, of computer science and philosophy."

Hmm, Keenan thought. *That's an unusual combination.* Snapping back to reality, he quipped, "Great. He's an expert in two ways to bore me to death."

Synthia smiled and patted him on the shoulder sympathetically.

• • •

When Keenan flew out of the network of blue tunnels, he found himself surrounded by water. He was in a small boat being rowed ashore by a young man with golden hair. He tried to engage his guide in conversation, but the young man acted as if he were a fixture of the boat, rowing steadily and ignoring Keenan completely.

The Alexandria Project consisted of a cluster of small buildings surrounding a central skyscraper. To his right he could see the lip of a natural amphitheater that descended down into the island. The boat banked slightly to the left, and he could see their destination. It was a small dock at the base of a small lighthouse. The lighthouse appeared to have been carved from a rock spire; an outer winding staircase led to a large shimmering crystal at the top.

The boat rocked gently as it bumped up against the dock, and the young man jumped out to tie it off. Keenan suddenly realized he had been sitting and that he needed to tell his avatar to stand up before he could walk. The boat pitched back as he stood up quickly, but the strong grip of the young man kept him from falling backward into the water. Keenan was lifted unceremoniously out of the boat and placed down onto the dock with a thud. Keenan noted that despite this rough handling, his avatar's trench coat and fedora remained unwrinkled. He smoothed out his real shirt absently before walking toward a small archway at the end of the dock.

As he passed under the archway, an alarm sounded. Two guards stepped out of the rock face and approached him swiftly. Before he had a chance to defend himself, one guard had torn off his coat, while the other began patting him down. Keenan tried to shove the second guard away, but he was frozen in place. Seconds later, the first guard found the revolver and dangled it in front of Keenan's face accusingly.

"Weapons are forbidden in Alexandria!" the guard rumbled.

"I'm a detective in the CMPD." Keenan tried to flash his badge before remembering that it was in his coat, and that he couldn't move. "As an officer of the law, I'm authorized to carry a side arm."

The guard's programming was limited, and after a moment's hesitation he repeated, "No weapons!"

A third man, who'd been watching the proceedings from the top of the lighthouse, descended the spiral steps quickly and brushed the guards aside. He was tall, thin, and very tan. His hair was even more golden than the boatman's, and his eyes reflected the blue of the simulated ocean. The man wore a simple robe tied with a thin braid.

"You'll have to forgive the guards; we didn't have a chance to inform them of your arrival. Still, I'm afraid we do have rather strict policies regarding malicious code, no matter how well intentioned. If you turn your gun over to the guard, I promise it will be returned to you upon your departure."

The man was smiling, but it was clear Keenan didn't have many options. He nodded to the guard who was still holding the gun in front of his face. The guard grunted and stuck the barrel of the gun into the front of his robe. Keenan wasn't sure how to clean a virtual gun, but he was going to ask Synthia when he got back to the office.

"Thank you, Detective. Allow me to introduce myself," the man said. "I'm Dr. Glassner, head librarian and project coordinator for the Alexandria Library."

Keenan reached out a hand, discovering he again had control of his character. "Detective Daniel Keenan."

As a gesture, the shaking of hands in Surreality seemed wooden and conveyed little of the subtle meaning it could in real life. Still, Glassner smiled and shook his hand for a few seconds, then dropped it abruptly. "So, you're here about my former partner."

Keenan nodded. "Specifically, his murder."

"If only that were true," Glassner said. Sensing Keenan's silence, he continued, "Just a bit of humor. I'm sure Franklin Haines told you all about his takeover of the company we built together. I trust you can understand why I might find his virtual death amusing, perhaps even gratifying."

The two had begun walking toward the central tower, and the guards disappeared back into the rock face. "That sounds like a pretty clear motive to me, especially since what we're really talking about is the theft of eighty million in assets."

Glassner shrugged. "Why pretend otherwise? But it's not money I want, Detective, it's a legacy."

"How so?" Keenan asked.

"Franklin wants to turn Surreality into just another form of entertainment, a video game. When we created Surreality, it was supposed to be so much more than that. Think of it." He stopped and put an arm around Keenan's avatar. "You can create anything you can dream of here. The possibilities for research alone are staggering. You can collaborate with colleagues and scholars from around the world as if you were in the same room, touching the same experiment."

"How is that any different from what you can already do on the Internet?"

Glassner shook his head. "The Web is still just a screen. No matter how fast our connections get, we are only looking at pictures of each other. There's no sense that you are actually in the same place as anyone you are talking to. In here you can move, you can interact, and you can build, without worrying about procurement budgets or even safety regulations. If an experiment blows up in here, you can just tweak the simulation."

That might have been handy in high school chemistry, Keenan thought idly. "But Haines didn't agree with your vision?"

Glassner dropped his arm and started back toward the tower. "He said it wasn't profitable, and he convinced the board I was steering the company toward financial ruin. Franklin's only ever seen this world as a fantasy, a place where you can satisfy your most hedonistic desires. His casino is only the beginning."

"Where were you during the Arcadia premiere?" Keenan asked, trying to pull the conversation back onto less philosophical ground.

"I'm not sure. I wasn't on the guest list, though Franklin finds a way to make sure I know everything he's doing. What time?"

Keenan consulted his notes. "The twenty-first, around 6 p.m."

"Well, surely you've been able to get my login history from the Surreality Committee."

Keenan nodded. "We're working with the committee very closely during this inquiry, but I'm the kind of guy who likes to hear things directly from the horse's mouth."

Glassner smiled. "I was here, working in the library, as I am most evenings. This project demands all my time and energy."

"Are you married?"

Glassner shook his head. "My work is my life. I don't need anything else."

In Keenan's experience, most people who said that had either lost everything, or never had the opportunity to get it in the first place. He wasn't sure which one Glassner was.

They approached the base of the tower and stepped onto a clear disc, one of four that surrounded the spire on all sides. Keenan hesitated at first, and when he did get on, he moved as close as he could to the center of the disc. Glassner pressed a small control panel hidden in the stone, and the disc began rising quickly. Within seconds, they were hundreds of feet above the ground.

Keenan's stomach dropped just looking at the screen, while Glassner laughed, "Afraid you'll fall, Detective?"

Keenan was just trying to keep his view from tilting down. From this elevation he could see Arcadia in the distance; the construction programmers were still hard at work removing the rocks. Beyond the island he could see the bustling metropolis of Surreal-City. Synthia had told him that 'Surreal-City' was only a nickname, as neither Glassner nor Haines had gone to the trouble of naming it when they designed the first buildings. The city was one of the first maps written for Surreality, and had been expanded on by countless companies and individual users. Thousands of people walked down sidewalks, drove cars of every shape and size, and lit up offices in the numerous skyscrapers. Keenan wondered who exactly would come to Surreality to work at a desk job, but the sudden jolt as the disc stopped its ascent jarred him back into the unpleasant present.

Keenan turned and followed Glassner, who moved into a room at the top of the tower. Wide open-air arches afforded a view of the entire island. Atop the arches sat a domed ceiling, which vaulted some thirty feet above them. Glassner's modest desk was made of stone, in keeping with the island's style. In fact, his entire office was stone, right down to the chairs that even Keenan's avatar thought needed cushions. Keenan's host gestured toward a seat, and he took it awkwardly.

"Look, Detective Keenan, it's no secret why Franklin sent you here. I don't know if he actually thinks I did this, or he's just trying to disrupt my work, but it doesn't matter. I didn't kill Franklin Haines or steal his money, even if I'd like to shake the hand of the person who did. Whoever did this was—"

"Master class," Keenan groaned. "I've been hearing that a lot lately, but what would it really take to pull this kind of thing off? Could you do it?"

Glassner shrugged. "Truthfully, no. Franklin and I wrote the base algorithms for this place and created some of the early worlds, but nowadays he employs an army of programmers. I doubt there's a single individual who knows all you'd need to go completely undetected."

Except maybe this Tuxedo guy, Keenan thought.

"What would be involved?"

"Well, masking your IP address is easy, and your character can be modified to blend in with the scenery but still interact. It's the interaction that's the key. Surreality has an advanced physics model running in the background, tracking every gust of wind, every contact between characters. There are hundreds of subroutines running at any one time trying to make the environment as realistic as possible. Getting into Arcadia, murdering Franklin in that . . . theatrical way, and stealing eighty million dollars, without getting picked up by something, is next to impossible. Your killer might be able to hide from view, but their avatar was still in the room, so to speak."

If that's the case, then what the hell am I doing? Keenan thought. "So, somewhere there's a record of the killer's exact movements."

"Well . . . no," Glassner replied. "The physics model is refreshed every couple of minutes and cached for an hour on the user's computer, but none of it is stored permanently."

"Haines told me pretty much the same thing," Keenan replied.

"Even if you could get at the data, all it would really tell you is that someone was there, not who they were or where they were hiding."

Keenan knew exactly why he was on this case. There was no tech trail for the lab geeks to follow, and any other kind of a trail was already two weeks cold. There was no crime scene evidence, no body, and few leads other than speculation. This was the case they would use to hang him out to dry.

CHAPTER FIVE

After talking to Glassner, all Keenan felt like doing was stewing on the couch. Garfunkel leaned against him as Keenan stroked his head idly and emptied bottle number three of Yuengling. Had Daily known what he was handing Keenan? What it would mean if he botched this case?

Daily had put up a good front when the higher-ups pushed for Keenan's leave of absence. He'd said all the right things to defend his friend, "a damn good cop." But Daily could read the writing on the wall as well as anyone. The press had withheld the pictures of the woman Sinclair had brutally beaten to death. But they had been all too happy to paint the picture of a Columbus Metro cop killing an unarmed suspect. The full details came out a few days later, including the fact that Sinclair had been carrying a knife. But the damage had already been done, and the city wanted blood.

Publicly, the chief was behind Keenan, but that support would be short-lived. The shooting hadn't had even a whiff of racial motivation, unlike similar incidents in the last few years, and evidence collected at the scene of the first victim pointed to Sinclair as the killer. Officially, Keenan had responded with deadly force in the preservation of his own safety after the suspect drew a weapon. But there were questions. What was Keenan doing in that alley alone? And when he began making a pursuit on foot, why hadn't he called it in?

"Detective!"

Somebody was shouting at him.

"Are you listening, Hayes?"

Keenan moaned as he got off the couch and stumbled toward the computer. He swore he had turned the speakers off, but somehow Synthia was shouting at him. Keenan had picked up a new headset when he'd bought the beer. He'd had a little trouble figuring out how to plug them in, his speakers giving off a loud crackle when he'd tried plugging the mic jack into the speaker output, but eventually he figured them out. He switched off the speakers and slipped on the headset, adjusting the mic over his mouth.

"What do you want, Synthia?"

"That's a hell of a greeting. How did the interview with Glassner go?"

"Lousy. He probably did it, or hired whoever did. He also spelled out how it would be next to impossible to catch the killer, or thief, or whatever."

Synthia smiled an evil smile. "Now's not the time to be giving up, Detective. I just heard from my friend the bartender. Our penguin is back on the prowl."

Keenan chuckled. "That's cats."

"Really? I kind of liked the idea of prowling penguins. Anyway, before you go waltzing into the Source, I thought you might need this."

She produced a bulletproof vest from behind her desk. Keenan shrugged off his coat and took the garment from Synthia, expecting it to immediately snap onto his character. He stood for a few moments doing nothing until Synthia spoke up. "Well, put it on!"

Keenan took off his dress shirt and dropped the vest over his head. He'd managed to get his character's arms to go up through the holes, but they wouldn't come back down. The vest was completely obstructing his field of view. He tried to shake his character by walking around, hoping the vest would just fall into place. Instead he tripped over Synthia's desk, landing with what he imagined was a painful thud. He cursed as she laughed.

"You look ridiculous," Synthia said.

"Thanks for the help. Is this really the best you could come up with?"

Synthia threw up her hands and hopped off her desk. She ran her hands over the vest, and it transformed into a handkerchief which she caught in the air, then tucked into the pocket of Keenan's jacket. Keenan stared at her. "Why didn't you just do that before?"

"So I like watching you have a hard time. Does this come as a surprise to you?"

"Explain to me again why your designers made you so . . ."

"Charming?" Synthia replied innocently.

"Difficult."

"It's part of my designer's theory about the Turing test. He says all artificial intelligences are too polite, too eager to please, so they don't pass as human. Real people are grumpy. Make a cranky AI and you might be more likely to believe it's a human you're talking to."

"So your designers made you grumpy?"

"See, I know you're just trying to push my buttons, but you're going to be late."

Keenan had replaced the dress shirt and thrown on the jacket. He gestured at the neatly folded handkerchief in his pocket. "What's this for, anyway?"

"It's a patch, a security update for your character. It hasn't been officially released, or even fully tested, but it should offer you some additional protection in red zones."

"Protection from what?"

"From someone doing the same thing to you that they did to Haines."

Keenan shrugged. "Thanks."

"Watch your caboose, Hayes."

. . .

Keenan slowed to a stop as he approached the entrance to the Source. He was floating at the end of one of the blue tunnels that stopped abruptly at a red node. A message box flashed in front of him.

YOU ARE ABOUT TO ENTER AN UNSUPPORTED ZONE. CONTINUING MAY RESULT IN DAMAGE TO YOUR COMPUTER. SURREALITY IS NOT RESPONSIBLE FOR ANY LOSS OF PROPERTY OR DAMAGE INCURRED IN THIS ZONE. DO YOU WISH TO CONTINUE?

What the hell. Tom's been saying I need a new computer anyway, Keenan thought as he clicked Yes.

The message box parted, and he soon found himself surrounded by a storm of crimson. Whoever had designed this part of the loading code had done their best to portray the dangers of this area of Surreality. Below him he could see shadows passing by, some looking as if they were going to swallow him up. Keenan considered drawing his gun, but the shadows seemed to be keeping their distance for now. And he wasn't sure what his character-erasing gun would do to a tunnel between worlds, but he didn't really want to find out.

Fortunately, the trip was fairly uneventful, and a moment later he branched to the left and stepped through a portal to the Source.

The sky was dark, and a light rain fell all around him. The sound was kind of pleasant but gave the place a sinister look. Except for Surreal-City and his office, all of the maps he'd seen so far seemed to be some kind of island, and the Source was no different. All around him, bright white disks traced a jagged path before falling out of sight about thirty feet away. Keenan followed one of the disks cautiously, nearly losing his footing as the ground abruptly dropped away. He looked down and saw a sea of electricity. Lights flashed below him, stretching for what seemed like miles. As he looked further, he could see that the lights were actually circuit pathways, and the precipice was the edge of a computer chip. The ground beneath him was smooth and black, and glistened from the coat of rain.

He walked toward the only building on the small island, an industrial-looking bar with neon lights and small horizontal slits for windows. At the center was a large crimson door with bolts arranged in a diamond pattern. Two bouncers stood on either side of the door, their arms crossed and legs spread apart. Keenan tried to slip past, but the bouncer on the right stopped him.

"Hold on. We don't allow cops here."

Keenan smiled warmly. "Who said I was a cop?"

"That outfit looks like something drug out of the first-run dialogs. That makes you either a cop or a n00b," the right goon answered.

Keenan thought about asking what the hell a "noob" was, but figured it wouldn't help matters. "That seems like an over-generalization," he said.

"People who play this game for real like to personalize their character," the left bouncer said.

"Maybe I just like the outfit," Keenan replied.

"It is a rather fetching ensemble," the bouncer on the left said.

"It evokes feelings of fall, particularly one over a cliff," the first bouncer continued.

"Look, if I was a cop do you really think I'd be so obvious about it?"

The bouncer on the left shrugged. "Probably not. But we still have to frisk you."

At this Keenan tensed. He had his badge and side arm within easy reach. Given their conversational skills, it seemed unlikely these goons were mere programs like the guards at Alexandria, and they had found his gun in seconds. He tried desperately to think of an attack he could use, but came up with nothing.

The bouncer on the right muscled his way in and opened Keenan's jacket while the other one patted down his pants. The first one reached for something in the pocket where Keenan's gun should have been, but pulled out a flask instead.

"No outside booze," he said, unscrewing the cap and pouring the contents into his open mouth. Keenan was grateful for his avatar's placid face, since in the real world he would have betrayed his surprise. He wondered if his gun was replaced or merely transformed like the bulletproof vest had been. If the flask was the gun, had the guard unloaded it by drinking its contents?

The other bouncer grumbled from his position at Keenan's feet. "He's clean."

The two stood and parted with outstretched arms in seeming hospitality. "Enjoy the Source, we're always open!"

Both men began laughing, but Keenan wasn't in on the joke. Not wanting to tempt fate, he stepped through the crimson doors and made his way into the bar. The Source was awash with activity. Though it had looked small from the outside, it actually had two levels, with a spiral metal staircase leading down to a lower level. Most people seemed to be sitting around or taking in the scenery, a few chatting over drinks. Some of the more adventurous souls were out on the dance floor, though most looked like they should have paid a little more for their dance algorithms.

Tuxedo was not among those on the floor, though Keenan smiled at the idea of a dancing penguin. He scanned the room and found the hacker at one of the circular bars sipping something through a straw. The penguin was sitting in a pose more cartoonish than natural. Keenan picked out a seat a couple of chairs away and called the bartender over.

"What'll it be, stranger?" The bartender was dressed in a manner evoking the Wild West, but somehow the juxtaposition didn't seem unnatural. He gave no indication of recognizing Keenan or any acknowledgment of their arrangement. But Keenan figured it must be pretty easy for synthetic intelligence algorithms to play it cool when they needed to.

"Scotch, neat," Keenan said, trying to think of something appropriate for his private eye persona.

"That'll be fifty surs, partner."

A "sur," as Keenan had learned, was slang for Surreality Dollar. A window popped up asking him if he'd like to accept the charge. Keenan clicked Yes, and his avatar tossed a credit card onto the bar. The barkeep swept up the card, swiped it, and flipped it back into Keenan's palm in a single practiced motion. The drink appeared a second later. Keenan took a long sip before putting it back on the bar. Usually he didn't drink on duty, but he figured a virtual drink was unlikely to have much of an effect.

"In case you were wondering, I reprogrammed the bartender," a casual voice called over to him.

"Excuse me?" Keenan said, turning to address the speaker.

"It seems he had a habit of telling people where I was," Tux continued. "I thought about dressing him as a samurai warrior, but how would he serve drinks with a sword?"

Keenan didn't speak. This cartoon penguin didn't look particularly dangerous, but there were things Tux could probably do that would be worse than any beating from a muscle-bound goon. He opened his inventory window and kept the gun poised for a quick draw while Tux stared at him.

"Did your computer freeze, or have you just never seen a talking penguin before?"

Keenan shook his head. "That's not so strange. My college mascot is a killer nut."

Tux raised an eyebrow. "You must be Detective Keenan. Still getting used to your new skin?"

The muscles in Keenan's shoulders eased. Tux was playing it friendly to start. "For the most part. What about you? What makes you want to be a penguin?"

Tux smiled. His character's features were more expressive than Keenan might have expected. "This is the form that best suits my personality, just like you."

"Hmm," Keenan grunted. "So you know who I am. Do you know why I'm here?"

"You want to know if I had anything to do with Franklin Haines being eighty million dollars poorer." Tux took a sip of his drink. "I'm not your man, though I appreciate the compliment."

"Any particular reason I should believe you?" Keenan asked, taking a sip from his own drink.

"I don't know how much you know about me, but I'm not a thief. I've worked with all sorts of companies at one point or another. Even Haines. It's bad for business if I'm seen as a criminal."

"I wouldn't think so, since your business deals in corporate secrets."

"That reputation is ... greatly exaggerated. I assure you, Detective, I'm not breaking any laws, or at least not any you have jurisdiction to enforce."

Keenan didn't appreciate the less-than-subtle jab, though it did tell him something useful. Tux knew a lot about this case, including the people investigating it.

"Okay, if you didn't do this, who else could?"

Tuxedo shrugged. "Birds of my feather don't tend to flock together, but you're dealing with—"

"A master-class hacker?" Keenan interjected.

Tux shook his head. "They don't necessarily have to be good. They just need access. Haines got into bed with some fairly unsavory elements to get this Arcadia deal done."

"How would you know that?"

"I keep my ear to the ground," Tux leaned with his head, "so to speak."

"Did someone hire you to get dirt on Haines?"

Tux shook his head. "Come on, Detective Keenan, you were doing so well. Obviously I can't tell you who hires me or even if I'm on a job right now. But finding out secrets about one of the creators of Surreality can be its own reward."

"Is that why you were at the premiere, to dig up dirt on Haines?"

"Maybe I just like to gamble," Tux chuckled, which sounded like a rooster crossed with a canary. "Surreality caters to any fantasy, including ones that are illegal in the real world. It's legal to pay for sex acts, try illicit drugs, and even kill people. A crime is only a crime if it has an impact on the real world. And you're the first detective I've seen here."

"That's encouraging."

"Why do think I picked a Western bartender? This is the new Wild West; the law hasn't caught up with half the things happening on Twitter, let alone this place."

"Is this where I say 'there's a new sheriff in town'?" Keenan quipped.

Tux grinned. "Maybe, but you'd need a different hat."

"I'm not sure where to get one," Keenan replied truthfully.

Tux laughed again. "I like you. You're not a gamer, and you're not a hacker like me. So why did your department give this case to you?"

Keenan knocked back the rest of his drink. "Tech boys a lot like you took a shot at it and came up empty. Sometimes the old methods are the best methods."

"I couldn't have said it better myself," Tux said. "Don't get me wrong, I'm a child of technology just like the rest of the people here. But the difference is there are a few of us who still have a creative spirit, an inquisitive mind. I suspect we're a lot alike."

"Oh?"

"Sure. For instance, I bet you'd like to know as much as I do why there were a bunch of Polos at the Arcadia Casino opening."

"Polos?"

Tux shook his head. "I think it stands for 'Power Lords' or some shit. They're identity thieves mostly. They run spam attacks, set up fake websites and fake worlds inside Surreality."

"Does the Surreality Committee know about them?"

Tux shrugged. "Probably, but it's hard to make anything stick. They operate mostly out of red zones where the committee doesn't know what's going on."

"And they were at the Arcadia Casino?"

"Exactly," Tux replied. "Casinos and organized crime have a long and storied history, but Haines wouldn't have let them just crash his party."

"You got in, didn't you?"

Tux smiled. "I'm the best, Detective. Most of these Polos couldn't string two lines of code together to say 'Hello world.' If they were there, Haines knew about them, one way or the other."

Keenan leaned in. "You said Haines was working with some 'unsavory elements' to get Arcadia up and running. Do you think these Polos are involved?"

"Almost certainly, but I lack some of the real-world resources to prove it conclusively. Not everything is stored electronically."

Keenan narrowed his eyes. "What are you driving at?"

Tux leaned back comfortably. "Isn't it obvious? I'm proposing a partnership. I help you track down one of these Polos in the real world; you ask him about his involvement with Haines and pass anything you learn along to me."

"You don't seriously expect me to agree to that, do you? For one, you're a suspect who had means and opportunity, if not motive. And second, this is still an official police inquiry. I can't hand my files off to a civilian."

"And I would never expect you to. Just make sure you fill out all your paperwork, and I can do the rest, I assure you. The trick is getting you to look in the right direction."

"So far I don't see a direction, just another blind alley," Keenan replied.

"Come on, I've read about you, Keenan. Surely you can see a couple of steps down the line. If the Polos invested money in the Arcadia venture, and all of that money has been stolen, then it's not only Haines's money that disappeared. The Polos are probably putting pressure on Haines to get that money back, and they won't be squeamish about using violence as an incentive.

Whoever attacked Haines may not have killed him, but they may have triggered the events that will.

"And I'll do you one better," Tux said, pulling out a small tablet. "You need a crime scene, I can get you one." He tapped a control on the side of the tablet and an image of Arcadia Island popped up, complete with Haines's strangled corpse.

"Where'd you get this?" Keenan said.

"It's not finished, just a preliminary reconstruction from data I mined off witnesses. Half the people who attended the Arcadia premiere were seeing Surreality for the first time, and they haven't logged back into the accounts they created. There's a surprising amount of data to be found, even in erased sectors and missing files."

Keenan had to admit Tux was good, but why was he so interested in the Haines case? And why would he want to help Keenan? He doubted there was anything that was truly beyond a determined person's reach, especially someone with such obvious talents as Tuxedo. So, what did he need with a plain old metro detective like Keenan? It didn't smell right to him, but he didn't see that he had a lot of options.

"What's your price?"

"I already told you, just information. I'll be in touch when I have more, but you need to get going."

Keenan was jerked out of the conversation by the sound of his phone ringing. Garfunkel was barking at him, which he usually only did when Keenan was asleep. He logged off abruptly, his avatar vanishing while Tux smiled and tossed a couple of surs onto the bar.

As Keenan picked up the phone, he realized it was pitch-black outside. *Surreality can really play tricks with your sense of time*, he thought.

The voice on the other end of the line was Daily. He was breathing heavily and seemed to be at the end of his patience. "Where the hell were you? I tried to call you three times!"

"Long story," Keenan replied. "What's going on, Tom?"

"There's been an incident. We need you to get down to the Columbus Athenaeum right away."

"What happened?" Keenan asked, already grabbing his gear.

"Franklin Haines has been shot."

CHAPTER SIX

After his third pass around the statehouse, Keenan wondered if he would've been better off walking. The streets were packed with news vans, police cruisers, and more than the typical crush of people in downtown Columbus on a Thursday night.

If he'd been at the station he would've taken one of the cruisers, but working from home meant driving his own car, a boxy early 90s Ford Taurus that had no right to still be on the road. Cutting over a curb, he was able to force himself into the garage, jamming his car up next to one of the obstructed spots near a cement pole. He didn't even bother locking it as he jumped out and ran for the stairs that led back to street level.

The Athenaeum was bigger inside than it looked from the street. At one point it had been three separate buildings, one of them a Masonic Temple. This meant a maze of corridors and a wide variety of internal architectural styles. There were a number of ballrooms and small chapels for weddings, and plenty of places for someone with bad intentions to hide. Keenan strongly suspected the maze of corridors and hallways rearranged itself every time he was down here.

Several uniforms had blockaded the main entrance, trying their best to keep back the reporters and looky-loos. Keenan shoved through the crowd, but one of the younger officers put up a stiff hand as he got close to the barrier.

"No unauthorized personnel, sir. Step back."

Keenan cursed as he realized his badge was not in his jacket; then he heard a voice from the top of the stairs.

"It's okay, Braxton. Let him through," Tom Daily called, waving to Keenan.

The young officer apologized, but Keenan was already past him. "How many new people did Columbus Metro hire while I was gone?" he said as he caught up to Daily.

"Braxton's been on the force for nearly a year, Dan. Since he obviously meant so much to you, I'm shocked he doesn't remember who you are."

"Thanks, buddy," Keenan said as he pulled open the heavy metal doors to the lobby. The room was surprisingly quiet given the number of people. Several men in fine suits and women in long gowns were leaning against wood-paneled pillars, or sitting in tall crimson chairs at the edges of the room. A few had been laid out on the couches in obvious shock. To his right Keenan could see that a few of the metro cops had commandeered the side offices, and were interviewing and processing out the witnesses who were in better shape.

"What's the damage, Tom?"

Sonya Caliente answered for him as she walked up to meet Keenan. "About time you got here, Dan. It's a real mess. We've got two dead and at least twenty injured, including Haines."

"The shooter?"

"He got out onto the street through one of the service hallways. Private security gave him some chase, but they lost him on Broad Street."

"That's practically around the corner!" Keenan said, disgusted.

Caliente gestured behind her at a burly man recovering his breath in one of the chairs, his uniform shirt untucked and his face red and sweaty. His gun hung loosely from a belt that looked like it was about to give up the ghost.

"You'd think Haines would be able to afford better," Keenan remarked.

"I don't know. If I lost eighty million, it might make me pinch a few pennies," Caliente said.

Keenan chuckled. "How's Haines doing?"

"You can ask him yourself. In fact, I think he wants to talk to you."

Keenan rolled his eyes. "Great. I was kind of liking this whole interviewing-people-in-my-pajamas thing."

"Sounds like he's not all bad," Tom said. "Reports from some of the witnesses have Haines spotting the shooter just before he opened fire and diving to protect his wife. He took a bullet in the arm."

"More like a graze, but to hear him tell it, it's like the shooter blew off his whole arm," Caliente said. "Still, that's better than my ex-husband. He would have just let me get shot."

"Not likely," Tom said. "Then he'd have to put up with you haunting him."

Caliente was nine months past a fairly nasty divorce. Her ex-husband had argued that her job and her hours made Sonya an unfit mother. Somehow he'd gotten one of the less scrupulous judges to agree. Caliente was appealing the ruling, but the process had been tied up for months. And the truth was, her job didn't give her much time to make a defense.

"I've got better things to do in my afterlife then hang around that loser," Caliente said.

"Don't we all," Keenan replied. He walked toward the Olympian Ballroom a little reluctantly, shrugging on the disposable protective gown and gloves one of the officers handed him. With all the commotion, it wasn't likely there would be much evidence that hadn't been trampled by half a dozen feet, but he might get lucky.

The ballroom was a war zone.

Keenan stepped inside quickly and slammed the doors behind him. He could tell that the benefit had been an elegant affair, even as he surveyed the room full of overturned tables and chairs. Everything had been covered with pristine white linen. It was now stained with blood, bits of food and champagne, and shards of glass from shattered flutes.

He was standing at the end of a long red carpet. Above him, strings of decorative white lights ran between Corinthian columns. Two rows of wrought iron accented chandeliers hung from the ceiling. They had been dimmed for the reception, which now allowed the strings to flicker and send beads of light in a thousand different directions, highlighting the grisly scene below.

The wood floor beneath his feet creaked as he slowly moved into the room. The only other people there were two uniforms on the second-floor balcony, and a few remaining guests at a table to his left. Two bodies lay hastily covered by one of the white linen tablecloths behind it.

"Detective Keenan!"

Haines had spotted him. He was seated at the center of the main table, with an EMT on either side treating his arm and checking his vitals. Even having read Haines's file, Keenan was taken aback at the man's youth. Surreality had followed an initial trajectory similar to the most successful technology companies: a couple of young men with a good idea that exploded in a few years.

His young wife sat beside him. She was pale, more from shock than complexion. Her white strapless dress was stained with her husband's blood, though she herself appeared unharmed save for a few bumps and bruises. She didn't seem to register Keenan as he approached them.

"I'm Detective Keenan," he said, extending a hand.

SURREALITY

"Nice to finally meet you face-to-face. Are these the kind of results we can expect from the CMPD's finest?" Haines said, gesturing at the room.

Haines was clearly angry. How much of that anger was directed specifically at Keenan, and how much of it was searching for the first available target, Keenan couldn't tell.

"Mr. Haines, I assure you we're doing everything we can."

"I've gotten nothing but assurances from your department for the last two weeks. How much longer do you expect me to sit quietly and wait for you to do your job?"

"I understand your frustration, Mr. Haines," Keenan said. "Is there anything you can tell me about your assailant, maybe a description?"

Haines shook his head. "I only saw him for an instant before I was hit. He stepped out from behind that pillar," Haines pointed behind Keenan, "and just opened fire."

"What about you, Mrs. Haines?"

She looked up as if seeing Keenan for the first time. "I'm sorry, I didn't see anything."

Despite her obvious shock, her voice was steady and low. Her green eyes met his for a moment, then quickly looked away.

"That's all right," Keenan said, turning back to Mr. Haines. "We're interviewing the rest of the benefit guests as we speak. Someone will have a description we can use."

Haines nodded grudgingly. "I expect results, and soon."

The EMT treating Haines's arm interjected with a few more questions, and Keenan took the opportunity to escape to the company of the uniforms upstairs.

The stairs to the upper floor were marble and echoed under Keenan's feet. The gold-plated handrail subdividing the stair contrasted the wrought iron of the guardrails. Masonic symbols were carved on each face of the newels, though the paint was chipping away in places. Keenan turned left and hopped up another short flight of steps to the upper balcony.

Numbered yellow tags littered the floor where the shooter had stood. In the space of thirty seconds he had emptied thirty-six rounds. Keenan rested his hand on the balcony guardrail, taking in the killer's view. Haines was either very lucky or the shooter was a terrible shot. Was this another warning, driving home a point the Arcadia attack had failed to make?

He turned and walked toward the set of double doors that had likely been the killer's mode of escape. Behind them a short dark hallway ended in another set of doors a few dozen feet ahead, with a stairway leading up to his left.

Keenan approached the uniformed officer closest to him. "Excuse me, Officer . . . ?"

"Connor, sir."

"Right," Keenan nodded. "Could I have your flashlight, Connor? I'd like to take a look down this hallway."

"Of course, sir." Connor handed him a black flashlight that probably doubled as his nightstick. Keenan switched on the light and let the heavy door latch behind him. The killer would have covered the distance in a matter of seconds. In the dark it would have been difficult to see the other entrance, and Keenan grinned when he saw the faint drops of blood on the carpet.

Bet the bastard bashed his nose, Keenan thought. *It might be broken.*

The doors hadn't slowed the killer down much, despite his injury. From the splinter marks around the deadbolt, Keenan could tell the doors had been locked before the killer kicked them in. He traced the old door with the tip of his gloved hand. There was a definite indentation. *At least we've got his blood and shoe size*, Keenan thought before pushing open the door.

The service hallway was narrow and ran along the edge of the ballroom into the rooms beyond. He turned right, following the hallway around a corner until he reached a set of stairs that led down to the kitchen, laundry rooms, and other offices. Above him he could hear the clunking of feet from impatient guests whose shock had turned to indignation.

A faint breath of cooler air drew his attention to the metal door cracked open about twenty yards in front of him.

Keenan's breathing shortened. He wanted to flip on the lights, but he had no idea where to find a switch. With each step he could hear his heart pounding. *I'm really out of shape if a couple of flights of stairs wind me*, he thought, keeping Connor's flashlight trained on the door as he advanced. Unthinkingly, he kicked the door open and spun out into an empty alleyway.

Except it wasn't empty.

The rain was ice-cold and stung with each drop. The tunnel formed by the two brick buildings seemed to stretch for miles. His every step echoed against the cracked pavement. The alley was dark, lit only by a few hanging lights on the Athenaeum side, though most were busted out. He felt a familiar weight at his hip and remembered that it was his gun, fully loaded and glistening in the thin light.

Someone was laughing hysterically. Keenan could not locate the sound. It bounced back and forth across the buildings, sometimes sounding right next to him and other times at the far end of the alley. Most of the windows were dark and dusty, or boarded up. The sound had to be coming from the street, but he was alone. He drew his gun.

His heart went cold in sudden recognition, the laughter penetrating his mind. That laugh, like a wild jackal, was Sinclair.

But Sinclair was dead. Keenan had killed him. And yet he was still laughing.

The laughing rose up to his left, and he fired. The gun was deafening, the sounds of the blast cascading off every surface and pushing him back. The laughing increased again, and again he fired. This time the reverberation knocked him off his feet and sent him crashing to the rain-slicked pavement. The gun tumbled uselessly out of his hand.

"Dan. Are you all right?"

New sounds rushed into focus, pushing aside Sinclair's voice. Keenan stumbled as Caliente put an arm around his shoulder. He wasn't sure if he had actually fallen or if he had been standing the whole time. He felt disoriented and a little bruised. His knuckles were white from gripping the flashlight so tightly. His gun was nowhere to be seen.

He loosened his grip and waved her off with his other hand. "I'm fine."

The streets were bone-dry. The laughter was gone.

Caliente looked concerned, which made Keenan worried. What had he looked like when she came into the alley?

"Really, I'm fine," Keenan said. In truth, Keenan was seeing the scene for the first time as it really was. Fortunately, eight years of being a detective gave him some unconscious instincts.

"I was just tracing the killer's movements. It looks like he turned left out of the alley, ran down Lynn Street, then along past St. Joseph's before disappearing somewhere on Broad. Maybe the traffic cam will have picked him up getting into a getaway car."

"I've already got the techs pulling the cameras and doing the calls out to social media," Caliente said. "A busy night like this, there might be someone on the street who snapped a picture. Find anything interesting?"

His eyes fell to a dumpster about fifty feet away. The lid had been clamped down with a metal bar, but the door on the side was still open. Already half-sunk in a slurry of rotting food and broken bottles was the long lens of a camera. With an escaping suspect, any object of interest would need to be cataloged and bagged, and this didn't look like the sort of camera that would get tossed out behind a banquet hall.

Caliente spotted the camera too and grinned. "Isn't it the rookie's turn to go dumpster diving?"

"Even after being on leave for two months, I'd hardly call myself a rookie," Keenan said.

"On the contrary, I'm now two months your superior," Caliente flashed back with evil glee.

"I don't think that's how it works," Keenan said, already walking toward the dumpster.

Fortunately, time spent absorbed in Surreality had made him neglect meals, otherwise the involuntary gagging reflex he experienced as he reached for the lens would have brought up more than air. Gingerly, he pushed aside the remnants of two hundred pappardelle dinners and discovered the lens was attached to a camera.

Caliente held a plastic evidence bag open at a distance from her body, into which Keenan roughly dropped the camera. He sloughed off his gloves into the open dumpster and grimaced.

"I think they have another batch of that pasta left if you're hungry," Caliente quipped. "They only had time to serve half the guests before all the fun started."

Keenan growled as Caliente laughed and patted him on the back.

• • •

It was three in the morning by the time Keenan got back to his car. Somehow he'd managed to stay buried in the maze of the Athenaeum and dodge some of the more zealous local reporters.

Their shooter was a man in his mid-twenties, average height, average build, and with either blond or brown hair depending on the lighting; in other words, half the college students and interns in the greater Columbus area. The camera and a fake press pass had afforded him access to the benefit, though neither had been carefully scrutinized by "security."

Keenan debated sleep, but he was meeting Tom for breakfast in only a couple of hours, and Synthia would want an update. Garfunkel was asleep when Keenan carefully opened the door. The dog lifted his head in brief acknowledgment before letting it fall back onto the leather sofa. Keenan felt ahead in the dark for the kitchen and tripped over the futon, cursing and stumbling into his brick feature wall. His right foot throbbed as he forged ahead toward the fridge. Given his disorientation, making coffee in the dark seemed an unwise and hazardous enterprise, but his stash of diet soda was still intact.

"Shouldn't you be in bed, Hayes?" Synthia asked as he dragged himself into the office. He grunted and fell into a seat behind his desk.

As usual, Synthia was perched at the edge of her desk, and Keenan wondered if code had even been written for her to sit in a chair. She was holding a pencil poised over a sketch pad, moving it in small swift strokes.

"I didn't know you could draw."

"There's a lot you don't know about me."

Keenan thought for a moment, then said, "This is gonna sound rude, but . . ."

"Why would I need to know how to draw?" Synthia finished.

"Yeah," Keenan answered sheepishly.

"All part of being human. I have hobbies like anyone, and while you mortals sleep, I can practice my art."

"Can I see?"

"It's not a finished product," Synthia said, looking it over before answering. "But, all right."

He walked over to her desk and sat beside her, needing a moment to find the right perch. Apparently balancing on corners wasn't something Surreality avatars did by default. She handed him the sketchbook, still open to the page she had been working on. Rendered in gray scale was the plateau of the shooting range. The sky was full of clouds, some wispy, others thick like cotton. The waves were crashing high against the rock, and he could even see the light mist of the spray of water. The whole image looked as if it were shaded with tiny dots, rather than continuous strokes.

"This is pretty good," Keenan said as he flipped the page.

"That next one is actually a companion piece," Synthia said.

Upon turning the page, Keenan was met with an image of the balloons, each with teeth like he had seen in his dream. In one of the gaping mouths he could see the end of someone's leg, and what looked like a pinstripe suit rather like the one he was currently wearing.

"Very funny."

"I think this is some of my best work."

"I agree," Keenan said, handing the book back to her. Synthia looked puzzled as to whether he had given her a compliment or not.

"So it seems you've got a live one now, Hayes."

Keenan grunted again. "Excuse me?"

"The benefit shooting has been all over the news, not to mention all of the forum chatter."

"Are you saying I didn't have to stay up and brief you?"

Synthia smiled. "Since I can't accompany you to the crime scene, I need to find other ways to keep myself in the loop, something that became a lot easier after tonight."

Keenan shrugged. "Murder has a habit of getting people's attention."

"Are you all right?"

"I wasn't on scene when it happened."

"That's not what I mean," Synthia said, her tone becoming serious.

"You been talkin' to Caliente?" Keenan's mind briefly drifted back to the alley.

Synthia looked surprised. "No, should I have been?"

Keenan shook his head. "It's nothing. I got a little out of breath climbing all over the Athenaeum. I've been sitting on my couch for too long, though I don't think trying to solve a case in front of my computer is going to make that any better."

He wasn't sure if Synthia bought the line or not. It was all he intended to offer a computer program at the moment.

Synthia continued, "I'm just concerned. This is your first major case since the Sinclair incident and it's already in the news."

Keenan's glare grew frosty, though Synthia had no way of sensing it. "How do you know about the Sinclair case?"

Synthia seemed to pick up on his agitation even without a visual cue. "I told you before, I was fully briefed on this case and on who I'd be working with, including your recent history and the reasons for your leave of absence. For the record, every report I've read says you didn't have a choice but to shoot Sinclair. He was armed and cornered, and obviously violently disturbed."

"I don't want to talk about it," Keenan said. He nearly added 'not with a damn computer program' but wasn't sure how Synthia would respond to outright hostility. It wasn't really her fault, he supposed. Her concern and her inquisitiveness were something programmed into her. But if he didn't want to talk about the case with his friends, he sure as hell wasn't going to spill his guts to someone who wasn't actually there.

"That's fine," Synthia said. "But if this Haines thing doesn't get cleared up soon, the press is going to make this story about you."

She was right and Keenan knew it, and he didn't have much time. "What's your point?"

"That I'm your partner and I can help you, not just with the Surreality stuff, but with anything that spills over into the 'real world.' And buddy, you look like you could use all the help you can get."

Keenan cracked a small smile. "I thought you were my secretary."

Synthia shoved him in the arm. "Do you really think they'd waste a sophisticated AI like me just so you could have someone to answer your phone?"

"Since when have you answered a phone?"

"I'm talking to Caliente right now," Synthia said.

Keenan looked at Synthia. She was sitting on the edge of her desk, the sketch pad to her right and the pencil still in her hand. "You're talking to Caliente right now?"

"Yes."

"How?"

Synthia sighed. "What part of synthetic intelligence algorithm is unclear to you? I'm capable of parallel processing, just like real secretaries. If it helps your visual, though . . ." Synthia put down her pencil and picked up the phone on her desk. She crossed her legs and leaned to hold the phone in between her head and shoulder. "Better?"

"I suppose. Did I just hear you call yourself a secretary?"

Synthia ignored him and began taking notes. A few moments later she put down the phone, still laughing to herself as she stared at her notebook.

Keenan looked at her inquisitively. "What was that about?"

"Nothing. Caliente was just calling to make sure you took a shower before coming back into the station," Synthia grinned.

Keenan had already scrubbed his arm pretty vigorously at the Athenaeum, though it still felt like he had bits of marinara under his fingernails. "Was that it?"

Synthia shook her head. "Traffic cameras are apparently a bust. Your techs pulled the tape and got nothing but static. Some kind of jamming signal went out just before the time of the shooting. It knocked out cameras for a five-block radius."

Keenan raised an eyebrow. "How in the hell did he do that? Those things are supposed to be shielded from interference."

"Evidently our shooter has some skills beyond inflicting mayhem."

"Or maybe he wasn't working alone."

CHAPTER SEVEN

That is the last gut buster I'm ever eating, Keenan thought as he dragged himself through the front door of his apartment. The "gut buster" was a creation of Jack & Benny's and included three kinds of breakfast meat, cheese, hash browns, a potato pancake, and an egg, all smothered in country gravy. At the moment these were congealing into a solid lump at the pit of Keenan's stomach that made moving a bit unpleasant.

He dropped a couple of extra sausages into the dog bowl, and Garfunkel sucked them down appreciatively. When describing how dogs eat, "chew" is not a word you often come across. His mother kept telling him it was bad to give the dog people-food, that Garfunkel would just continue to beg, but Keenan didn't really care. It was probably best he shared with the dog anyway; otherwise his time on leave might really catch up with him.

The breakfast with Tom had been productive. Tom confirmed what Synthia had told him about the traffic cameras, though some of the techs were still holding out hope that they'd be able to pull something out of the scrambled signal. Tom, however, wasn't optimistic. They'd had a bit more luck with the camera Keenan had found in the dumpster. The outside had been wiped clean, but they'd been able to lift a partial fingerprint from the SD card. They were running it now. Hopefully the guy was local, or the search could take days.

The SD card itself contained a couple blurry shots of the Athenaeum crowd, and one clear photo of Haines from what looked like the shooter's position. Why the killer had taken the picture was anyone's guess, especially if he knew he was going to ditch the camera in his escape. It was possible he'd intended to pocket the SD card and just hadn't had time, intending to keep the photo as a trophy or as a way to remind Haines just how vulnerable he really was. Whatever the reason, it would help their case for a warrant when the prints finally came through. Tom had sounded frustrated but upbeat during breakfast. They were both the sort of men who liked complicated problems, and it felt good to be talking shop once more.

Keenan's answering machine was lit up again, though this time the caller wasn't Synthia.

"I've got something for you, Detective. Meet me at the Surreality Zoo at nine o'clock." Tuxedo.

Keenan checked his watch. The meeting was in about twenty minutes, barely enough time for a shower. He hadn't thought about the hacker since their meeting last night; his thoughts had been consumed with the shooting. Tuxedo almost seemed to have known about the shooting before it happened, causing Keenan to wonder whether he could count this avian avatar as an ally or an adversary. He'd worked with shady characters before, but none who could hide behind a mask. Keenan could read people, but could he read an avatar?

Ultimately, there was no choice but to hear what the bird had to say.

Tux hadn't been specific on where to meet inside the zoo, so Keenan wandered to the place that seemed most likely, the Arctic exhibit. The zoo hosted a wide variety of animals, both real and imagined. He was impressed by the level of detail; he could see the hair on the gorillas and the spots on the cheetahs. Upon arriving at the Arctic exhibit, Keenan stopped and stared at the penguins. He wondered if sometimes Tuxedo jumped in and slid down the chutes of ice, swimming from ice block to ice block.

"Why weren't you at the entrance?" a voice said from behind.

Keenan turned around to see Tux wearing a Hawaiian T-shirt and sunglasses, sipping something cool and refreshing from a long novelty glass.

"I thought I'd meet you somewhere you'd feel more at home," Keenan replied.

"Glad to see you haven't lost your sense of humor, Detective. I picked the zoo because it's one of the most trafficked spots in Surreality, outside of the city. It makes it easier to blend in."

"With who, exactly?" Keenan said, looking between the real-life fake penguins and the cartoon that stood in front of him.

Tux chose to ignore him. "I found a couple of names that weren't on your list."

So far Keenan had had just as much luck with the list of IP addresses as the techs, which is to say, none. Most of them were people who had created accounts for the first time, specifically for this event, and nobody looked like someone with the knowledge to pull off the untraceable theft of eighty million dollars.

"Anybody interesting?" Keenan asked.

"Absolutely." Tux nodded. "Though tracking them down was more difficult than I originally anticipated. A couple of two-bit Polos I can give you for free, but for the rest I will require a finder's fee."

Keenan smirked. "I'm disappointed, Tuxedo, I thought you were only in this for information."

Tux grinned. "A bird's gotta eat."

"How much are we talking?" Keenan asked.

"Fifty thousand surs," Tux responded coolly. This was about five hundred real dollars; probably a bargain, if Tuxedo could be trusted, which was still a pretty big if. The homicide department wasn't going to be thrilled if too many expenses were incurred on a virtual case, especially with a high-profile shooting already eating up resources.

"How do I know the list isn't just the names of your grandma's bridge club?"

"My grandmother plays poker, and my reputation depends on reliable information."

"Thirty thousand surs. From what I hear, birds don't eat that much," Keenan countered.

Tuxedo smiled. "How 'bout we settle on forty-five thousand?"

"Or we could settle on me taking you in for corporate espionage."

Tux lifted his sunglasses and winked. "Not the most friendly attitude, Detective Keenan, but lucky for you, tenacity is a quality I admire. Thirty thousand it is."

He handed Keenan a notepad. "The woman you're interested in is Ms. Nancy Klein."

"Who's she?"

"She's the most desirable and expensive woman in Surreality. She doesn't tend to make appearances on public servers, but not only was she seen at the Arcadia premiere, she was also seen in the company of our two Polos."

"Do you think they hired her?"

"Doubtful," Tux replied. "She isn't a common hooker. A couple of identity thieves working in a crew wouldn't have enough to afford her."

"But Haines might."

Tux nodded. "She might even give him a discount. After all, bagging one of the creators of Surreality has got to be a boon for her business."

"But why take the risk?" Keenan asked. "It's not like he's even getting the benefit of an actual mistress."

"Don't discount the pleasures of the virtual until you've tried them. Surreality offers some unique ways to be interactive. Franklin Haines spends more time in Surreality than anyone. Maybe he doesn't have time for anything else."

Keenan thought back to Haines's young wife, stained by her husband's blood from a bullet that might have hit her. It wasn't the first time Keenan had seen an unfaithful man who genuinely seemed to love his wife, but they were always the most confusing.

"Where do I find Ms. Klein?"

Tux sucked down the last of his drink. "It just so happens I have a way in. One thing, Klein's establishment caters only to the most exclusive of clientele, so I would lose the trench coat if I were you."

"Oh," Keenan said, "and what would you suggest?"

"A tuxedo. And not some cheap knockoff you can pick up from any vendor, but the genuine article. You want to be able to see the threads, not just smooth textures painted on."

That's great, Keenan thought. *Another thing my graphics card or my budget won't be able to handle.*

. . .

Fortunately Tux knew a few places Keenan could rent a tuxedo, though they didn't come cheap. The tailor calculated Keenan's measurements by loading his model data and switching his standard clothing for the tuxedo. The threads looked as smooth and indistinct on the tux as his other clothes, but Keenan supposed he would have to take the tailor's word for it. He deposited a couple thousand surs as payment, plus twenty thousand in collateral in case he picked up a virus in a red zone. He then made his way to the address Tux had given him.

Ms. Klein's establishment didn't look like any club Keenan had seen before. It was a mansion with carefully manicured gardens that stretched at least half a mile from the main house. The transit tunnels had deposited Keenan on a bench under a wrought iron lamppost. A stone path to his left led up to the house, and stars glistened above in what seemed to be a perpetual night.

On either side of the paneled doors, two guards stared straight ahead like they were auditioning to be statues. Their suits, shades, and earpieces fit the Secret Service more than your typical bouncer, and certainly didn't match the decor. They let him through without searching his clothes, even holding the door open, before closing it noiselessly behind. This was a welcome change from how the last set of guards had treated him, but somehow this didn't put Keenan any more at ease.

A merlot-colored carpet led to a small white desk, behind which sat a scarcely dressed woman perched precariously on a stool. Seven draped entryways lay in front of him, three on each side and one in the back. He supposed the far room would be Ms. Klein's and moved in that direction when the hostess stopped him.

"What's your pleasure, sir?" she began in a lilting voice, not even acknowledging Keenan's attempt to barge in. "We have a wide variety of sensual delights for your simulated self to enjoy."

She wore a black ruffled lace corset that accentuated her generous virtual bosom, but her lips drew most of his attention, moist and full and rose red. Her thighs were bare but for the garters connecting her black fishnet stockings.

"You look like a forties type. You like your women mysterious but feisty, yielding only to your will. Maybe harboring some kind of terrible secret she can tell only you."

"I'm not looking for secrets; I'm just looking to talk to Ms. Klein," Keenan said.

"I'm sorry, sir, but Ms. Klein is by appointment only. She's probably a little out of your price range anyway, though that is a very nice rental."

Keenan grumbled to himself. Tux had assured him the rental would pass. Maybe he didn't know as much about these kinds of places as he'd let on.

"Relax, honey," the woman said, getting off her stool and putting her hand on his chest. "I wouldn't mind taking care of you myself."

Keenan put his hands on her shoulders and gently pushed her back. "I appreciate the offer, but I really need to see Ms. Klein."

Apparently Keenan had issued some sort of challenge. The woman drove herself closer to him, till she was at a distance that in real life would have rendered him far less objective. "Ms. Klein is booked solid, and I could satisfy you in ways you couldn't dream of."

"Your offer is very flattering, but I'm afraid I must insist. Now where is Ms. Klein?"

The hostess backed away—annoyed, he thought at first—but when she raised her arm to point behind him, a different interpretation became evident. The doors burst open and the two guards that had been standing out front lunged in Keenan's direction.

Keenan drew his gun and fired wildly, diving for cover behind the hostess's desk. Miraculously one shot managed to hit the mount of a large chandelier that hung in the main lobby. Under normal circumstances the chandelier would have crashed to the ground, sending shards of glass in all directions and hopefully knocking down one or both of the guards. Unfortunately for Keenan, the chandelier merely vanished into thin air. Evidently his gun didn't just erase characters, but objects as well.

He cursed and shoved the hostess forward into the adjacent room. The hostess screamed as the guards continued firing. The small desk exploded behind them into splinters of wood, and the blast threw them into one of the party rooms.

Keenan clicked his tuxedo into his inventory and switched back to his trench coat, not wanting to lose his security deposit. He had a few seconds to survey the room before the guards entered.

The "party room" was a frenzy of activity, and it took several moments before anyone noticed Keenan and the frantic hostess. The room was a swarm of blues, greens, reds, and blacks, little of which came from clothing. Elves, nymphs, dwarfs, and all kinds of fantastic creatures were engaged in activities not suitable for fairy tales.

Keenan shot the hostess a look. She shrugged and said, "We do cater to every interest."

Mercifully, Keenan didn't have time to respond. The guards tore the curtain down as they entered, spraying the room with gunfire, indiscriminate about their targets. Stray gunfire hit several of the feather beds, raising a cloud of white plumage between Keenan and the two gunmen. His view was further obstructed by the frenzied patrons suddenly running around the room, most of whom hadn't collected themselves enough to realize they could just log out. He shoved past a winged nymph and dove for cover behind a bed that had contained a pair of humanoid cats.

The guards began mowing down whole sections of the crowd. Those that didn't log out in time were thrown to the floor, unable to move. This cleared the path for Keenan to fire from his crouched position, striking the leftmost guard in the leg.

The guard tried to walk toward him, instead moving in a circle as the controls for his right leg went out. Fortunately for Keenan, the rest of him quickly disappeared.

Enraged, the other guard fired in Keenan's general direction. A torrent of bullets struck the spot that moments ago had been Keenan's head. Luckily Keenan had managed to dodge behind one of the marble pillars that divided the room. The narrow pillar did little to conceal him, and the guard quickly shifted his fire. Shards of the column knocked Keenan off balance and back onto his hands.

Keenan twisted and fired, missing the guard and taking out a bed from beneath two very focused succubi instead. A moment later the column shattered, showering Keenan in dust and blowing any cover he might have had. The guard aimed slowly, moving pointedly toward Keenan. On his last stride he tripped over something unseen, which sent his gun flying. Keenan wasn't sure what had just happened, but he wasn't about to complain. He grabbed the guard by the collar and dragged him to his feet.

"Who are you, and why have you so rudely interrupted these fine people's evening?" Keenan asked.

The guard stared at him blankly, unwilling or unable to speak. Keenan took his pistol and hit the guard in the jaw. Unfortunately this wasn't as useful as Keenan had hoped. The guard began dissolving right before his eyes. Keenan glared, frustrated, at his gun, which apparently didn't require bullets to make people disappear.

Most of the patrons had left for quieter corners of Surreality, willing to forgo the rest of their session till another time. The hostess was frozen in place where Keenan had left her; she seemed to be in shock.

"I take it the guards aren't programmed to do that?" Keenan asked.

"Sometimes we do have to escort someone out, but our server just kicks them off," the hostess stammered. "The guards are supposed to be just for show. I didn't even know they had guns! I can't believe they shot so many of our clients!"

Keenan realized the guards had ignored him until he started insisting to see Ms. Klein. Clearly someone didn't want him poking around.

"They'll recover," Keenan replied flatly, "and now you're going to tell me where Ms. Klein is."

The hostess shook her head. "I don't know. I haven't heard from her in days. She usually gives us notice when she goes on vacation, and even then she usually logs in from her laptop to satisfy our more select clients, for an added fee, of course."

"Of course," Keenan smiled. "Do you know who she is—who she really is, I mean? What does she do?"

"I have no idea," the hostess replied. "If anyone knew who she was in the real world, it would bring an unbearable amount of inappropriate attention from those less rooted in reality. Ms. Klein enjoys this private hobby of hers, one for which she has an unusual talent. She does not want anyone in the outside world to judge her, or get the wrong idea."

"In other words, you don't know if she's missing or just hasn't logged on in a while."

The hostess shook her head again, and Keenan hit one of the beds in frustration. He supposed her explanation made sense. People acted differently in Surreality than they did in real life, though which was their true personality was harder to guess.

"Was there anything unusual that happened the last time you saw her? Something she did, a client she entertained, anything?"

"I know she was planning to attend the Arcadia premiere. She took some of the new girls with her, but she split off with a couple of men shortly after she arrived. "

Those must have been the Polos, Keenan thought.

"Do you typically bring new girls to prominent events like Arcadia?" he asked.

The hostess sighed, "We're always hiring new girls. We're hopelessly understaffed, and the lifestyle can be a little rough on newcomers. Clients can be very demanding, particularly when the limits placed on them by society and physics are removed. Of the six girls we hired before Arcadia, two haven't shown up for work since. I can get you all their names, but I'm afraid I don't know more than that. Anonymity is helpful for all in this profession."

Keenan murmured his thanks and helped the woman to her feet. She met his gaze and smiled. "Are you sure I can't do anything for you?"

Keenan put on his fedora. "Another time perhaps."

"What's your name?"

"Hayes. Coleman Hayes."

"That's a funny name for a detective, Hayes."

Keenan decided to log out rather than reply, suddenly grateful for the ability to just disappear. He leaned back in his real chair, inhaled slowly through his nose, and rubbed his eyes with his hands. He'd been up for more than thirty hours.

This was the second shooting in as many days, and in some ways it had felt no less real. He'd thought the game would feel different, especially since there were no stakes. He couldn't get hurt, but his heart had still pounded in his chest. The mouse was sweaty from where he'd gripped it tightly, and Garfunkel was nuzzling his hand, trying to position it on top of his head.

Keenan slowly relaxed as he petted the dog. He crossed over to the couch, the dog following close behind, and resumed petting as he leaned into the cushions. He turned onto his side and bent his knees, forming a little crook into which the dog leapt and curled up. Keenan was almost asleep when the phone rang again.

"You get it, Garfunkel," Keenan groaned as he rolled onto the floor. The bulldog's head had been resting on his calf and hit the couch with a thud, which startled the dog and caused Keenan to chuckle.

"What is it, Caliente?" Keenan barked into the phone.

"Easy, buddy, you're not the only one who hasn't had a good night's sleep."

"I'm sorry, Sonya. I get a little punchy after my twelfth cup of coffee."

"Twelve? I don't get cranky until at least eighteen. Rookie."

"I'd hardly call that sugary swill you drink, coffee. You got something to tell me, or is this just a social call?"

"I thought you'd want to know about one of the uninvited guests to Franklin Haines's party." He could hear her grin through the phone.

"Oh? You get an ID on our shooter?"

"Not yet, but you might be interested in who else decided to show up."

"You gonna tell me before I fall asleep?" Keenan asked.

"Robert Glassner, Haines's ex-business partner."

Keenan was suddenly wide awake. "He wasn't on any of the witness lists."

"He must have slipped out when the shooting started," Caliente replied. "But it just so happens our shooter snapped a picture of him. I think we've got our second man."

CHAPTER EIGHT

Caliente had taken the liberty of updating Synthia on the shooting at the Athenaeum. Apparently the two of them were already thick as thieves, something Keenan didn't think boded too well for him.

"That's what Glassner looks like?" Synthia said, holding up a digital copy of the photo the shooter had taken.

Keenan thought of Glassner's avatar, the golden-haired athletic man he'd met at the Alexandria project. Someone was obviously overcompensating.

"Do you think he started losing his hair after he and Haines split up, or when he started his daring life of crime?" Synthia mused.

"We haven't proven anything yet, Synthia. For all we know he just wanted to crash the benefit for the free food."

"Hardly. That was a five-thousand-dollar-a-plate function."

For five thousand dollars I'd expect a little better than pasta, Keenan thought, shuddering as he recalled the congealed mass he'd had to rummage through.

"Be that as it may, all we really know is he was on the scene. I'm just going to Alexandria to talk to him."

"Want me to tag along? I could charm the answers out of him while you nail him to the wall," Synthia said enthusiastically.

"I think I'll save you for when I really need you," Keenan replied.

"Like you needed me at Klein's place? When were you going to tell me about blowing up one of the most prominent underground establishments in Surreality?"

"Hey, for the record, I'm not the one who started shooting."

"No, apparently all you had to do was ask about Ms. Klein and they decided to rough you up."

"Yeah, that about sums it up," Keenan sighed.

"Well, I'm sure you'll be pleased to learn that your little misadventure was a trending topic within twenty minutes on Twitter. I personally like #pr0nfail, though #privatesdick is a contender as well."

"How about #hefiredhissecretary?"

"No need to get snippy, Hayes," Synthia said. "The manufacturer of those guards is swearing up and down that their behavior was not part of their programming. Apparently it's better to be hacked than admit you made faulty merchandise."

"I've always thought so," Keenan said. "Did you find out about Klein's from the forums, or have you been spying on me the whole time?"

"I couldn't have spied on you even if wanted to," Synthia said as she spun off her desk and slumped down into her chair. Leaning on her elbows, she continued, "Klein's place is locked up tight to keep prying eyes out. It wouldn't be good for her business if someone broke in and tried to blackmail her clients. I doubt even a hacker like Tux could get in."

"So if you wanted to know what was going on in a place like that, you'd have to go in yourself."

"Almost certainly, and the server is likely to block any kind of recording programs you tried to take with you."

Keenan handed Synthia the list of new employees he'd gotten from the hostess. "These women were with Klein at the Arcadia premiere, and several of them haven't returned to work since. It's possible they were only working for Klein to dig up some dirt on someone, and got out when they found what they wanted."

"You think it's Haines," Synthia observed.

"I don't know. Think he'll tell me if I ask?"

Synthia laughed. "Fair enough. Do you want me to get Tux working on this list?"

"Yeah," Keenan said, "and he's doing it for free this time. The rental place wouldn't take my tuxedo back. They said something about 'infected code.'"

"Want me to have it dry-cleaned?"

"Nah. That would be a waste of your considerable talents."

"Why, Detective, I think that's one of the first nice things you've said to me," Synthia said, a smile spreading across her face.

"I get sentimental when I'm tired."

• • •

Alexandria was quiet when Keenan arrived a few minutes later. He'd bypassed the boat and the gateway, and materialized at the base of the tower.

"Don't stand there!" a distressed voice called out from behind him.

Keenan looked down to see he was standing on top of a pancaked Glassner. He looked like he'd been flattened by a steamroller. Grisly details were rendered in a cartoonish way, his eyes wide like saucers, his face caught in obvious surprise. He quickly sidestepped, though not before leaving a conspicuous footprint on the avatar's robe.

"Sorry, didn't see you there." He turned to address the speaker and was amused to see Glassner's new avatar was wearing his real-life appearance..

"It's about time you showed up, Detective."

"Pardon?" Keenan said. "Dr. Glassner, I'm here because I have some questions, though I guess the first one is what the hell happened?"

Glassner looked up and Keenan's eyes followed.

"Oh," Keenan said, taking a moment to appreciate the scene above him. Glassner's office had been tilted 45 degrees off its original axis. Looking around, he could see the stone desk, chairs, and a broken telescope scattered around the body.

"See, if it were me, I would have tilted the whole building, like the leaning tower of Pisa," Keenan said, chuckling to himself. "I take it you were up there when this happened?"

"Yes," Glassner said grumpily. "I was sitting at my desk when the whole room began shaking. My avatar started to slide, and I tried to brace myself, but all the furniture was sliding as well. When I hit the ground, I was logged off, and when I tried to log back in, Surreality said my avatar had been erased. I logged in with one of my older accounts and found this." He pointed to the disk that had once been his body.

"If your avatar's been deleted, then . . ." Keenan began.

"Yes, my assets have been stolen as well. The sum may be more modest than Haines's loss, but most of Alexandria's finances were being run through me. Without that money, we're sunk within the week."

"Was anyone else logged into Alexandria at the time? Did you see or hear anyone?"

Glassner shook his head. "I was definitely alone in my office. There may have been a few students in the lower levels, but they were gone when I logged back in."

"I'll need their names if you can get them," Keenan said.

"I'll try, but I'm having trouble accessing all of my administrative rights with this avatar. Everything was associated with the other account," Glassner replied.

Keenan looked up again. "Any chance I can get up there?"

Glassner nodded. "The lift seems to be in perfect working order, though I can't guarantee it won't disappear beneath your feet."

That's reassuring, Keenan thought. The clear glass was unnerving enough without the thought that he could suddenly plummet to the ground. If this was the same hacker who had attacked Arcadia, then it wasn't likely there were any hidden traps, but maybe the thief was evolving.

"You're coming with me," Keenan said, wrapping an arm around the stout dwarf of a man and pushing him toward the elevator. "I still have a few questions."

The two men stood suspended in the virtual air, held up by nothing, staring at the tiled dome. Keenan hadn't noticed the first time he was here how intricate the facade was. The dome was divided into quadrants, each containing a mural in a different style. He thought he recognized part of the ceiling of the Sistine Chapel, as well as a charcoal sketch rendering of what looked like the original Library of Alexandria. The third quadrant featured a mural from an Egyptian tomb, a plaque beneath the section saying it came from the Tomb of Huy. The last was Van Gogh's *Starry Night*. The clash in styles was jarring, even more so when looked at from an angle.

He leaned to look at the broken edge of the floor. The office appeared to have been peeled off quite neatly, as if it had merely been resting on the tower below it. Keenan envisioned a giant hand pulling upward on the opposite side and dumping out the contents like dirt from a bucket.

"Are you just going to look, Detective Keenan?" Glassner said impatiently.

In truth there was little else Keenan could do. He certainly wasn't stepping into the office, as he had no desire to become a pancake himself, and he didn't have any tools to collect data from the scene.

"I'm just trying to get a better sense of what happened. For instance, I'm wondering how you came to be at Haines's benefit last night."

If avatars could sweat, Glassner's forehead would be drenched. "I believe you're mistaken. I—I haven't seen or even spoken with Franklin in months."

"And yet you were his first suspect."

"We didn't part on the best of terms, as you well know."

"So you can understand, then, why I'd be curious about you crashing his fundraiser," Keenan continued, ignoring Glassner's denial.

Glassner threw his hands up. "All right, I was there, but I didn't shoot anybody. I didn't even see what happened."

"Where were you?"

"I was in the restroom when I heard the gunshots. I panicked and ran, and kept on running till I got back to my car."

Keenan would have expected Glassner to cower in one of the stalls at the first sound of gunfire rather than make a break for it, but people could always surprise you.

"And you didn't think to report what you'd heard to the police?" Keenan asked.

"There were hundreds of people on scene. One more witness wasn't going to do you any good. I was just happy to get out of there."

"Did you see anything as you were 'getting out of there'?"

"No. It was all kind of a blur, actually. Just reacting on instinct I guess. Like I said, I didn't see the shooter."

But the shooter saw you, Keenan thought.

"Why were you there in the first place? Why did you want to talk to Haines after all this time?" Keenan pressed.

Glassner's tone changed. "Actually, I wanted to talk to Katherine."

"Katherine?" Keenan said, puzzled.

"Mrs. Haines."

"Why?"

"She's quite the graphic artist. She designed that cherry blossom effect, the one Haines used to build Arcadia. I was hoping to get her help with some of the expansions to Alexandria, both from a design and practical perspective. She's always been better at developing indexing algorithms than me."

"You know her personally?"

"I should hope so. She is my sister, after all."

CHAPTER NINE

"Glassner is Franklin Haines's brother-in-law?!" Synthia exclaimed after Keenan filled her in on the details of his interview. "That seems like the sort of thing you should have known already."

"Katherine Haines is actually Glassner's stepsister. His mother married her father about ten years ago," Keenan replied.

"So, Surreality was a family business till Haines kicked his brother-in-law out. I'll bet that makes Thanksgiving a bit awkward."

"The two men haven't spoken in months, but Glassner keeps in fairly regular touch with Katherine, or he did until lately."

Synthia leaned forward. "What's changed?"

"The Arcadia project was taking up a lot of time and energy the last few weeks before the premiere. It's one of those things where they only come up for pizza and coffee."

"Kind of like you on a case," Synthia observed.

"I'm more of a Chinese guy, myself," Keenan replied.

"So are you going to talk to her?"

Keenan nodded. "According to Glassner, Mrs. Haines had agreed to meet with him during the benefit. If she confirms that, then Glassner's reason for being there checks out."

Synthia shook her head. "She's more than just an alibi witness. She can give you the inside scoop on Haines and Glassner. Katherine Haines has known both of these men from the beginning of their partnership to the end. If she's close with her stepbrother, I'll bet she had some thoughts on how her husband edged him out."

Keenan smiled. "That thought had occurred to me, Synthia."

"Good, because I think I'm through the last of her assistants and should have her on shortly," Synthia said.

She pressed a control on her phone. "Your phone's going to ring in a minute." Sure enough, he could already hear it warbling from the other side of the room. Keenan slid his chair out and walked to the phone, falling backward in a practiced motion onto the couch as he did so.

"Mrs. Haines?"

"Yes. Hello again, Detective Keenan."

Her voice was remarkably steady for someone who'd been shot at the previous evening. Then again, the wife of the CEO of a major technical firm probably had to know how to be comfortable in almost any situation.

Keenan, on the other hand, wasn't quite sure what to say. He tried the direct approach. "I have a couple of questions about your husband's case if you have a few minutes."

"Yes, of course, Detective. Anything I can do to help."

"Given your schedule, would it be easier for you to come by my office here in Surreality?"

"Actually, I was just about to step out to lunch. Would you mind meeting me instead? There's an outdoor café near my husband's office."

"What sort of café?" Keenan asked.

At this, Garfunkel perked up. He was probably the only dog in the world who knew the word "café." He also hadn't been walked yet, and the trek downtown would be a good way to work off both their breakfasts.

"Do they like dogs?"

• • •

Garfunkel was running back and forth and whining. Typically he was sedate when getting ready for a walk, but at that moment he was a little white blur. Keenan was putting on a clean white shirt, since he was still wearing the one from the day before, and shaving off the day's growth of stubble.

Garfunkel darted in the bathroom and tugged at Keenan's pant leg. "All right, all right, we're going already! You know, I forgot to ask if she even likes dogs. She might be a cat person."

Garfunkel gave him the pathetic look that only bulldogs and beagles can, and Keenan patted him on the head. "There, there, I was just kidding, boy. Everybody loves dogs, especially you."

His tail wagged happily, and Keenan walked into the kitchen to get his leash. No sooner had he clipped it onto Garfunkel's collar, than his arm was nearly pulled out of its socket. He grabbed his keys as he slid across the room and somehow got the door locked before being dragged into the street.

He had to run to keep up with Garfunkel's pace. Surprisingly, the bulldog seemed to know exactly where he was going, and Keenan's only involvement was to make sure the dog did not run out in front of traffic. This caused even further damage to Keenan's arm, and he massaged it with his other hand while they ran.

When they arrived in Bicentennial Park at the southern end of the Scioto Mile, Keenan was confused. In front of him was the "jewel of the mile," Milestone 229, which was decidedly not a dog place. He wasn't exactly uncomfortable there, but it was definitely not his scene. Increased development in the downtown wasn't a bad thing, but he was running out of dive places where he could eat for just five bucks.

"Over here, Detective Keenan," a female voice said from behind him.

It turned out Mrs. Haines's "café" was a street vendor parked at the edge of the mile. "Café del Monte" was written on the side of the cart. Beside it stood Mrs. Haines, wearing an understated hunter green skirt suit. Her hair, on the other hand, was loose, long and billowing in the wind.

"Mrs. Haines, it's nice to see you again."

"And you," Katherine responded. "I see you're not wearing your trench coat and fedora this afternoon."

"Your husband told you that, eh?" Keenan said, caught a little off guard. "I apologize if it seems unprofessional."

"Surreality tends to bring out a little of the romantic in people. It's only natural."

Garfunkel barked impatiently, and Keenan looked down. "Right, I'm sorry. I should have introduced you as soon as we got here. Mrs. Haines, this is my dog, Garfunkel."

She knelt down and began stroking Garfunkel's head and scratching behind his ears, which made his tongue hang out. Keenan looked down at the happy bulldog's face. "Enjoying ourselves, are we?"

"You have a wonderful dog. I believe he suits you."

"Yeah, we seem to get along all right. He hasn't chewed up any of my shoes lately." Looking around, he said, "Is this where you usually get lunch?"

"Why not? The open air is more private than a restaurant where the waiter hangs over you every minute. And I love this part of the city. You can play chess, take a walk through the park, or just watch the water going by."

Garfunkel pawed at Keenan's leg. Keenan looked down and patted his dog on the head. "All right, boy, we'll get something to eat. It was cruel of me to make you wait, I see that now."

Mrs. Haines laughed and ordered a toasted roast beef sandwich, exchanging a few pleasantries with the owner. Keenan opted for a meatball sub, with a couple extra for the "meatball with legs." Garfunkel didn't acknowledge the jab and accepted the food happily. It occurred to Keenan that this was probably one of the few places where Katherine Haines was treated as a normal human being, rather than the wife of one of the most influential people in the city.

They walked along the curved promenade next to the river. To the right were numerous fountains with water spraying out of the mouths of fish. In his younger days, Garfunkel might have jumped up into these fountains and played with the brass fish. Actually, he still might have, were he not so engorged with meatballs and marinara.

"Does your husband ever come here?" Keenan asked, finishing his sub and crumpling up the paper.

Mrs. Haines chuckled as she shook her head. "The press has a way of finding him when he's out in public. That's why he likes to take vacations on remote islands and hidden beaches, though it's been a while since we've done either."

"Arcadia's been keeping you both pretty busy," Keenan observed.

"Yes, Franklin's been working day and night for a year and a half, mostly from home. He's less distracted that way."

"And what about you?"

"Arcadia is more my husband's work than mine. Franklin likes to handle most of the technical aspects himself, though he occasionally will call me in to consult on the design elements."

"Like those cherry blossoms," Keenan said.

Katherine smiled. "A little dramatic, especially for a casino, I'll admit."

"Is that the kind of work your stepbrother was looking for?"

Mrs. Haines smiled coyly. "So I see you've worked out that my husband's 'greatest rival' and I are related."

"Are you and Dr. Glassner close?"

Katherine nodded. "We became good friends. Our parents started dating when we were in college. Both of us took great amusement in how ... adorable our parents were. My father had been through a messy divorce a few years prior, and Glassner's mother was widowed, yet they both fell in love like they were teenagers. It was oddly ... refreshing."

"So you've kept in touch even after his falling-out with your husband?"

"Franklin and Robert are both idealists in their own way. It's what attracted them to each other as friends. It hurt everyone when their partnership broke. It can be hard to hold onto friends as you go higher in business, and I didn't want to lose the friendship I had in Robert. Maybe some part of me wanted to keep him in our lives so that he and Frank could reconcile, but the last few days make that seem unlikely."

"And he was set to meet you at the Athenaeum?"

She nodded. "Robert's expanding the library caverns below the island. He wanted to run some ideas by me for transparent lighting in the cave ceiling. Candles down there are a little dim."

"Caverns?"

She nodded. "Next time you're there you'll have to ask him for the grand tour. It really is quite extraordinary."

The three of them stopped for a moment at the Broad Street Bridge, turning to lean against the concrete railing. The heavy food had finally settled in Garfunkel's stomach, and he was content to lay his head down on his paws and stare at the seagulls. Katherine's eyes were closed, enjoying the cool breeze. It was peaceful, quiet, and a little too cozy for Keenan standing next to a married woman. He decided to change the subject.

"It must be nice having your husband work from home most of the time."

Katherine Haines looked at him with her piercing green eyes. "You're not much of a gamer yourself, are you, Detective Keenan?"

"Not really, though from what I've seen, Surreality is hardly a game."

"Indeed. My husband enjoys fully immersing himself in that world. He got one of those Oculus Rift things recently, sees the whole of Surreality through glasses and noise-canceling headphones. He says it's like he's really there."

Keenan squirmed a little uncomfortably at the thought of his trench-coat-wearing detective being up close and personal with Franklin Haines. The distance afforded by a screen and the third-person perspective made the outfit seem less ridiculous.

"Have you ever tried the Rift?"

Katherine shook her head. "I prefer to spend only as much time in Surreality as I have to. I'll often take my work out here, sitting with a netbook in the open air. The last thing I want is a computer that ties me to one place."

"If you feel that way—"

"Then why am I a programmer in the first place?" Mrs. Haines laughed as she finished his question. "I like using logic to solve real-world problems, something computers are very good at. But most of all, I like to create art, to explore the ways in which the beauty of this world can be simplified into an equation or an algorithm."

"But doesn't it take something away from beauty to boil it down to a sequence of numbers?"

Katherine shook her head. "On the contrary, it shows that the world is organized, that it isn't all random. True randomness is nothing but a blur of noise. It takes order for something to be truly beautiful."

"I never thought about it that way," Keenan said.

"Most people don't. Some people think it takes away from the miracle of life for it to have been designed, programmed. I disagree. Randomness is chaos, and chaos without order leads to entropy, decay, and nothingness. Even Surreality has wonders that transcend the equations that govern it."

So far those "wonders" seemed to be a snarky intelligence algorithm and a fanciful brothel.

"It doesn't look all that different from anywhere else to me," Keenan said. "People gamble, drink, hook up, and get murdered, just like the real world. Not much of an escape."

Garfunkel barked at a seagull that'd landed within what he considered his territory. Katherine leaned down to pat his head. "You have a very happy dog, Detective."

"That's because he's well fed," Keenan said.

She looked up at Keenan. "I doubt it. Love takes more than being well provided for." Mrs. Haines looked at her watch and picked herself off the ground. "Sadly, I have to be going. Was there anything else you needed?"

Keenan shook his head. "Not unless you can remember anything else about the attack last night."

Katherine frowned. "All I remember is being knocked down when Franklin jumped in front of me. I didn't see anything until it was all over. I'm sorry there isn't more."

"That's all right. We'll find this guy."

"I'm sure you will. Thank you both for the nice walk."

"Our pleasure."

She smiled, turned to leave, then paused and turned back to say, "If you enjoy choral music, there's a performance at the Palace Theatre tomorrow evening. You're welcome to join me if you'd like. Franklin hasn't left the house since the shooting, and I hate to go alone."

Keenan was not particularly keen on choral music, or any music performed in a theater for that matter. The idea of sitting in tiny chairs for hours on end just listening . . .

"That's a very generous invitation, but I really should be working on the—"

"Splendid," Katherine said, ignoring him. "I'll send your secretary the details."

Keenan groaned inwardly. "I look forward to it."

He spent an extra few seconds watching her leave, then shook his head. He looked down at Garfunkel, who wagged his tail, evidently ready for the return trip. Keenan scowled playfully. "You're just happy you don't have to go the theater."

Loud chimes emanated from his coat pocket, a sound he wasn't used to hearing even when he was on regular duty. His work cell was an older flip phone that he held onto despite his fellow officers' repeated attempts to get him to replace it. The last thing a guy like Keenan needed was a "smart phone" or a data plan. He was just surprised he'd actually charged the damn thing.

"Enjoying your walk?" The now-familiar sound of Synthia's voice blared from the other end of the line. "Nice café you took the lady to. You really know how to show a girl a good time. I know a great little fish and chips stand if you're interested, or I hear Schmidt's has a cart."

"Hey, don't knock a Bahama Mama till you've tried one. And are you tracking me or something?"

"I set up the appointment, remember? And there's no way they would have let you bring Garfunkel into 229."

"He's better company than you. Did you call for a reason?"

"I hear you're going to the opera. I was just calling to express my sympathies."

"You don't like opera either?"

"Too ordered. I spend a lot of my day being a set of equations. I like things that are more raw and emotional, like Perry Como."

Keenan wondered if that was Synthia's creator's cruel idea of a joke, or if she'd determined her own tastes.

"Anyway," she continued, "I'll rent you a suit."

"I own a suit," Keenan said, indignant.

"No you don't, at least not one fit to be seen next to Katherine Haines."

"I'm hanging up now."

"That's fine. Just thought you might want to know that Caliente's waiting back at your apartment. She said something about drinking all your beer."

"You know, a good secretary would have led with that."

"'Partner,' Hayes, and don't you forget it."

• • •

On the way home, Keenan swung Garfunkel through Goodale Park since the patient bulldog had gone a while without a decent tree. Usually at this time of day the park was filled with groups playing ultimate Frisbee or taking a walk by the pond, but that day it seemed strangely empty. As they sidled up to one of the trees in Garfunkel's domain, the only other person they saw was a young man sitting on a bench with a tablet.

The young man seemed absorbed in what he was working on, to the exclusion of the sights and sounds around him. Curious, Keenan allowed the sniffing Garfunkel to tug him closer to the man, hoping to catch a glimpse of whatever commanded his attention. Upon examination, Keenan saw with startling clarity the world he'd been thrust into for the past few days.

The man was moving around a virtual representation of the park, though on the screen he flew above the trees. *I didn't know you could fly*, Keenan thought. The young man looked up, having finally noticed Keenan's attention, and gave him a look that communicated displeasure at the disruption. Keenan smiled quickly and nodded toward the dog, before finding somewhere else interesting for Garfunkel to sniff.

The two were exhausted by the time they turned up Keenan's street, so much so that he'd nearly collapsed through the door before he heard the cheery sound from above.

"About time you got back," Caliente said, getting up from her deck chair and leaning over the side of the railing. "Got anything in your fridge besides Yeungling?"

Garfunkel was tugging at his leash to get inside, so Keenan cracked open the door and let the bulldog run loose while he talked to Caliente from the street. "My guard dog will be with you in a minute. Who let you in, anyway?"

"Your super. He has a better fridge than you." She dangled a couple of lemon berry shandies over the railing.

Keenan wrinkled his nose. "You drink anything straight and bitter like the rest of us?"

"If you don't want one . . ."

"Aren't you on duty right now?"

"Just came off the same thirty-six hours you have. Taking a little relax and recharge before I'm on again. Care to join?"

Keenan walked into the apartment, turned a corner, and walked up the steps to the porch. Caliente handed him the bottle and he took a grateful swig. Truthfully, anything was refreshing after breathing High Street air for a couple hours.

"At least this isn't the plain lemon stuff," Keenan said. "That stuff tastes like Pine-Sol."

Caliente grimaced. "Do you have a basis for comparison?"

"Not one of my prouder moments, Sonya. Let's just leave it at that."

"For now," she said after taking a longer swig, "but if there's a story to that, I want to hear it someday."

"Some things are best left a mystery."

"I'll bet Daily knows," Caliente said, her eyes flashing with mischief, then turning serious. "Are you feeling okay?"

"It's just been a little while since I pulled hours like this."

"Not since the Sinclair case," Caliente said.

"It's not like that. Maybe I'm not as young as I used to be."

"Bullshit," she said. "You're as old as I am, and I'm practically a teenager."

"I'd forgotten," Keenan replied.

"Well you'd better remember." She put the bottle down on the hardwood. Garfunkel took a few steps over to it and sniffed before turning his nose up and heading back to his master. "But I'm not talking about that. The other night, behind the Athenaeum, you looked like you'd seen a ghost."

"I didn't give that security guard enough credit. Running up and down all those stairs can be very tiring."

"Something makes me think our shooter didn't think so, and neither did you. Listen, you don't have to tell me, but Daily's worried about you."

"Tom's always worried about me. He thinks I've been a bachelor too long."

"Cut the crap, Dan. I'm your partner, remember, and I can read between the lines as well as the next gal. I'm not sure Tom felt you were up to this case before, but it's even worse now that it's become a matter of life and death."

"And a matter for the press," Keenan added.

Caliente nodded. "I know you're up to this. But at some point you're going to have to convince Tom and the deputy chief of that."

"So what would you do?"

She looked at him hard. "I'd take the damn psych eval. I'd tell them about the dreams, because there are always dreams. And if you're still reliving the attack like you were in that alley, then I wouldn't say a word."

Keenan smiled and leaned back. Even without seeing him for two months, Sonya knew him better than anyone.

She wasn't wrong. Dreams were a natural part of processing the attack, and the shrink would be expecting them, would probably be suspicious if they weren't there. But what he'd felt in that alley was something else. A man with a clear conscience didn't hallucinate, didn't conjure up the ghost of the man he killed to torment himself. That's what they were all worried about, even Caliente. They were worried that he'd been emotionally compromised, that he'd been looking for an excuse to shoot Sinclair, and he'd just been lucky enough to be handed one.

They weren't wrong to be worried. He had those same thoughts.

"You're probably right, Sonya. Never been much for shrinks."

"Hell, neither have I," she said, knocking back the last of her drink. "Probably one of the reasons my marriage ended. My ex-husband used to talk about counseling, but I didn't think a counselor was going to tell me anything I didn't already know myself. It's not that hard to identify the problems in a marriage, but it's another thing entirely to fix them."

"You think it would have made a difference?" Keenan asked.

"Hell no," Caliente smiled. "The man was a prick. He was just looking for another way to build a case against me so he could take my children. Once I get my kids back, I hope to never see his sniveling face again."

"I'll drink to that."

CHAPTER TEN

"You sure take a gal to all the nice places, Hayes."

Synthia and Keenan were standing in the middle of Tux's reproduction of the island and Arcadia Hotel, just moments before its demise. The fowl hacker had dropped it off while Keenan finished beer number three with Caliente.

"You wanted to be more involved in the case, didn't you?"

Synthia raised an eyebrow. "Nice sentiment, but we both know I'm here because you can't make head nor tail of how to manipulate the environment."

"Isn't it enough that I need you?"

Synthia grumbled something under her breath that Keenan didn't quite hear. "What exactly are we doing here, anyway? Tux already gave you his report."

"Which so far hasn't resulted in us finding one of these Polos out in the real world, or any of the girls who were working for Ms. Klein."

"Okay, granted. But what do you think you can do that Tux can't?"

Keenan shrugged. "Call it force of habit. I'm used to looking at crime scenes myself, and I got this case in the first place because techies like Tux couldn't get anywhere with it."

The island on which Synthia and Keenan stood was barren. Keenan's coat blew around him as a light breeze worked its way across the land. The grass rustled softly underfoot as they walked. The air carried a sense of foreboding, though Keenan dismissed this as his imagination.

As they reached the middle of the island, a small platform appeared in front of Synthia. The console looked similar to a video mixer, and as she manipulated a couple of knobs, the clouds began to move faster, then people began to materialize.

"Bring them in at half speed, would you?" Keenan said.

"Of course," Synthia nodded.

The crowd was growing all around them. Keenan moved over to where Synthia was standing, narrowly avoiding a certain rude penguin on his way to the podium. "How does Surreality govern where people appear? With a crowd this size, some people are going to bump into each other."

Synthia gestured in front of her. "Each world has a couple of nodes where people appear by default, and they're used in a random rotation. Even then you can run into each other, but the underlying software makes the bump look as smooth as possible. You're bumped but not shoved, so usually you can just keep walking."

"And that's all code running in the background?"

Synthia nodded. "All part of the physics engine."

Keenan frowned. "What's that again?"

"Think about it like this. While we may bend them a little to allow for hovering and paper-thin structures, this world follows the same laws of physics as 'the real world.' Every interaction is governed by a common framework running in the background of every environment."

Keenan remembered Dr. Glassner saying something similar in their first interview. "This framework is something like hundreds of subroutines, right?"

"Right," Synthia agreed, "though the number of subroutines is actually several thousand. Each individual algorithm is developed over the course of months by a team of engineers. Some are built by Haines's company, and others from proprietary physics engines like Havok. There are frequent updates to add new features and fix bugs, and some algorithms even tweak themselves based on the emergent gameplay of users."

Keenan thought for a moment. "Tux said that you wouldn't have to be a master-class hacker, just someone with access to go undetected, though even then you'd still be tracked by dozens of programs."

"So all we have to do is figure out which programs the killer turned off, and which he couldn't. Easy peasy lemon squeezy." Synthia grinned mischievously.

"Ever the optimist, aren't we, Synthia?"

"I'm a realist, Hayes, a useful quality in a place built around fantasy."

The cherry blossoms had started to fall all around them. The effect was mesmerizing. Every petal fell seemingly at random, gleaming white before landing in place. Every detail seemed carefully orchestrated and yet organic, beauty for beauty's sake. Rather than feeling the effect wasted on something as mundane as a casino opening, Keenan felt it elevated the proceedings. Even though the crowd would only see this once, Katherine Haines had taken great care to put her own stamp on Arcadia.

And so had the killer.

"Remarkable, isn't it?" Synthia said, taking a moment to watch for herself.

"It is," Keenan agreed. "I would have thought a computer animation like this would look more artificial, more like a pattern, but each leaf seems to follow a random path to the ground."

Synthia shook her head. "Machines can't generate true randomness. What you're seeing is a very clever algorithm, most likely fractal-based."

"Fractal?"

"It's a repeating geometric pattern, governed by a simple set of equations but leading to great complexity with just a few iterations. The advantage is that calculating the position of the leaves is easy, and appears natural. Most things that look complex are cheats and can change with a small adjustment of variables. Watch this . . ."

Synthia reached up and took off her hair. Underneath was a perfectly smooth ovoid surface. She tossed the wig up into the air. It hovered a couple feet in front of her and began growing to several times its original size.

"See the individual hairs, Hayes? Each strand of hair is governed by a couple of sinusoidal equations." Anticipating Keenan's question, she clarified. "Curves. I adjust the shape of the curve by changing some of the numbers around."

A long equation in white appeared in front of her, and she flipped a couple of the variables up and down like tumblers. The hair began to wave as if blown by the wind, then to stretch and contract as if viewed in a funhouse mirror.

"The cherry blossoms are no different, just a little more complex," Synthia said, putting her hair back on. Looking at herself in her compact, she reached out to the equation and adjusted the numbers till her hair was back to normal.

"Is that a trick your creator built for you to show off at parties?"

"Sort of," Synthia replied. "I have an adaptive nature, which means I'm able to write my own software, and I have a limited ability to manipulate my own environment and appearance."

"So in other words, you made it up."

"I wouldn't be much use to you, or to myself for that matter, if I couldn't learn and adapt in the same ways you do. That's why my creator agreed to me working with you in the first place. He thought detective work would expand my capabilities in some interesting directions."

Their conversation was interrupted by the booming voice of Franklin Haines, slowed down but still exuberant as the simulation played forward.

"You want to learn about detective work? Let's see the murder," Keenan said. "Can you take out the audio and slow it to one-quarter speed?"

Synthia nodded and the scene slowed. Keenan walked up the stairs to the left, Synthia following a couple feet behind. Before they were even halfway up the stairs, the dancers appeared, one of their ample bosoms rendering just inches from Keenan's face. He dodged instinctively, but she just passed through him. Keenan turned and looked quizzically at Synthia.

"We're on a different layer than they are right now. They're being processed as ghost images while we have direct control over the environment."

"Could the hacker have done something similar?"

Synthia shook her head. "This is just a simulation, not the actual Surreality environment. I turned off the solid form of the characters so we could take any vantage point we liked, even buried in the uncanny valley of one of Klein's girls."

"Very funny," Keenan replied, taking the rest of the stairs two at a time. They stopped a few feet away from Haines in profile. He had just finished his speech and was taking a moment to look down at the crowd with satisfaction. Haines's smile looked flat and artificial, almost as if it had been painted on. Even as he smiled, the impressions of fingers were beginning to form around his throat. As Keenan and Synthia watched the simulation slowly move forward, the young CEO's face began to turn red, and he staggered forward.

"Freeze it here," Keenan said, leaning over the railing until he was facing Haines. "It looks like the killer was standing right in front of him. The placement of the fingers suggests the killer was reaching up."

"Quite a bit, since to stand there he'd be hovering about twenty feet off the ground," Synthia said, looking down.

"Well that's one rule of physics they broke," Keenan grinned.

"So what does this tell you, anyway? If they're hovering in the air, there's no telling how tall their avatar is in Surreality."

"Right," Keenan said, "forensics doesn't do us a lot of good in here, but there's one thing these finger impressions tell us. The killer looked Haines in the eye at the moment of death."

"That's an intimate position," Synthia mused, "personal even."

"And nothing like our Athenaeum shooter," Keenan observed.

"Maybe he could get closer to Haines in Surreality than he could in the real world," Synthia said. "He wouldn't have gotten out of that ballroom alive if he had just walked up to Haines and shot him."

And killing him with commands on a keyboard is really no different than killing from a distance, Keenan thought. He wasn't sure how to think about Haines's fake murder in relation to the real shooting. If he treated it like a theft, then it didn't make sense for the thief to come back and take potshots at Haines later. And why make a show of Haines's death at all? The added touch of strangling him must have been harder than just taking the money.

"You're right, but it still feels different somehow," Keenan said. "The killer here was meticulous, strangling Haines, stealing the money, and destroying Arcadia in one simultaneous stroke."

"And taking Ms. Klein. The Arcadia premiere was the last time anyone saw her," Synthia observed. "Someone had a message they wanted Haines to hear loud and clear."

"Can we find Klein and the new hires?" Keenan asked.

The crowd vanished with the exception of six young women scattered evenly throughout the crowd in groups of two, and Klein in the front row directly below the balcony. From Haines's vantage point, Keenan could understand why she would be in demand.

"I'd thought they'd be the dancers," Keenan said a little sheepishly.

"Those are just playthings, window dressing as it were," Synthia said. "They probably didn't have a dozen lines of dialogue between them."

Keenan pointed to the woman in the front row. "How many people would know this is Klein?"

"Her clientele is very select and she hardly leaves the dark net, so very few, I would think."

Though she doesn't exactly blend into the crowd, either, Keenan thought. "Are these girls the new hires?" he said, gesturing at the other women plucked out of the crowd.

Synthia nodded. "We've been able to trace all but these two," she said, pointing to two women standing about twenty feet back from Klein. "If they've logged back in, Tux hasn't been able to find them. The others live all over the country, so they don't fit well with our Athenaeum shooter or any accomplice."

"But they still could have taken Haines's money," Keenan said.

"Granted," Synthia said, "Tux said something about putting a trace on their bank accounts but didn't want to get into specifics."

Keenan frowned. "I'd expect not, since that kind of thing requires a federal warrant." He didn't really expect Tux to find anything, since these four girls had apparently reported back to Klein's establishment. There was a lot of paperwork and jurisdictional posturing involved in bringing the FBI into a case like this, which would be the last thing the CMPD or Keenan needed right now. Tux could at least let him know if it was worth the trouble.

"Let's see the other two from the beginning."

Synthia ran the simulation in reverse to right before they arrived on the island. It didn't occur to Keenan till the floor disappeared that this would result in them standing twenty feet in the air, and he threw out a hand in surprise. Instead of falling like a stone, however, they floated gently downward, Synthia chuckling to herself all the way down.

"You might have warned me," Keenan growled.

Synthia just grinned and pointed to the node where Klein and the missing women had first appeared. The three women walked in tight formation as the simulation ran forward again. Their faces were front the entire time, even as they occasionally sidestepped to avoid an invisible person in the crowd. A few rows back from the front, the two women stopped, and Klein kept walking until she was standing directly in front of Keenan.

"Can you add anyone in Ms. Klein's immediate vicinity?"

Two clean-cut men wearing simple but fashionable button-up shirts and khakis appeared on either side of Klein.

"Those two look like just about every other default avatar in Surreality," Synthia said.

"Those'll be Tux's Polos. He gave me their screen names but hasn't had any luck on tracing their home addresses. Take it back thirty seconds," Keenan said, "let's see where these two came from."

Klein was standing with the two missing women again. As they made their way to the front, one man joined alongside from the right, then the other stepped into place a few feet later. When the two women stopped, the two men and Ms. Klein walked together till they were all right up front. Everything was smooth, without anyone breaking stride.

"That didn't look quite as clear-cut as I would have hoped," Keenan said.

"What did you expect, these guys to pull out their guns and grab her?"

Keenan shook his head. "I guess not, but you'd think there'd be something indicating duress, even a misstep or a gesture."

This was the element of Surreality that kept Keenan the most off-balance. While at times people seemed to react just as they would in the real world, their expressions were completely hidden behind the mask of their avatar. There were no subtle body cues to pick up on, no hint that something was going wrong.

"What about after the attack?"

Klein and the two men stood attentively, watching Haines's speech and the casino appearing around them. Klein seemed to be placed so that Haines could easily see her, but she faced forward, avoiding his direct gaze. When the walls started to crack and rubble began to fall, the three ran out of the lobby as a unit, completely ignoring Haines's fate. Klein's girls attended to themselves, logging off instead of running for their employer. Klein and her escorts were gone a second later, winking out before a large chunk of rubble landed on top of them.

The scene froze again and Synthia walked up beside him. "Things get a bit fuzzier from here. The number of people logged in recording the scene drops off sharply at this point."

"She left with those two men, presumably unwillingly since no one has heard from her since, though it's hardly conclusive.

Haines and Klein don't even look at each other. If her capture or presence is supposed to be some kind of threat, he's playing it awfully cool."

"You could always ask Haines if he knew Klein was here," Synthia offered.

"The deputy chief's going to have me off the case soon enough without giving him any more help. 'Why am I digging into Haines's personal life when I should be trying to find the money?' or some other such malarkey. The thing of it is, he might be right. I only have Tux's word that Klein had something to do with Haines, and he was a little thin with the details."

"Why would Tux send you on a wild goose chase?" Synthia asked.

"If I can prove Haines was having an affair with Klein, then Tux will have ammunition he can use against Haines at his discretion. Same goes for the Polos; if it ever came out that Haines had taken money from them or was working with them on Arcadia in some other way, his career would be ruined."

"Something Dr. Glassner wouldn't be too sorry to see happen. *He* could be Tux for all we know." Synthia's eyes widened.

Keenan shook his head. "I doubt it. Glassner said he wasn't much of a hacker elite, and he doesn't seem like the kind of man who would get off on taking down corporations for hire. He genuinely seems principled, which probably explains why he's no longer at the top of the company."

"He could have hired Tuxedo."

"Possibly, or Tux may be acting in his own interests. Still, Tux is our best source for information at the moment. We just have to make sure he's giving us more than he's getting."

The two stood staring at the rock that moments ago had been Ms. Klein and the Polos. Synthia spoke first.

"Maybe Klein's leverage," she mused. "If Haines was having an affair with her, and if these Polos were tied up in her business, it might be a perfect way to get Haines to give them a piece of the action. Haines lets the Polos in on the Arcadia business, or his affair with Klein goes public. Abducting her might be as simple as protecting their interests, to prevent Haines from buying her off himself, or worse."

"Maybe." Keenan frowned. "But why would they blow up Arcadia then, if their money's in there too?"

"It could have been Haines himself, either to get out from the Polos' influence or as some kind of publicity stunt. The attack on Arcadia has made this little venture national news, instead of something confined to the Surreality forums. The murderer or thief or whatever we're calling them may have actually done him a favor."

"If that's true, the Polos aren't going to let Haines just walk away with his money and theirs. They'd send him a message."

"Like a real shooting?"

"Exactly."

"So all you have to do is find your shooter."

"Simple as that, eh?" Keenan grinned.

CHAPTER ELEVEN

Keenan's head was pounding. Or was it the door?

He peeled his cheek off the desk from where he'd fallen asleep. His ears were hot and red from the headphones, which were cocked at an odd angle. He tossed them off and stared at his front door, unsure what to make of the sounds behind it. Garfunkel had already padded up to the front of the apartment, and Keenan wondered, not for the first time, if he could train the dog to answer the door.

"Coming!" Keenan said as he got up.

He opened the door to find Caliente leaning against the doorjamb.

"I've been banging on your door for nearly five minutes. I was going to try flashing it next."

"What exactly would that accomplish?" Keenan asked.

"It would get your super's attention for starters."

"So . . . I should close the door and wait a couple more minutes?"

"Just let me in, *pendejo*."

Caliente walked into the apartment and fell down on the couch with a heavy thud.

"So what brings you barging in?" Keenan asked, shutting the door.

"Just making sure you come up for air once in a while. From the look of you, I'd say you were up all night."

Keenan turned around to look at the clock in the kitchen. He wouldn't have much of a case for yelling at Caliente for coming too early.

"I got some sleep, I'm just not too clear as to when or how much."

Caliente tossed him something, and Keenan reacted reflexively, having to bobble the object several times before getting a firm hold of it. He turned it over, still unable to discern what it was. It looked like a small plastic thermos.

"It's coffee," Caliente answered. "The latest in modern technology. Press the button on the bottom and it heats the contents to their proper scalding temperature."

"Thanks," Keenan said, pressing the button and feeling the can grow warmer. He popped the top, and a spray of steam nearly burnt his hand.

"See what I mean?"

Keenan took a sip, blowing several times to ensure he didn't burn anything else. The liquid tasted syrupy and sweet, nothing like coffee. "I don't know how you can drink this mocha stuff."

"That's white chocolate amaretto, actually," Caliente said, taking a deep sip of her own can. "Best way to start the day. Drink up, Dan. We've got someone to see."

Keenan took another small sip and winced as he burned the top of his mouth. "Who?"

Caliente smiled devilishly. "The roommate of our Athenaeum shooter."

"Partial finally got a hit?" Keenan said.

Caliente shook her head. "Not exactly. Our connection to the fingerprint databases must be the slowest in the state. Fortunately, the roommate called in a missing persons report. When one of the uniforms noticed this guy's description matched our shooter, we ran the prints on a lark and got our hit. It seems this kid never left his dorm room, even for classes."

"So who is he?"

"Michael Chaffin, a junior at your alma mater."

"He goes to OSU?"

Caliente nodded. "Studying journalism, if you'd believe it."

"Ohio State hasn't had a proper journalism department in years; they just rolled it into the School of Communication."

Caliente frowned. "I thought the school had a daily newspaper."

"About all that was ever good for was a cheap umbrella in the rain."

"Well, whatever the state of the paper, it might explain how he faked a press pass. We got a warrant to search Chaffin's dorm room based on the photos on the camera and the partial print."

Keenan whistled. "Judge Bryson was being nice to you."

"I'm not without my charms," Caliente said. "Chaffin lives in Canfield Hall on south campus. The roommate's meeting us there in about half an hour."

"Does he have any idea his friend is a person of interest for our banquet shooting?"

"I don't think so. I figured I'd leave that part up to you."

Keenan nodded. "News that your roommate is a murder suspect is always better in person."

He tried to chug down the rest of the sickly-sweet coffee, sticking his tongue out after barely two sips. Caliente laughed.

• • •

The drive to campus took about twenty minutes, most of the delays due to the number of cars parked in the street and the habit of most OSU students to walk into oncoming traffic without a second thought. Keenan had been tempted on more than one occasion to spend the afternoon writing jaywalking tickets, but generally thought better of it. Parking at least was ample, if you were willing to walk, the new South Campus Gateway having been built a few years after Keenan's time.

Canfield Hall was part of a circle of connected buildings at the intersection of Neil and 11th Avenue. Morrison Tower and Mack Hall flanked it on either side, with the women-only Fechko House sitting in front. It was difficult to tell from the street where one building ended and the next began. Across the street was the legendary Adriatico's Pizza, arguably the best on campus, though Keenan had always preferred "Fly Pie." The inviting smells from inside tempted Keenan to push back the interview, but breakfast would just have to wait.

Chaffin's room was on the third floor and was the only three-person suite in the building. Apparently the third roommate had dropped out after the first week of the semester, and housing hadn't found a replacement yet. It took several minutes of knocking before the door opened. The young man on the other side was thin, with greasy hair, a day's stubble, and dirt under his fingernails. The room smelled of alcohol and a few other fumes Keenan didn't recognize.

The young man smiled at Caliente, and Keenan cleared his throat. "We're with the Columbus Metropolitan Police Department. We're here about a missing persons report you filed."

"Oh good, I was beginning to think you guys weren't showing up," the young man said, still staring at Caliente.

"We're sorry if you've been kept waiting," Caliente replied. "This is Detective Keenan and I'm Detective Caliente."

He's going to say it, Keenan thought, *and I'm not responsible for what happens next.*

"Oh, *muy caliente.*" The young man hadn't quite grasped the fact that Sonya was carrying a gun.

But Caliente was never that predictable. "You're not so bad yourself. What's your name?"

"Steve," he replied, suddenly shy.

"Well, Steve, mind telling us which room is your friend's?"

"No problem." He gestured for them to come inside. The room was in a condition similar to its remaining occupant. Leftover bits of food and trash were scattered around the room. Ahead of them was the "common area," such as it was: a couple of chairs and a mini-fridge were its chief features. The cushions had been repaired multiple times with duct tape, and the two chairs had been shoved together to make a rudimentary couch, facing a TV probably picked up out of a dumpster. Keenan found himself comparing it to his apartment, particularly his last couple of months of bachelor living, though at least he had a better couch.

The larger room to the left was their host's room, making the one on the right Chaffin's. Also to the right was a small private bathroom, which the occupants must have been responsible for cleaning, given its current state. Keenan discreetly shut the door and walked toward the room on the right.

"That's his computer over there." The roommate gestured to a white tower sitting on a small desk. Caliente walked over to it and slid into the chair. She whistled as she examined the back of the case.

"What is it?"

"I think we've found a clunker older than yours, Dan."

"Very funny."

"I'm serious, this looks like a model from at least ten years ago. I'm not sure it'd even connect to the Net."

Keenan turned to Steve. "Do you have a computer yourself, maybe one you and your roommate shared?"

The kid shook his head. "Don't need them much, and if I do, I use the ones in the lab. I do paintings mostly."

He gestured behind him to his own room, where several canvases were stacked up, displaying views that could just as easily have resulted from dropping the paint can from three feet above the canvas. Open paint cans explained some of the fumes Keenan had noticed earlier.

"Very nice work." The kid grunted in appreciation as Keenan continued, "Have you ever heard of Surreality? Did your roommate ever talk about it?"

"Nah man, he wasn't a philosophy major, he was into journalism."

Caliente and Keenan exchanged looks as Keenan continued, "The one I mean is a game, one where you can live out an alternate reality and explore a virtual world."

"We don't have many games, though we have gotten some girls to come over for Twister before."

Keenan had a feeling this guy was huffing more than paint fumes. Caliente had moved on to going through dressers and closets, trying to find anything out of the ordinary. Chaffin didn't have much in the way of clothing, other than the typical assortment of T-shirts, khakis, and sandals. Caliente bagged one of the sandals for comparison with the shoe indentation on the door in the Athenaeum, while Keenan decided to try another tactic.

"You said your roommate didn't go to class much. Do you have any idea what he did most of the time?"

"I don't know, really. I spend a lot of time over at my girlfriend's apartment, but he must never leave 'cause he's always here when I get back."

Keenan didn't care to speculate what sort of girl might be attracted to a guy like this, though it was a little tempting. "What time do you usually get home?"

"Oh, pretty late at night. He's usually in bed then."

"So you'd say you're not really sure if this guy goes to class or not."

Steve looked down at the floor. "Guess not."

"Thanks, you've been very helpful," Keenan said, happy to let the kid go back to torturing his canvases. He walked over to Caliente to see if she was faring any better.

"What makes you think this kid was even using Surreality?" Caliente asked as Keenan sat down next to her.

Keenan shrugged. "If we think Chaffin is the same guy who attacked Haines at Arcadia, then he'd have to have some kind of access. Ditto if he was one of the Polos trying to send Haines a message by shooting up the banquet. Then again, he could just be some random nut."

"Well, he's not doing much with that old heap," Caliente gestured, "but I did find a card to one of the computer labs a few buildings from here. The card gives him twenty-four hour access, but it isn't his."

"Whose is it?"

"It's an old card," Caliente said, handing it to him, "must have been in and out of his wallet hundreds of times."

"I can read a first name, 'Diane' maybe," Keenan said, squinting.

"Diane's his ex," the roommate called from behind them. "The three of them are always hanging out together."

"Three?" Caliente asked.

"Diane and Jeannette, his current girlfriend."

"Any of these ladies have a last name?" Keenan asked.

"Um, not that I can remember."

Keenan doubted Steven even remembered his own last name. He turned to Caliente. "Find any pictures, anything that might give us a description besides our friend Picasso back there?"

Caliente shook her head. "The desk is clean. Most people are storing everything online these days anyway. His Facebook page is a dead end too. Anything of real value he's keeping hidden."

Keenan rubbed his chin. "They might be students, we can check with Admissions if you've got nothing else."

"Oh, I was saving the best for last." Caliente banged the top of the computer tower and slid the side panel off, laying it on the table. Taped to the inside was an envelope which Caliente removed and opened, spreading its contents over the desk.

Keenan whistled. "There must be at least five thousand dollars here."

The roommate's interest was suddenly piqued. "Michael never told me he had that kind of dough. He always made me pay for pizza."

"The nerve of some people," Caliente said, pulling out the warrant and handing it to Steve. "If we find him, I'll be sure he buys your next dozen pies."

While Steve reviewed the warrant, Keenan leaned over and whispered to Caliente, "I'm assuming he didn't have a job where he could earn this kind of cash legitimately."

Caliente shook her head. "No job, no grandmother dying and leaving him an inheritance, and no trace of this money in his bank account or credit cards."

She passed the money to Keenan, who readied an evidence bag. Keenan thumbed through the bills, all twenties, crisp like they were brand-new. He frowned as his eyes drifted toward the serial numbers.

"Sonya, look at this." Caliente leaned on his shoulder, her head only a few inches from his. "The bills are sequential, and brand-new. He must have had another account somewhere and gotten the money out in a hurry."

"Insurance? Payoff for somebody else?" Caliente offered.

"Maybe."

Their voices were lowered, as the roommate was not being too subtle about trying to listen in. Caliente tilted her head toward the door and Keenan nodded. As they were about to leave, Steve stopped them.

"Hey. Don't I know you from somewhere?"

Keenan didn't bother turning around. "Unless you're a seventh- or eighth-year senior, I doubt it."

"No, weren't you on the news or something?"

Shit, Keenan thought, *somebody spotted me at the Athenaeum after all.*

"Aren't you the cop who killed that guy?"

Caliente reeled but Keenan put a hand on her shoulder. He turned around calmly. "I believe you're mistaken."

"Yeah, I recognize you. You took down that bastard who kicked in his wife's face."

"She wasn't his wife—" Keenan started, then thought better of it. "We have to be going."

"It's a bum rap you being put on suspension, bet you're glad to be back."

Keenan's voice was flat. "Thanks, I am."

"I'd've stepped on his throat, or chopped off his nuts or something. That kind of scum doesn't deserve to walk this earth."

Keenan wondered if Steve's violent reaction would extend to Chaffin if he turned out to be their banquet shooter. "Trust me kid, you wouldn't have."

"You don't think so, huh? You don't think I'm tough enough? I'd make the bastard beg for mercy. Is that what you did, make the guy remember what he'd done before you sent him to hell?"

Keenan stared coldly into the kid's eyes. His ears were buzzing from blood, and his vision was narrowing. In the back of his head he heard that laughter again, like this was all so damn funny. Finally he answered.

"No."

He turned abruptly, bumping into Caliente as he stormed down the hallway. He was all the way onto the street before she caught up to him.

"Hey, I thought we were getting a slice," Caliente said.

Keenan's voice was still flat. "Not hungry."

Caliente stepped in front of him. "Since when does a good detective not have room for pizza? Did that kid get to you?"

"No," Keenan growled. "Drop it, Sonya."

Caliente squared her shoulders and crossed her arms. "No. I'm tired of watching you beat yourself up. Thought I'd take a turn."

"Oh?" Keenan's lip curled in a half smirk.

"Hell yeah, like where do you get off not telling me you'd found that Sinclair bastard?"

"You'd been pulled onto another case."

"Bullshit. You and I started that case together. I saw what that creep did to that poor young woman, same as you. What, were you afraid if I came along there'd have been twelve bullets in his chest instead of six?"

Keenan was silent for a while. "No sense ruining two cops' perfectly good careers."

Caliente shook her head. "I could've taken care of myself. Hell, we could have taken care of each other. But you didn't give me the chance."

"I'm sorry."

"What is it about this case that's messing you up so much, anyway? Is it that you shot a man, or that it kept you out of action for so long?"

"I'm not really sure, Sonya," Keenan said, shifting his weight from one foot to the other.

"That's okay. Just remember who your friends are."

She kissed him lightly on the cheek, then patted the other with her right hand.

"Now how about that slice?"

• • •

An hour and a half later he was back in Surreality, standing outside the amphitheater on Alexandria Island. He'd arrived home to find his dog waiting impatiently for food. Caliente's abrupt appearance had thrown off the morning routine. Fortunately Goody's was open, and he was able to apologize to Garfunkel in proper fashion with a couple strips of bacon and an English muffin. Admissions had been closed for the weekend, so Caliente was going back to the station to check the online databases for Chaffin's two friends.

The pit of his stomach was acid—from the sickly sweet coffee or from slice number three, he wasn't sure. He contemplated brewing a proper pot, but his stomach had turned against him, so he opted instead for a clear soda and the healing action of carbonation. Garfunkel had rebounded and was now full of energy, which unfortunately would have to go unspent for the moment.

Once back in Surreality, he'd passed on the names of Chaffin's associates to Tuxedo, who said he'd try to have something for him by the end of the day. This left Keenan little to do besides check in with Glassner, and see if anyone who'd seen him take a swan dive off the tower had returned to Alexandria. At the moment he was regretting that decision.

"I think the toga is a bit much."

He'd brought Synthia along so she could interview witnesses while he poked around. She'd been delighted at the prospect, and had switched to the toga before Keenan could turn around. *In a place where you can change clothes instantly, I guess there's no need for modesty.* The outfit wasn't particularly historically accurate; it revealed more of Synthia's bare shoulder and legs than was customary.

"Spill something in your lap, Hayes, or can't you keep your eyes off me?"

Keenan said nothing, but moved his avatar to look off to the side. A number of people were gathering in the small teaching theater. Glassner had mentioned to Keenan that he gave several of these seminars a week to the researchers and academics who chose to gather in Alexandria. Some were students, some came to debate high-minded ideas, and some came only to see what all the fuss was about. Synthia made a quick scan of the crowd. "It looks like most of the people who were around for Glassner's face-plant are here now."

"I don't suppose we can get him to dismiss class early."

Glassner was standing on a rock in the center of the theater, which at his current height would have brought him up to Keenan's shoulders. As he was speaking, most of the crowd were taking careful notes, though Keenan wondered if their real selves were paying attention.

"We live at the dawn of the next age of human interaction. Social networking has advanced to the point that we are friends with everyone. We all have a voice, whether it is a blog, a tweet, or a six-second Vine. We are freer to make ourselves heard than ever before, to build our online platforms to promote ourselves.

Even Surreality was created out of our deep desire to be connected and to express ourselves. Our forum is everywhere, and the potential for discourse is beyond anything Aristotle or Socrates could have dreamed.

"And how do we use this potential? To create memes.

"We celebrate the banal, or the humorous. When we do engage with the deeper issues of society, we shout past each other, giving voice to our most extreme opinions without hearing what others are saying. There is a digital dark age coming, my friends, but it is not one in which our technology will fail us. Rather, we will fail ourselves. Our voices will grow louder even as we have less and less to say. We will cease to be. We will merely exist.

"That is why we are here. There is so much left to be said, so much more to be discovered. And the words of our past must be cherished again. It is my hope that this library, and those who study here, will not sink into the sea or burn in a fire like its namesake, but will shine as a beacon for a future that consists of more than #YOLO."

There was muted laughter, and Keenan rolled his eyes. "Laying it on a little thick, isn't he?" he whispered to Synthia.

"He said yellow wrong."

"What?" Keenan asked.

"Nothing. Shhh."

Glassner continued. "We are dedicated not only to the preservation of the past, but the creation of the future. For all of the advancements we have made as a species, we have not answered the most fundamental of questions. Why are we alive? Why do we have a mind that asks such questions? And what will happen to us when we die? I know that among you, and those that will follow, are the people who will help us to begin to answer those vital questions.

"I am not saying that we should shun technology; after all, I helped create this world in which we have all gathered. I merely mean that technology should serve us, not we it. Our time is something we give away at far below its fair market value. I only ask for a small piece of that time, and I ask you to use it to think or to research or to dream."

Glassner rose from his stone, and the students began to shuffle out of the amphitheater. Many winked out immediately, and Keenan hoped that none of those were the witnesses he'd sat through the speech to interview. The rest were moving toward the main library and the surrounding buildings. Looking around, Glassner saw Keenan and began walking toward him.

"Great," Keenan whispered.

"Relax, Hayes. I've got you covered. I have a list of people we need to talk to, and I can get started on that while you and Dr. Glassner chat."

"No Synthia, wait!" Keenan whispered sharply, but she was already gone.

"Detective Keenan. Good to see you again."

Keenan turned to see Glassner standing behind him. "And you as well, Dr. Glassner. I see you've chosen to maintain your original appearance."

Glassner chuckled, something Keenan hadn't been sure the man was capable of. "I was living in my own kind of fantasy world. I just had a harsh reminder of that, and it's one I intend to take to heart." The two began following the line of students. "Since you're here, why don't we take a tour of the rest of the library?"

"Your sister mentioned something about a cavern," Keenan offered.

"Indeed—another of my sister's proud accomplishments—one that must be seen to be believed."

Keenan gave way to the inevitable. "Lead the way."

They stood on another clear disc, and Keenan braced himself as the platform dropped and the sky disappeared. He was surrounded by solid rock, with no discernible light source. The screen adjusted, and soon he was able to make out his surroundings more clearly. Glassner chuckled again.

"As you can see, the tower is only the tip of the iceberg, so to speak. We are descending into the main archives of the library."

The view expanded, and the disc carried them down into a cavernous room. The chamber was vast, its diameter stretching the whole length of the island, and it descended hundreds of feet below. The floors were organized in a rough lattice, with gaps in the floors that showed the stories below. Shelves lined every path of the lattice, filled with books of every shape and size. Long rolling ladders traveled the shelves to help reach the highest content.

The room was lit by thousands of small orbs that lined the paths and the ends of each shelf, giving off a warm glow, like candlelight. The ceiling emulated the lattice structure of the floor, with panes of crystal between dark metal frames.

"This is the greatest repository of knowledge in human history. Everything from hundreds of libraries has been scanned and stored here, with more being added every day. We've already carved into the rock beneath this island several times, and we're due for another expansion if everything keeps pace."

Keenan looked around as they continued to descend. "It's all very impressive, but why have the room at all? Isn't this all stored in a database somewhere?"

"Actually dozens of databases, across three datacenters, but you're right. This could all be distilled down to a single terminal, but where would be the pleasure in walking through the stacks, knowing that you're surrounded by the knowledge of countless ages? As we go deeper we also go older, like an ice core. We've already traveled more than a thousand years into the past. Below us we have representations of ancient papyrus, stone tablets, and placeholders for books lost in the original fire of Alexandria; titles we only know about from brief references in surviving texts."

Glassner laughed again. "I'm sorry, Detective. It's been my habit of late to give speeches. How did you like my talk this afternoon?"

"It was very . . . interesting."

"Very diplomatic, but I'm not so easily bruised. What do you really think?"

"I think you're right that people seem to be spending more time on social media and less time being social. But wouldn't the best response to that be to encourage them to spend more time in the real world, and less in the virtual?"

"In an ideal world perhaps, but we must meet the people where they are. Technology is not inherently bad for us, just some of the things we do with it. I'm merely trying to show people the ways in which technology can take them away from what really matters, and to help them refocus on what does."

"And hopefully raise some funds in the process," Keenan said. "Maybe get a couple of your students to contribute to your Kickstarter campaign."

"It's true, my 'death and rebirth' has put some things into perspective. We're hungry again, but I think in the long run that will keep us from becoming complacent."

The lift stopped and Glassner stepped out onto the lattice floor. "Come here a moment, there's something I want to show you."

Keenan stepped off the disc and was surprised to find dirt instead of crystal between the walkways of the floor. He was at the bottom of the library, further evidenced by the dim light. All the shelves had a layer of dust. Keenan reached out to touch one, and was surprised to see a thin layer of gray film transferred to his fingers. The dust faded away after a few seconds, which was just as well since Keenan had no idea how to wipe his avatar's hands.

He rounded a corner and saw Glassner standing in front of a shelf that held twelve clay tablets.

"This is the oldest part of the library, and contains one of our first acquisitions. These tablets are replicas of the Epic of Gilgamesh, dating back to the seventh century BC. The story itself may be an untold amount older. Go ahead, touch them."

Keenan moved his avatar forward to pick up the first of the tablets. His character had some difficulty lifting it at first, but he was soon able to see the writing clearly, the indentations of the letters casting small shadows on the tablet. He reached to place it back, but misjudged the shelf, and the tablet dropped to the floor, shattering into a hundred pieces. He cursed, but Glassner only laughed.

"Relax, it's only one of the oldest relics in human history. We've still got eleven of them." He gestured with his hand, and the shattered pieces rose from the floor and reassembled on the shelf. "It scares the hell out of the new students."

"Indeed," Keenan nodded. "I think I'll go and check on how my partner's doing. Thanks for the tour."

"My pleasure, Detective."

Keenan moved back to the disc, which rose toward the surface, stopping abruptly as it punched through the ground. Keenan's eyes took a moment to adjust to the brightness of the sunlight, or the change in contrast on his screen, anyway. He stepped out into the courtyard and pulled out the pink phone Synthia had given him.

"For a detective, you're not very observant," said a voice from behind.

Keenan turned and saw Synthia, toga replaced with a London Fog trench coat and a cigarette burning between her teeth. Her eyes danced from beneath a gray fedora, and instead of a compact she held a notebook. The trench coat cut higher than Keenan's, ending two inches above the knee.

"Not bad, Synth."

"Thought you might get a kick out of it," she said, cigarette bouncing between her teeth. "I talked to the students. Big fat zero there. Nobody saw anybody, not even each other. Turns out, few of them are even cleared to go near Glassner's office."

"That wouldn't have stopped whoever tore that tower open with a can opener."

"You're right, but it doesn't do us a lot of good. I did find something interesting, though. Apparently Glassner had a private meeting in his office with a woman a couple of days after the Arcadia incident."

"Couldn't it have been one of the students?"

Synthia shook her head. "They always meet Glassner in the amphitheater or one of the classrooms. The only people besides Glassner who go up to his office are the staff, and she wasn't one of them."

"Get a description?"

"Nope. Nobody saw her up close, and she hasn't been back since."

"That sure gives us a lot to go on."

"What? Now you go back down and ask Glassner who the woman was."

Keenan thought for a moment. "Let's hold off on that. Just talking to someone new is hardly a reason to grill him. I'd like to see what we can find out on our own. Feel like going back to the office, toots?

"Whatever you say, dick."

"That's Private Dick."

CHAPTER TWELVE

By the time they got back to the office it was late afternoon. Synthia hung her new trench coat up beside her desk, then resumed her perch at its edge. She cocked her head to the side for a moment, then picked up her notebook.

"Katherine Haines's office called several times while we were out."

"Damn. I forgot that was tonight," Keenan said.

"That's why you have me, Hayes. Everything's already arranged. Your tickets are available at the box office, and the show will be starting in about ninety minutes. Your tux is ready, and the rental place is only a couple of blocks from the theater, so you should be able to manage on foot, but I'd get going if I were you. Traffic downtown this time of night can be a bear."

Keenan was about to protest when Synthia interrupted him.

"All the instructions have been e-mailed to you, including how to properly assemble your tuxedo in time for your date."

"It's not a da—" The screen clicked off and Keenan cursed again. Evidently Synthia had the ability to log him off if she liked. With an effort he dragged himself in front of his closet. Garfunkel looked up at Keenan as he threw on a clean undershirt and white dress shirt, and jumped into black socks. "Sorry buddy, but I don't think she rented a suit for you."

Keenan printed out Synthia's directions and headed for the door. The statehouse would be as good a place as any to hide the old jalopy, but it would be filling up quickly on a weekend with shows. Fortunately, the place Synthia had chosen to rent the tux from had everything ready, including the shoes he'd forgotten to bring, and a more appropriate shirt. He'd had difficulty finding the order till he realized his secretary had put it in under his screen name, "Coleman Hayes."

He changed in his car and considered it mildly impressive when he arrived only twenty minutes late. It had started raining as soon as he stepped out of the garage, the collar of his coat providing little protection from the chill. Several times he had to jump backward as fast-moving cars kicked up a wall of water that threatened to ruin any positive effect the tux might have. He ran across Broad Street, though the smooth soles of his dress shoes made the pavement more like an ice rink.

The Palace Theatre was located at the base of the LeVeque Tower, with a long row of clear glass doors facing the street, underneath a large marquee announcing the venue's name in red. Directly ahead was a double set of red-carpeted marble stairs curving outward at both ends into the building's shared lobby. Keenan checked his soggy coat and walked up the stairs.

Before a show, the long hallway would be filled with a crush of people, but now it felt all too conspicuously empty. The curved neoclassical ceiling high above made the room feel even more cavernous, though the Palace was considerably smaller than the Ohio Theatre a couple of blocks away.

Another set of stairs and a turn to the left brought him to the mezzanine level. Even in the darkened theater, Keenan could see the high dome above them, latticed like the middle of a sunflower, and patterned so that it was difficult to tell exactly how deep the dome was. The hall was a sharp contrast to where he'd first met Katherine Haines, and even though he'd been here occasionally when he was growing up, he felt out of place. He wondered for probably the tenth time exactly why she'd asked him to come. He was even less sure why he'd agreed.

From the mezzanine he could step down into Katherine Haines's box via a narrow walkway on his left. He had a feeling the ushers were about to tell him he was in the wrong place, but they let him pass with only a slightly disapproving stare. At the bottom of the narrow hallway was a pair of scarlet curtains leading into Haines's box. Another usher handed Keenan a libretto, which he pocketed, doubting very much he'd be able to follow the words anyway. The usher parted the curtains silently, and closed them swiftly behind Keenan as soon as he'd passed through.

Haines's box was uncomfortably prominent, hanging just in front of stage right. Personally, he didn't understand why you'd pay more to watch the show from the extreme left rather than the center, but he supposed that wasn't the point. Katherine Haines was alone, save for a bottle of Cabernet and two glasses. She wore a crimson dress with her shoulders bare. The dress would have nearly touched the floor if she had been standing, but it was cut up the side to reveal a generous amount of thigh. Her hair was pulled up, and a thin diamond necklace hung from her neck. Her skin was pale and glowed under the low light.

Keenan looked longer than he should have without saying anything, but when she turned and smiled she met his eyes directly.

"Good evening, Detective. That tuxedo suits you."

"Thanks." Keenan considered commenting on her dress, but had a feeling she already knew what he thought of it. He was becoming aware of how high above the floor they were. It felt like he was standing on the edge of a cliff. He felt exposed, even though the box was dark.

She offered him a glass of wine, but he declined, doubting that alcohol would lessen his anxiety at the moment.

The music had yet to begin, the curtain only starting to rise as Keenan sat down. The chorus was small and stood silent for several minutes. Suddenly the room was filled with sound. Keenan had been expecting an orchestra, but the chorus produced enough sound for a group three times their size. The hall felt designed just for them, as the notes breathed in the room after each pause.

Mrs. Haines sat forward in her seat, head tilted toward the audience. Keenan thought he could see tension that eased as the music began. The piece was soft and sad, and he could not recognize the language. The melodies were smooth and subtle, the chorus savoring every note. He wondered if Mrs. Haines had always loved music, or if it had been a passion she'd acquired along with her husband's fortunes. The effect it had on her temperament seemed to indicate it was more than a recent interest.

"My husband used to take me here, one of the trappings of his life that didn't take long to get used to." She took a sip from her glass.

"Your husband enjoys this kind of music?" Keenan said, grateful she had spoken since he had no idea where to break in. The music seemed to continue forever, one movement blending into the next.

She nodded. "We both studied music in college, though not as our primary focus. A lot of computer scientists and programmers take music, actually. It helps to have something that forces your mind to think in a different way. When we began seeing each other, he would take me here often, though back then we couldn't afford these seats."

"And lately?"

"Not as often, but he doesn't mind when I go by myself."

"If you don't mind my saying so, I was half expecting your office to call and cancel."

She took another sip. "Is that what most people do when they go through something traumatic, sit at home where it's safe? Maybe Frank would rather I be home, but all I'd do there is think about the benefit. Here I can relax and forget about everything. Is that so surprising?"

"I guess not. Has your husband said anything else about the case?"

"He's not terribly pleased with you."

Keenan chuckled. No surprise there. "What do you think?"

"I think he'd hate whoever took the case. But he doesn't really mean it. It's just hard having to rely on someone else to solve your own problems."

They were quiet and listened for a couple more minutes until Keenan asked, "What sort of piece is this?"

"It's fairly modern, but from an ancient East Orthodox tradition. It's a canon, a series of prayers to God, repenting our sins and asking for his grace. Most composers, including this one, leave out the second ode from the canon."

"Why's that?"

"It contains Moses's rebuke of the Israelites, and doesn't paint God in the most merciful of lights. Sometimes God forgives our sins, and sometimes he punishes us."

"Some sins deserve to be punished," Keenan replied flatly.

"Not a surprising view, considering your profession. Is that the way you feel about the man you shot?"

Keenan's heart stopped.

"I'm sorry," Mrs. Haines said quickly. "I don't mean to be so personal."

"It's all right," Keenan said. "Cops don't go into a situation like that thinking it will end in a man's death. I didn't plan to shoot Sinclair in that alley. It's just what happened."

"But still, isn't it justice that a man who could do a thing so evil is dead?"

Yes, Keenan thought. Out loud he said, "I don't answer those questions. It's up to the courts to decide what justice is. I just enforce the law."

The music had grown softer; the low bass of the men crying out to God sent a chill down Keenan's spine. The women sounded like they were weeping, their voices strong but on the verge of breaking. The sound drove away all thought, all attempts at conversation, demanding the heart of the listener. Keenan observed Katherine, who had turned toward the chorus, her eyes closed and her breathing slowed.

"I don't know how anyone could mistreat something so beautiful," Keenan said.

Mrs. Haines turned, Keenan realizing he'd said that out loud. He wasn't sure if he'd been talking about the woman Sinclair had beaten, or the woman sitting uncomfortably close.

"Beauty is just another possession, Detective. Given time, anything is disposable." She met his gaze as if studying him. "But not to you."

It took his cheek several seconds to register the kiss, his brain several more to process it. It didn't feel like Caliente's friendly kiss of encouragement. This carried warmth and lingering sensation even after she'd leaned back in her chair.

"You're a good man, Mr. Keenan, the right one for this case, of that I am sure."

Keenan suddenly really needed that drink, but not here. "I have some work back at the station. I really should be going."

"You're leaving?" she said, sounding disappointed.

For my own safety.

"I'm afraid so. We're getting close on our shooter, and I need to see if anything came in. I'll let you both know as soon as I find out anything."

"Thank you for all your help."

Keenan nodded quickly and practically ran back up the stairs. His face felt warm, and he was grateful for the rain as he stepped outside.

. . .

Keenan didn't feel like going home, but there weren't many places he felt like going in a tux. At night the police station would be quieter, meaning he could slip into regular clothes without too much commentary on his current outfit. More importantly, he planned to retrieve the bottle of Jack Daniels that was hopefully still stashed in his desk, assuming Daily or Caliente hadn't nicked it.

He was kicking himself for leaving so abruptly, while at the same time feeling relieved. If he was lucky, there'd be no official reason he'd ever have to see her again. His arm carried the lingering memory of something soft and warm pressed against it. It had been a long time since he'd been close to a beautiful woman, able to take in her smell, her soft breath. Not since . . .

Keenan shook his head. There was no sense thinking about that now. A drink, or three, would set him straight.

The station was dark, but a few of the offices showed a glow under the doors, probably a few of the techs running an analysis or playing D&D or something. The officer out front gave him a thumbs-up. "Good to see you back, Detective."

Keenan smiled politely, then ducked into the bullpen. Daily was out, as were most of the other detectives. His locker—with clean, or at least different, clothes—was in the lounge. He could see a light from underneath and he quietly swore to himself. He didn't really want to talk to anyone, but the damp tux was starting to feel heavy and uncomfortable. He opened the door.

"You will please keep your hands on top of the desk. I intend to search your office."

"This is a pretty good movie, Dan, though why Bogart doesn't hit him again I don't understand," Caliente said, a bag of microwave popcorn lying in her lap. She looked him over in the tux. "You look sexy. How was your date?"

"It wasn't a date." Keenan threw his jacket over a chair.

"That's not what the lipstick on your cheek says," Caliente said, tossing another piece of popcorn in the air and catching it in her mouth.

Keenan instinctively wiped at his cheek while Caliente laughed.

"She kissed you? I was just kidding around."

Keenan glared at her. "Not funny, Sonya. I'd appreciate it if you didn't spread that information around. I wouldn't want it to be misunderstood."

"No need to get defensive, Dan. I've been spending a lot of this year being celibate against my will. I know the feeling."

"That's not it."

"Whatever you say, my lips are sealed. Now what am I sealing them about?"

Keenan sighed. "It wasn't a big deal. She was just expressing her gratitude for my hard work on the case."

"You? You've hardly done everything!" Caliente scoffed playfully. "I'm expecting some full-on *besos* for all the hours I've put in."

"I'll see what I can do. What are you still doing at the station?"

"Going over the illustrious record of the young Michael Chaffin. We checked all his university accounts, but they've been wiped clean. No web history and nothing in his personal cloud. E-mail box was empty too, but the university was able to give me a backup of the last couple of months. I've been poring over those with no luck for the last few hours, and decided I needed a break before I got back into them. Plus, I don't know if I've ever actually seen this movie."

"You're kidding, right? This is one of the greatest crime movies of all time."

"Not surprising coming from someone who runs around in a trench coat and fedora."

"That's beside the point. Bogart's the kind of investigator we all wish we could be, someone who busts down doors and knocks people around till he gets the answers."

"And all the women would leave their husbands for him."

"His partner's wife at least waited till her husband was dead."

"Flimsy example, since it's obvious she loved him long before that."

"What's your point, Caliente?"

She tossed a couple pieces of popcorn at him. "Who needs a point, it's just fun to rile you up."

He grumbled and tossed the popcorn back at her.

"So what are you doing here, anyway?" Caliente asked.

By way of answer Keenan slipped out to his desk, returning to the break room with the bottle of Jack Daniels. There were no glasses, and Keenan was hesitant to drink whiskey out of a plastic cup, but beggars couldn't be choosers. He grabbed two cups and poured out a couple of shots.

"As good a reason as any," Caliente replied. The two raised their glasses and knocked the shots back. Caliente pounded her chest as her head came back down. "That does not mix well with popcorn. How are you feeling?"

"Fine. Remind me to chase this with Pepto or I'll have heartburn for hours."

"I like a man who can handle his whiskey. Feel like finishing this movie with me?"

"Sure, I could use a refresher course."

He grabbed a handful of popcorn, which Caliente playfully tried to swat out of his hand. He scooted his chair alongside hers and pulled his bow tie apart.

"And don't give away the ending."

"Wouldn't dream of it," Keenan said as he leaned back.

• • •

Keenan awoke with a shooting pain in his neck. His body felt clammy and he realized he was still wearing the tuxedo, which was looking a little worse for wear, between getting rained on and being his pajamas. He didn't remember when Caliente had left—or whether he'd made a conscious decision to sleep at the office. He rubbed his neck and staggered to his feet, his thighs stiff and raw from sitting in a hard chair all night.

Fortunately, after a fresh change of clothes, he was able to feel almost human. He hung up the tuxedo, hoping that most of his sins would be covered up by a good ironing, and walked out in search of coffee. It was early in the morning and the sun had barely begun shining through the windows, but the office was already a blur of activity. He made his way to the lab, where he knew they brewed the good stuff, and found Caliente leaning over a computer with two technicians sitting on opposite sides.

"Morning, sleepyhead. You didn't give away the ending but you nearly snored through it."

The technicians stifled a laugh and Keenan grunted, reaching for the pot and a Styrofoam cup. "Morning yourself, Caliente. What brings you to the land of Middle-earth?"

"Finding Chaffin's alter ego."

"So he does have a Surreality account?"

Caliente smiled. "Yep. We're walking in his shoes right now."

"How?"

One of the technicians answered, "From the SD card in his camera."

"Wasn't that blank?"

"We thought so too, but it turns out he had a hidden partition. We didn't spot it at first since he was using a 32-gigabyte card, and the amount of storage varies from manufacturer to manufacturer."

"English, please," Keenan said, hoping his first sip was making his mind sharper.

Caliente answered, "It's typical marketing, like when you buy a bag of chips that's mostly air."

The technicians grimaced at this. "Actually, it's because the manufacturer redefines what a gigabyte is."

Keenan put a hand on his shoulder. "I liked hers better. What does it mean for our case?"

"Because of the gap, your guy was able to hide a portable version of the Surreality program in what we thought was nonexistent memory. It was only when we compared it to another SD card of the same brand that we noticed the difference in size. Fortunately the partition wasn't encrypted, probably because he wanted to be able to easily use the card on different computers, so we were able to restore it to visible memory."

Keenan leaned in next to Caliente and looked at the screen. They were walking down the streets of Surreal-City near the park.

The screen passed in front of a small downtown bar, then shifted as they stepped through a portal onto the shores of Arcadia.

"We're building a list of known associates and a movement history, but there's a couple you're gonna be interested in right now."

Two windows popped up next to Chaffin's avatar, showing virtual headshots of two attractive young women.

"Look familiar?"

Keenan put his cup down next to the monitor. "Those two look a lot like Ms. Klein's missing girls."

"How much you want to bet these are Chaffin's friends, Diane and Jeannette?" Caliente said.

Keenan slugged down the rest of his coffee. "Let me have a copy of that card. I'll have Tux take a look at it, see what else he can find."

"Tux?" Caliente asked.

"Oh, he's just this penguin I know."

The technicians exchanged an amused look, then logged out of the account and transferred the contents of the SD card to a CD. Keenan grunted a brief thanks and left. Caliente followed and caught up alongside.

"What are you going to do?" Caliente asked.

"For the moment, breakfast. Care to join me?"

"Can't. I've got another appointment with the lawyer this morning, trying to undo some of the damage from my ex-husband and that *culero* judge."

"Any luck?"

Caliente shook her head. "Not really. I've seen my girls maybe three times in the last two months. Visitation is on a fixed schedule, and you know how this job is. On paper it looks like equal custody, but the reality is anything but."

"Anything you need?"

"Other than a promotion and a schedule that doesn't change week-to-week?"

"Best I can offer is dinner."

Caliente grinned. "Fair enough. But someplace you can't get one of those Reubens. The smell of sauerkraut makes me sick."

Keenan laughed. "Fine. I was feeling more Italian anyway."

"So what are you doing with that?" Caliente said, pointing to the disc.

Keenan smiled conspiratorially. "If Chaffin's in hiding, he probably won't risk going directly to these girls' homes. He'd need to schedule a meet somewhere, meaning Diane and Jeannette are probably waiting for him to contact them in Surreality."

"You're assuming he isn't already holed up with one of them."

"It's possible. He certainly had an accomplice to help him get away from the Athenaeum, but my guess is they split up afterward. Chaffin would know he couldn't go back to the dorm room, so he'd need someone else to get the money he stashed."

"So you're going to use Chaffin's account to schedule a meet with the girls in Surreality?"

Keenan shrugged. "It's a bit of a long shot, but it might work."

"You've had worse ideas," Caliente said.

"That's what I like about you, Sonya; you're such a positive thinker."

CHAPTER THIRTEEN

Keenan spent most of the afternoon working with Tux transferring Chaffin's avatar to Keenan's account. Tux had rigged a quick-switch button so Keenan could revert to his Hayes appearance if things got dicey. Evidently this involved some significant recoding of Surreality's account management functions, which Tux explained in great detail. After a while Keenan learned he could just lean back and sip his coffee with the volume on his headphones turned down while Tux rambled on.

Chaffin didn't have that much in terms of wardrobe for his avatar. The suit Keenan finally selected made him look like some kind of gigolo, a rumpled sport jacket with the shirt open halfway down his chest. Still, it wasn't like the tuxedo had done him any good either. The meeting was set for that evening at seven thirty p.m. Ms. Klein's was holding a cabaret show, put on by no less than Ms. Klein herself. The general public was unaware of her disappearance, allowing her to continue to perform with a different girl at the controls.

As he approached the villa, he noticed the distinct lack of guards. Security was now being managed by a few cameras discreetly hidden throughout the building. He passed through the doors without difficulty, and was taken aback by the scene in front of him.

The room had not been restored to its previous state; rather, it had been transformed into a club reminiscent of the Roaring Twenties. The chandelier was gone, replaced by soft lighting on either side of the hallway. The hostess was dressed the same as before and did not appear pleased to see him. She moved out from behind her podium and pressed up against him as if he were a preferred customer, but she spoke in a low whisper with words that were less than welcoming.

"I thought I told you not to come back here."

So, Chaffin was a known quantity at Klein's, Keenan thought. *Not surprising, considering his girlfriend and his ex worked here.*

"Relax, it's me," Keenan said. He tapped the control Tux had rigged for him, briefly flashing his own avatar before returning to Chaffin's shape.

"You!" The hostess didn't seem pleased to see either of the faces he wore. "Last time you were here, you scared away half my clientele. I was only able to get the rest back by throwing this little shindig."

"Too bad they're not getting the real thing."

"Yeah, and they better not find out about it from you, honey."

"I don't want any trouble. I'm just here to watch the show."

"Wearing somebody else's skin," the hostess said, tilting her head.

"Maybe I'm just kinky," Keenan offered.

"You gonna watch, you gotta pay." After swiping his credit chit she softened. "You got any special requests?"

"Depends, does the girl playing Ms. Klein know 'Stormy Weather'?"

The hostess smiled. "I'll see what I can do."

Keenan walked to the left and passed through the curtained opening. Several rooms had been merged together to create an elaborate jazz hall, complete with bar and stage. It was dark, the only light coming from tiny candles on each table and a spotlight focused on a lone microphone. A women walked up, pulled the mic to her, and began to sing.

Her dress was thin and gauzy, wrapping around her body, covering most, but allowing her skin and shape to shine through. Her hair was in black curls, and her skin looked painted blue. Keenan imagined the effect would have looked more detailed if he'd ever bothered to install the hardware Tom had given him.

The music was not jazz, but closer to the electronic music he'd heard at the Source. So far this had been the music of choice in the places he'd visited, and he wondered if it was the common music of the world, or whether Surreality had the same variety of music as anywhere. The sound seemed too polished to be live, but the manipulation of the avatar was a talented performance. Throughout the song, a ghostly afterimage of the singer would appear in the crowd and sing the backup, enticing customers before disappearing and moving across the room to the next person.

As he observed this, the singer appeared in front of him. She walked forward as if to embrace him, singing a couple of bars before vanishing again to encircle two men at a far table.

He breathed out, feeling goose bumps forming on his arm, and grabbed a corner table. Another hostess, this one wearing a light purple skirt and little else, sat down in Keenan's lap and asked if he would like a drink or anything else she could offer. He accepted the drink, hoping Tux's patches to his avatar would keep his character relatively sober.

Looking around the room, he remembered what Synthia had told him about avatar gender. Many men chose to play as women, and vice versa. The other tables were a fairly diverse mix of both, though Klein's employees were all women, at least in appearance. Life in the Short North was certainly an education in all forms of gender identity, but there was a certain elegance to Surreality's approach. You could just be whatever you wanted, and it would be automatically accepted.

His view finally fell to a table off to the left of the stage, behind a large grand piano that sounded like a synthesizer. Two women were seated at the table, a blonde and a tall redhead, both wearing sleeveless gowns with strips of material crossing their breasts. The redhead met his gaze, then stood up, her friend following soon after. The two weaved their way through the crowd, brushing against Keenan before walking through the exit.

He threw a couple of surs on the table and followed the two women at a discreet distance. As he stepped out of the lounge, he was surprised to find the two women were gone. The hostess spotted him and nodded to a room across the hall.

Passing through the curtain, Keenan found himself in a small room with two beds. Braided lamps hung from the ceiling and lit the silk beds in soft red light. The sheets themselves seemed to have higher thread count than pixel count. The curtain closed and took on the appearance of a fourth wall, sealing off the room from the rest of the villa.

As soon as the wall was sealed off, the two girls hugged him. Fortunately, they were too pleased to see him, or Chaffin's avatar anyway, to notice that Keenan did not hug them back. The gesture had saved him the trouble of figuring out a way to make direct contact with the women's avatars. Another one of Tux's modifications that he'd taken great pains to explain was a little infiltrator program—transferred through avatar contact—that was now tracing the girls' real-world locations. Tux had offered some suggestions on "fun" ways to plant the virus, which Keenan thankfully did not now have to consider.

"So where's Michael?" the redhead said, breaking her embrace. "'Cause he wouldn't be caught dead in that outfit."

Keenan had to think fast. "He thought it was too dangerous to come himself, so he sent me in his place."

The redhead sat down on one of the beds, leaning back and crossing her legs. "Nice try, but you don't sound like that drug-addled roommate of his, and Michael doesn't have any other friends. Not anymore."

Damn. Keenan thought. *That didn't last long.*

He pressed the toggle switch and donned his Hayes appearance.

"Who are you?" the blonde asked.

"He's a cop," the other girl said, "with a bit of a forties fetish."

"I'm Detective Daniel Keenan of the CMPD. We're looking for Michael as a person of interest in a shooting a couple of nights ago."

"The Athenaeum," the blonde said. "I heard about that. Do you think Michael's involved?"

"I'm not sure. That's why we need to find him, something I was hoping the two of you could help me with."

"Why should we help you?" the redhead said. "We can log out anytime this conversation gets boring and you'd never find us."

A message popped up in the right of Keenan's screen. Tux's tracer did quick work.

"I'm afraid you're wrong about that, Jeannette. I have your credit card information, your home address, and where you are logging in from. Are you at least on the second story of the Mickey-Dee's on campus? A family restaurant is no place to be logging in to a club like this."

Unsurprisingly, Jeannette had no qualms about swearing in a public place either.

"Yeah, I'd be kind of mad at me too. But the truth is I just want to help you."

Part of Keenan admired the skill with which Jeannette's avatar gave him the raspberry. Not just the articulation of the spread fingers, but the movement of the lips in a toot-tooting shape. Evidently her answer was "Thanks but no thanks." Her avatar disappeared a moment later.

"I suppose you'll want to leave too?" he said, turning to Diane.

She shook her head. "I don't know where Michael is. Jeannette's the one who's been helping him."

"Helping him with what?"

Diane turned away from him and walked toward one of the lamps. She twirled one of the hanging braids absently.

"He's her boyfriend now. Michael's one of those 'Polos.' I think Jeannette might be too."

"Where's Ms. Klein?"

Diane looked confused. "She's onstage."

"The woman pretending to be her is very good, but there's nothing quite like the original. Ms. Klein was with you and Jeannette right before she disappeared, at Franklin Haines's Arcadia opening. Then, a few weeks later, your ex-boyfriend decides to shoot up one of Haines's benefits."

"I don't know anything about that. All Jeannette asked me to do was help her hand off Ms. Klein to a couple of her associates at the premiere, but she never told me why."

"If you had to venture a guess?"

"Michael told me the Polos invested heavily in Haines's casino. I think taking Ms. Klein was a way to protect their investment."

Keenan nodded. "Then Arcadia crumbled to the ground, along with all its assets. When Haines's money disappeared, so did the Polos'."

"I think Michael was supposed to send Haines a message to get the money back. I didn't know he was going to kill those people." He could tell she was crying, even though her avatar's face was blank and expressionless.

"I work in a call center, hardly a glamorous job," she continued in between sniffles. "Michael offered me more than I could make in a year to help them. I didn't see what the harm was in kidnapping someone's avatar anyway."

If the Polos had anybody of Tux's skill, then capturing Klein's avatar may just have been a way to get her location in the real world. He wasn't sure what kind of leverage she bought them, over Haines or otherwise, but without knowing who she was in the real world, he was unlikely to find her.

"I understand," Keenan said.

"So what happens now?"

"Is there any way you can get in touch with Michael?"

She shook her head. "Jeannette's probably already told him you found us. He's not going to take my call."

She might be right, but Chaffin would want to know what she told Keenan, and take the opportunity to tie up any loose ends.

"I need you to try," Keenan said gently. "Ask him to meet in a public place. We'll have a protective detail on you, so you'll have nothing to worry about."

She twirled the braid of the lamp again. "What about me?"

"I hate paperwork," Keenan said. "You help me find Michael, and I think we can leave all of this in the imaginary world."

Her avatar smiled. "Deal."

• • •

Keenan rolled off the couch, landing on the floor with a loud thud. He groaned at the rude awakening and pulled himself onto his hands and knees. He turned his head to the right and heard three loud pops in succession. Garfunkel's panting face met his a moment later, and he closed his eyes as the dog licked his nose. He crawled back into a sitting position, Garfunkel jumping beside him. He began to scratch behind the dog's ears while rubbing his own neck.

Daily had called, wanting to catch breakfast again, and it occurred to Dan that he still didn't have any real food in the apartment. He fed Garfunkel what little edible food was left, then walked down the hall and onto the street.

The air was humid, summer's last hurrah apparently, and made Keenan feel even more in need of a shower. His hair was unkempt and did not improve much as he ran his fingers through it. Living virtually the last couple of days had distracted him from his usual regimens of shaving—or brushing his teeth, he noticed as he breathed into his hand.

Keenan walked to the diner, though 'shuffled' might have been a more accurate term. Tom had sounded cheerful, which Keenan never appreciated in the morning. He didn't get to cheerful until after cup number three, on good days.

He'd requested a couple of undercovers to keep an eye on Diane, though he'd had a devil of a time justifying why he wasn't bringing her in as a material witness. As soon as he walked her down to the station, she was useless in luring Chaffin, at least on their terms. In her apartment with everything as usual, they might stand a chance of getting him to come out of hiding.

Keenan pushed these thoughts aside as he stumbled through the diner doors.

"Morning, Dan. Sleep on the couch again?" Tom shouted from the counter.

"I hate having to wash my sheets," Keenan growled and slid in next to him.

"So how's the case?" Tom asked.

"Coffee first," Keenan replied. Fortunately, the waitresses here knew him well and already were pouring him a cup. "Leave the pot." The waitress smiled at the old joke, as Keenan took a long sip that warmed his chest.

"So how is it going?"

"Slowly. So far I've got two virtual murders and thefts, two more shot in the Athenaeum, and a missing virtual escort."

"They must've skipped you to the advanced level. Did you say two murders?"

Keenan nodded. "Dr. Glassner was attacked a few days ago. Same MO, mostly, at least so far as Alexandria's funds being drained."

"Alexandria?"

"Long story."

"Do you think it's the same suspect?" Tom asked.

"I don't know." Keenan rubbed his temples. "Haines's death had an audience, and for that matter, so did the attack at the Athenaeum. Glassner was killed in private, no witnesses."

"Do you think Glassner's trying to throw you off his scent for attacking Haines?"

"Maybe," Keenan mused. "But I don't think so. There are so many threads to this case, I'm having a hard time seeing all the connections."

"I'm sure you will," Tom said. "By the way, your tuxedo is still hanging in your locker at the station. You might want to air it out before returning it."

Keenan's response was interrupted by the woman behind the counter asking for their orders. Tom ordered a short stack, while

Keenan asked for sausage, eggs, and grapefruit. The waitress refilled both cups of coffee and Tom blew on the fresh cup.

"Listen, Dan, you been feeling okay?"

"Aside from a stiff neck and a red face, I feel pretty good. Why d'you ask?"

"Nothing, forget it."

"C'mon, what's up?"

"I said it's nothing. Drink your coffee."

The waitress set their plates down in front of them, and Tom poked at the stack of pancakes with his fork before pouring the syrup. Keenan played with his eggs for a moment, then turned to Tom. "You sure there's nothing bothering you?"

Tom sighed and put down his fork.

"I got asked again about you today. You still haven't done your psych evaluation."

"Oh, is that all?" Keenan said flatly.

"This isn't just bureaucratic nonsense, Dan. You've got to talk out the shooting with someone."

Keenan took a sip of his coffee. "Didn't know we were calling it a shooting now."

"Poor choice of words, I'm sorry, but the sessions are important."

"A shrink's not going to tell me anything I don't already know," Keenan said.

Except maybe why he kept seeing Sinclair around corners and in dreams.

Tom shrugged. "How would you know? You've never been to one."

"Why do they have you doing this anyway, Tom?" Keenan said. "You think I need therapy?"

"I never said that," Tom replied. "But this was different than a regular case. You fired your weapon six times into the same suspect. I think it wouldn't hurt to talk out why."

"You weren't there. You don't know." Keenan took a bite of his eggs.

"Whose fault is that, huh? You never asked. Not Caliente and certainly not me."

"You would have just tried to talk me out of it."

"Out of what exactly, Dan?"

Keenan lowered his head. "Never mind."

"No, I think I know what this is about. You wanted Sinclair to confront you in that alley. You wanted to take him down."

Keenan dropped his fork on his plate with a loud clatter. "And what if I did?"

"We're not vigilantes, Dan. You don't get to run around like some noir detective in the real world."

"Lucky for you, I'm not playing in the real world anymore."

Tom sighed. "I want you back in the real world, but the only way that'll happen is if you really work this thing through."

Keenan pointed with his fork at Tom's chest. "Sinclair got what he deserved. I'm sorry you don't see it that way. And I won't let some shrink, the deputy chief, or you tell me any different."

"I was giving you the space to deal with this on your own, Dan. Apparently that was a mistake."

"Yeah, sure was. God, if only I'd listened to you sooner."

"Y'know what, Dan? Go fuck yourself."

"Same to you, buddy," Keenan said, taking another bite of eggs.

Tom left his seat and stormed out the diner doors. Some of the other patrons in the diner looked in Keenan's direction, but he ignored them. He waited a couple of minutes, then tossed a twenty on the counter, boxed up his breakfast and Tom's pancakes, and walked through the doors. He half expected to see Tom waiting outside, but he was nowhere to be seen.

Keenan's feet wouldn't take him back to the apartment. He needed fresh air and to hear the world without headphones. The argument in the diner had been building for the last few months, ever since Tom had found him in that alley.

Tom was the first on scene, first to see Keenan standing in the rain, his gun hanging loosely from his hand. Tom's gun was drawn, having expected to find Keenan in trouble, wounded or worse. Instead he found the suspect dead, his blood pooling on the pavement, a deranged grin forever etched on his face. Tom had put his hand on Keenan's shoulder. Younger officers would take care of the body, gather up shell casings and what little evidence managed to survive the rain.

To the cops running to catch up, even to Tom, it had sounded like six shots in succession, but Keenan knew the truth. There'd been an instant, after the first two shots, when Sinclair was still standing with two smoking holes in his chest. He hadn't even begun to bleed and he'd looked right into Keenan's eyes before Keenan's last four bullets took him down.

He didn't even know where the alley had been, and this bothered him. The alley represented a part of him that could be around any corner. His episode at the Athenaeum had certainly proved that. Keenan didn't want to see that part of him again, but there was no way of knowing which alleys he'd have to go down.

The park had no dark corners, and somehow his wandering feet had carried him there. The leaves rustled under a light breeze, the humidity of the morning succumbing to the charms of fall. He breathed deeply of the smell of leaves and of crisp air. Garfunkel would have been jealous if he'd known, but Keenan was glad for a little time alone. He wondered how often

Katherine Haines was alone, at the opera or even in her own home.

He was still unsettled, less about the kiss—which had probably been just a friendly gesture—and more about his own attraction. He told himself it had just been a long time, and the last one had ended so badly. Even if he had feelings for Katherine, there was no way to act on them, not without jeopardizing his career.

It might be worth it.

Keenan wasn't sure how long his cell phone had been ringing before he heard it. He was surprised it was even in his pocket. Caliente's voice was serious.

"We found Jeannette, but somebody got to her first."

CHAPTER FOURTEEN

The address was only about a ten-minute walk from the park, so Keenan decided to go on foot. The girl's apartment was a good deal nicer than his own, close as it was to downtown, definitely more than a typical OSU student would have been able to afford. Officers were waiting at the door to lead Keenan up. He pulled a couple of sausages out of his breakfast, then gave the rest to one of the uniforms.

Jeannette Beverly was a brunette, not a redhead. She was slumped against the wall of her apartment, a clean bullet hole in the middle of her forehead. Across the room on a coffee table was her laptop with her avatar still logged in. Her avatar was asleep, apparently having been inactive for some time.

Caliente stood up from her crouch beside the body and walked over to Keenan. "You think Chaffin did this?"

Keenan shook his head. "It's possible, but I doubt she would have been his target. She is his girlfriend, after all."

"Maybe they had a bit of a domestic. Lousy way to lose an argument. The medical examiner's had a quick look here and puts time of death sometime between two and four a.m."

"That's only an hour or so after I talked with her." Keenan knelt beside the body as Caliente tossed him a pair of gloves. He gently leaned Jeannette forward to examine the wall behind her. The wall was mostly clear except for a fine mist of blood. There was no exit wound on the back of her head.

"Must've been a small-caliber bullet, probably from over there," he said as he gestured to the coffee table.

"Not exactly Chaffin's MO," Caliente observed.

"Maybe, or maybe he believes in different tools for different jobs. I'm not seeing any sign of a struggle. Whoever did this was either a professional or someone Jeannette trusted."

"She definitely trusted Chaffin. There are pictures of him all around the bedroom. They actually made quite a cute couple, if you leave off the identity theft and homicide."

Keenan stood up and moved to her couch, which the team had covered in plastic.

"Here, use this." Caliente tossed him a roll-up keyboard, which he plugged into one of the laptop's USB ports. As crimes involving computers increased, detectives had started carrying their own peripherals to cope with different interfaces and to avoid tampering with evidence. Keenan had a bit of a hard time getting used to the keys but soon found himself able to move the camera around the Surreality environment. Synthia had been teaching him how to move in both first- and third-person view, and this helped him to take a panorama of the place where Jeannette's avatar had been left.

He recognized Ms. Klein's villa almost immediately. In fact it looked like the avatar's body had been left in the same room where he'd questioned her. On a closer examination, he could see a small bullet hole in the character's forehead in the exact same place Jeannette had been shot. Keenan logged her off after forwarding her character data to Tux. He wasn't sure if leaving her at Klein's place was intended as a threat or plain intimidation, but this was something Klein's hostess didn't need to see.

He turned to see the young woman being zipped into a body bag. It was all such a waste. This girl had thrown her life away for nothing, and someone had been more than happy to see that she did. He suspected that Klein's kidnapping was related to the attacks on Haines, but so far all of his witnesses were turning up dead.

Caliente put a hand on his shoulder. "It's not your fault, you know. You tried to reach out to her and she turned you away. She got herself into this mess."

Keenan nodded. "I know. But did all of this start because of some game?"

"C'mon, Dan, we already know this is more than just a game."

"This girl died because she got caught by a virtual detective."

Caliente grinned. "I'd hardly call you a virtual detective. More of a cheap imitation."

"Thanks, Sonya. Wanna grab coffee later?"

"I thought you promised me dinner."

"Coffee and food are not mutually exclusive. I want to go over anything forensics gets from the scene and whatever Tux might turn up."

"Fine. Maybe later your avatar and mine could take a tour of some of the more interesting corners of Surreality. I've always wanted to see you in a fedora."

· · ·

Keenan returned to his apartment with the bare necessities: Captain Crunch, frozen pizza, and IBC root beer. Garfunkel greeted him energetically while Keenan heated up the pizza. He took two slices, ate one, and tossed the crust to the dog. He set the other one down beside his keyboard and logged back into his Surreality office.

Keenan had asked Diane back at Ms. Klein's to meet him in the Surreal-City park in the morning. He would rather tell her about Jeannette in person, but that might tip off Chaffin if he was watching Diane's real-world apartment. Entering the park, he picked up a newspaper so as to try and look inconspicuous, but his lack of knowledge of the controls hindered that appearance. He finally ditched the thing and sat next to the girl on a bench looking out toward a small pond.

"She's dead, isn't she?" Diane asked when he sat down.

Keenan nodded. "We found her this morning in her apartment, and at Ms. Klein's."

"Is the same thing going to happen to me?"

Keenan shook his head. "We'll keep you safe, I promise."

"What about Ms. Klein?" she asked.

"We still don't know if the Polos nabbed her in real life or just her avatar," Keenan replied. "But I'm sure she's okay. We'll do everything we can to find her."

The girl looked out toward the trees. "I didn't really know Jeannette well. She and Michael had only been dating the last couple of months. Michael and I used to be together, about a year ago, but we hadn't really talked until he mentioned the Klein job."

"Is that when you gave him your keycard?"

She shook her head. "No, that was a year ago. He's been mixed up in the Polos for a while, buying a few drinks with a stolen credit card, nothing major. But then he started to want to move up the ranks. He was starting to scare me, and I wanted out."

"What brought you back?"

"A year's a long time, and money was getting tight. I still love Michael, you know, even though he was hers. I thought I cared about the bad things he did, but the truth is I would've done anything to get him back."

"And now?"

She propped her arms along the top of the bench and tilted her head back. "Well, Jeannette's death gives us more of an excuse to meet, right? I'm scared of what might happen to me, and I'm scared of being dragged in by the cops. Maybe I'm calling him so he'll talk me out of turning myself in for protection. He's a decent guy; he might try to save me."

Unless he killed Jeannette, Keenan thought.

"We'll take him in peacefully. We just want to talk to him. Your helping us may save his life," Keenan said.

"I hope so. Thanks."

Keenan rose from the bench and was about to walk away when he turned back to face Diane. "Just one more thing. Did you or your friend by chance talk to a man named Glassner?"

She thought for a moment, then shook her head. "I don't think I know who that is."

"That's all right, just curious. I'll let you know when I find anything."

The girl nodded her thanks, then winked out of sight. As if on cue, Keenan's pink daisy cell phone rang.

"That's quite a story she told you," Synthia said. "You really believe she didn't know what she was getting herself into?"

"I really wish you'd stop spying on me."

"All part of the job. I just wanted to make sure you weren't late for your flying lesson."

"Excuse me?" Keenan asked, not remembering scheduling that particular appointment.

"Maybe your partner is just trying to prepare you for any situation that might arise in Surreality."

"This wouldn't have anything to do with wanting to see me fall on my butt, would it?"

Synthia's voice was the portrait of innocence. "Perish the thought, Hayes."

• • •

Keenan had been curious about flight ever since he saw the young man in Goodale Park flying above Surreal-City on his tablet. Keenan had assumed flight might be a purchased feature, since most of the people he saw moving around Surreality just walked. Apparently, activating flight mode was just a simple matter of flipping one of the menu options at the bottom of his screen. He wondered why more people didn't fly if it was so easy, if for nothing else than to avoid foot traffic or to get a better view of the city.

Synthia had suggested he start in the middle of the city. Keenan wasn't sure if the added obstacle of the buildings would really be helpful in learning, but Synthia had somehow convinced him he needed the points of reference. He toggled the flight control, and in a matter of seconds he was hovering in place about ten feet off the ground. Keenan pressed up and was immediately met with a face full of pavement. A voice rang in his ear from Synthia, who'd evidently dispensed with the construct of the phone to talk to him. "Flight controls, Hayes. That means down is up and up is down."

"Right. Of course," Keenan said, his voice muffled.

Synthia stifled a laugh and Keenan brushed himself off. He kicked off again and began a slow controlled ascent, hugging close to the building in front of him. The building was subdivided into zones, with the first being a busy shopping center, then office spaces which were virtually deserted, and finally a detailed three-story restaurant at the top. Each level had balcony seating and offered an impressive view of the city, which stretched for miles.

Keenan attempted to stop but continued to accelerate upward until he was about a hundred feet above the building. The image on his screen began to shake, and at first he thought he was slowing down. What he actually was doing was bumping up against the sky, like a fly trapped under a dome. He wondered if the rest of these environments were similarly limited. Surreality was not a cohesive world, after all, but rather a collection of islands in a vast digital ocean. Space was at a premium, even if it could be infinitely created. Haines's company charged rent for every piece of virtual real estate, corresponding to portions of hard drives in server racks. The island Arcadia was built on was prime real estate, connected as it was to Surreal-City.

Bumping into the ceiling was making him disoriented. He turned and managed to accelerate downward and land on the restaurant's second level. Actually, land was a charitable word, but he was pleased with the fact he'd only knocked over a table, two chairs, and an umbrella. An annoyed waiter moved toward him almost immediately and, with a snap of his fingers, set the table to rights.

"You can't just land here; you'll have to pay thirty surs like the rest of the customers."

Keenan noticed a message in the bottom left of his screen showing his account had already been deducted the thirty surs. He sighed and addressed the waiter. "That's a neat trick you did with the tables. Why let them be knocked over at all, though?"

The waiter didn't particularly seem in the mood to talk, but he at least answered the question. "You can't expect the physics of a particular area of a world to be different than the rest of that area."

"Because the graphics engine isn't designed to handle multiple rules in the same environment."

"I suppose, sir. Were you planning on ordering anything?"

"No thanks." Keenan looked over the edge of the balcony. He thought about jumping down, but the thought didn't sit well. "Uh, which way to the elevator?"

"Straight back and to the left. Feel free to drop in anytime," the waiter said as he began running a rag over the table.

The elevator cost another thirty surs and followed the outside line of the building, facing Arcadia. Most of the debris of the island had been cleared, and scaffolding was in place where parts of the walls were being restored. What would have taken months to recover from in the real world was being rebuilt in a matter of days.

The doors opened into the lobby, and he walked back to the street. He stopped when he began to feel a tugging at his leg in real life. Garfunkel had gotten up and was pulling on Keenan's jeans. Keenan tapped the dog on the top of the head. "Not now, boy."

The dog continued to tug.

"Can I help you?" Keenan leaned around into the kitchen and looked for obvious problems like a lack of food or water, but all were taken care of. Even the litter was clean, which surprised Keenan a little since he couldn't remember the last time he'd checked it. Garfunkel wasn't letting him off the hook this time. He jumped into Keenan's lap. Keenan gently pushed him off, but the dog jumped right back.

"All right, you win. I've been staring at this thing for too damn long anyway." Keenan groaned as he got up and sat down on the couch, his avatar now standing in the middle of the street, being slowly shoved to the side by passersby.

He began scratching Garfunkel's back until the dog rolled over in full revelry. Keenan rocked the dog back and forth as he rubbed his belly. Keenan had tried to make a point of spending a little quality time with his dog during the case, in part for their relationship, and in part to relax himself. Something about this case was so addictive he was forgetting the simple necessities of life.

"Y'know, I hate it when you're right," Keenan said as he continued to scratch Garfunkel.

He'd seen pets in Surreality, but they looked like little more than ornamentation, a fashion statement more than a companion. These dogs were perfectly behaved, not tugging their masters from place to place, not relieving themselves in inconvenient locations, and not sniffing other dogs at inappropriate times. In other words, they were no fun. Somehow he'd thought this would be an area the program would emphasize. From the looks of it, though, the fantasy world of Surreality focused less on the mundane and more on grand feats like flying or making love to mythical creatures, or, for the truly daring, both at the same time. Dogs didn't fit in that world.

Garfunkel was oblivious to Keenan's mood, only looking up every now and again when it seemed Keenan was going to stop. He looked over at the coffee maker and cursed that it was empty. Fortunately, he was supposed to meet Caliente in thirty minutes, and he estimated he might be able to stay conscious just long enough. The dog, however, could not say the same, his eyes already closed in contentment, body half hanging off the leather couch.

Keenan smiled and got up slowly so as not to disturb him. He walked over to the computer, logged off, and shut the machine down, since it probably needed a break as much as he did. He was halfway to the coffee shop when he realized he hadn't changed his shirt since yesterday.

• • •

Keenan was surrounded by a variety of "third wave" coffee cafés, places that saw coffee as something akin to wine or good cuisine and took every step of the brewing process very seriously.

Keenan's favorite, or at least the one where he felt the least out of place, was in a converted garage just a couple of blocks south of his apartment. Keenan was by no means a coffee snob, and definitely did not fit the mold of the usual clientele, but he had to admire the quality of their craft every now and again. He had no idea what he was ordering, and usually tried whatever was second from the top on their list of artisan coffees of the day.

The bearded man who handed them their lifeblood winced as Caliente knocked back half the cup like a shot of whiskey. Keenan made more of an effort to appreciate the cleanly filtered coffee, though he too needed a deeper sip just to stay awake.

"Long day," Caliente said.

Keenan agreed, taking a seat at one of the chairs around a long wooden table. Caliente slid in next to him.

"Nice to know you'll dress up for a girl."

"You saw me in a tuxedo before."

"Yeah, but that was for a witness interview. I like a man who's not afraid to wear a two-day-old shirt."

Keenan sniffed. "Possibly three," he admitted.

Caliente laughed. "Don't worry about it. I'm just as bad myself these days. So when you going to take me on a tour of this world you're living in now? I've had my fill of this one for the day."

Keenan shrugged. "Not really much to see. Talking penguins, a new Alexandria library, and of course, dwarf-on-elf action."

"I can see why you've been spending so much of your time there."

"Oh, yeah, it's right up my alley." He took another sip. "Y'know, these last couple of months, being stuck at home, I almost bought one of those mystery adventure games, working with Hercule Poirot to solve a murder on the Orient Express or something. There are a lot of days this feels pretty much the same."

"I didn't know you liked Agatha Christie."

"I'm not all about hard-boiled private eyes. Poirot solved his crimes with a minimum of physical evidence, relying on logic and knowledge of human behavior. Both private dicks and Poirot remind me there are ways to solve crimes using your head and not a crime lab."

Caliente frowned. "You mean you're going to have to use your head to solve this case? Daily might be right to be worried about you after all."

She laughed and Keenan chuckled politely, the fight with Tom still raw in his mind. "Thanks, Caliente. That really boosts my spirits."

"Anytime, *mi compadre*."

"Find anything out about our dead girl?"

Caliente shook her head. "Nothing of value. She was a second-year student, hadn't chosen a major yet, but was qualified to do several."

"You think she was working with the Polos to pay off student debt?"

"No. She had a full ride scholarship. She didn't come from money but had the grades to pay her way. Most of her family lives in Indiana."

"Has anyone called them yet?" Keenan asked.

Caliente stared into her cup. "I did. They had no idea what their daughter was mixed up in, or even that she had a boyfriend."

"You okay?" Keenan asked.

Caliente shrugged. "I've made my share of those calls, though I wouldn't mind if you got the next one."

Keenan sat there thinking, breathing deeply of the rising steam. "What's a girl like that doing mixed up with identity thieves?"

"Who knows? Chaffin looks about the same on paper. He might have waited until they were closer to reveal his true nature. Once you've invested time in a person, it's really hard to walk away. I've seen plenty of cases of women who commit crimes for their husbands or their boyfriends just so they both can have a better life."

"Do you think this is one of those?"

Caliente looked thoughtful. "I'm not sure. Some women attach themselves to dangerous men for the thrill, or for the access to power, or to have someone to take the fall if their own plans go awry."

Keenan took a long sip, Caliente raising her cup to her lips at the same time. She hadn't exactly dressed up for the occasion either, T-shirt and jeans, but the look suited her. He found himself stealing a look a little longer than a glance, burying his head back in his coffee cup when she glanced back. Caliente grinned.

Her cell phone chirped, and a moment later, so did Keenan's. Keenan wasn't sure who was on the other end of Caliente's call, but Daily was on the end of his.

"We need you back at the station, Dan. Your new friend Diane called to tell us she just heard from Chaffin. They've set up a meeting tomorrow at ten a.m."

"And where is this little fiasco taking place?" Keenan asked.

"Our alma mater, specifically, the new Ohio Union."

CHAPTER FIFTEEN

The new Ohio Union looked more like a mall than the dingy old fifties relic Keenan remembered. The old building had been completely demolished, razed to the ground a few years after his tenure at Ohio State. He remembered spending many long hours in the basement of that old Union, in a room that had once been a bowling alley, but had since been covered with cheap carpeting and couches that were falling apart. The room was presumably for quiet study, but he doubted anyone got much studying done when he and Daily and all their old friends sat around laughing raucously, and eating Marc Pi's if they were brave enough.

This new building was open and clean, three stories high with a vaulted ceiling and long cast-iron chandeliers emblazoned with block O's. Around the perimeter of the first floor, carved into the tile, were the lyrics to "Carmen Ohio." A bronze statue of their school's mascot, Brutus Buckeye, sat on a bench near the entrance next to the first set of stairs. Even the handles on the front door spelled O-H-I-O. It was certainly a marked improvement, though maybe a little more school spirit than Keenan was used to seeing in one place.

Diane was in the middle of the first-floor common area. Tall tables and high stools lined the edges, while couches and round chairs were arranged in groups of four around short coffee tables which mostly served to keep feet and bookbags off the floor. Diane was on one of these couches, trying to casually flip through a magazine on her tablet and not look like she was waiting for someone.

On the second floor, in both Diane's and Keenan's direct line of sight, was Caliente, trying to look inconspicuous on a woven bench that looked like it had been put together with old seatbelts. She wore the same T-shirt and jeans she had worn in the coffee shop, and had augmented them with a canvas bag that concealed her side arm. Keenan was up on the third floor, looking down through horizontal metal rails at their witness. Daily was in the courtyard off the side entrance, and the rest of Diane's protection detail was spread around on the floor and at the various entrances.

"Comm check, Eagle Eye calling Salsa Verde."

"Dan, those are the dumbest code names ever." Caliente shot him a look Keenan could see across the room.

"Sorry. Tom, how are you doing outside?"

"Did you see what they did to Sloopy's?" Daily asked, momentarily forgetting the two men were still pissed at each other.

"I'm more worried about what they did to our basement. It's a damn culinary academy down there," Keenan replied.

"I know. And did you see those bright orange and red walls?"

"Gentlemen, I'll be happy to let you both take me on a tour if you'll be so kind as to shut up now. We do have an op in progress," Caliente interjected.

"Right you are," Daily said. "How are things looking on your end, Braxton?"

Braxton had stationed himself inside a CABS campus bus station just across from the west entrance. "No sign of our perp yet, but I've got a lot of activity here on the South Oval."

"Just wait till you've seen the North Oval in the spring, we used to call it the Oven," Daily laughed.

Braxton sounded worried. "Nothing like that, sir. We've got a fair amount of students headed straight for the Union."

Keenan checked his watch. "We're still in the middle of classes. How many are we talking?"

"Couple hundred at least; you should be seeing the first of them now."

On cue the main doors parted, soon followed by the south and east doors. Three steady streams of students were making a beeline for the student activities kiosk near the High Street side of the building. Students wearing bright yellow T-shirts appeared almost out of nowhere to meet them and begin organizing them in a more orderly wrapping line.

Keenan called down from above, "Caliente, what the hell is going on?"

"I'm not sure; I can't see anything with all of this traffic in the way. I'm going down to the floor."

"Roger," Keenan acknowledged, standing up from his chair and reacquiring Diane. The crush of people was filling up every open white space on the lobby floor, and Diane had tucked her feet up under herself to try to appear as small as possible.

"Dan," Daily said, "This is wrapping around the building. We've got students coming in from all directions."

"Does anyone have eyes on our guy?" Keenan yelled, edging his way around the railing toward the stairs.

"I don't see him," Caliente said.

"I'm coming inside," said Daily, "we need more eyes on the floor. Braxton, you come too."

Up on the third floor the noise was still pretty muffled, but on the ground it was a circus. There was a lot of playful chattering and excitement going back and forth. Students began sitting down wherever they were, even pulling out laptops or decks of cards. Evidently whatever they were standing in line for was going to take a while.

"It's concert tickets," Braxton said over the radio. "Don't people usually get those online these days?"

"OSU students get free tickets to a lot of events at the Schott, but you have to order them in person," Keenan said. "I once walked in the rain to see—"

Caliente's voice cut in. "I think we have trouble. I've got a male, about 5'11", moving toward Diane. He's in a blue hoodie. I think it might be Chaffin."

Keenan strained to find Caliente and Daily, and found them separated from their target by the wall of students. The young man in the hoodie approached Diane casually, not seeming to even notice the rest of the activity around him.

"Do not engage, repeat, do not engage," Keenan said. "We need to wait until we can get him outside."

Had Chaffin known about the concert tickets, or did he just have a knack for surrounding himself with plenty of civilian targets? Daily and Caliente were doing their best to blend in with the scenery. Braxton had positioned himself next to the statue of Brutus and was looking uneasy. The hooded man reached the couch where Diane was sitting . . .

And kept on walking.

He passed right in front of Braxton before heading up the stairs to the second floor study area.

"Negative ID," Braxton said. "He's not our guy."

Keenan's earpiece squawked from the shot two seconds later. Chaffin stepped out of a clump of the line and fired at Braxton. His first two shots missed, striking Brutus's oversized head, but the third hit Braxton in the shoulder, dropping him instantly.

The crowd reacted as one large chaotic mass, screaming and running in every direction. Chaffin fired several more rounds into the air before shoving his way into the crowd.

"Officer down!" shouted Caliente.

"Tom, check on Braxton and Diane. Caliente, you've got the shooter," Keenan said, already running for the stairs. The closest stairs off the third floor were an enclosed stairwell, but even through the thick walls Keenan could hear another round of gunfire, and more screams.

"He's headed toward the east entrance," he heard Caliente yell over the radio.

"Negative," said one of the uniforms stationed on High Street. "The line around the building and the crowd trying to get out are completely jammed. He's not getting out this way."

Keenan stopped as he practically jumped onto the second floor landing. He crashed through the set of double doors. "Keep an eye on those exits," he said. "I'm headed for the garage."

Garage access on the second floor involved crossing the main ballroom, but it was still faster than trying to cut through what was happening below him. The room had been laid out in a similar arrangement to the benefit at the Athenaeum, evenly placed circular tables in a staggered grouping, making running in a straight line next to impossible. He knocked over several chairs and heard at least one glass break as he stormed for the back of the room.

As he reached the stage he heard a lot of swearing and cursing over his earpiece, several words in languages he had never heard before, and a couple Caliente had taught him. Underneath this heated exchange were a lot of banging pots and pans.

"Caliente, where the hell are you?"

"All this talk of food got me hungry. I'm going to find a service entrance to the lot. Better get off the line or I'll beat you there."

Keenan pushed open another set of doors which slammed shut behind him as he crossed a small concrete bridge. He opened the second set of doors slowly and brought himself flat against the far wall in a practiced motion. To his left were the stairs to the upper floors, to his right, the open garage. The garage was eerily quiet when compared to the chaos of a few seconds before, but he could hear running footsteps on the far side of the deck.

Keenan felt the weight of his side arm at his hip. Daily had been reluctant to let him carry, but Caliente had argued that Chaffin was dangerous, and a cop without a gun in that situation was just another target. Keenan's arm shook slightly as he extended the gun around the corner, and he had to use his other arm to balance it.

He ran a few yards to the line of cars across from him and pointed his weapon in the vague direction of the footsteps. Metal clanging and a headlight shattering in the car next to him put the shooter farther to his right, and he turned and fired before ducking for cover as another hail of bullets sailed over his head.

Chaffin had pulled a handgun in the Union, something that made a big noise but didn't have a lot of firepower. The weapon he was using to pin down Keenan was considerably more threatening, firing rounds in three-shot bursts. If Chaffin had wanted, he could have turned the Accord Keenan was hiding behind into swiss cheese, but the shooter was already on the move again, heading for the opposite stairs.

"Caliente, tell me you're on the first floor of the deck. Chaffin should be coming your way."

"Negative, Dan, I've got nothing on either stairwell."

That left up, though Keenan wondered what the hell Chaffin was thinking. He didn't have a lot options on the ground, but there were even fewer five flights up. Keenan ran back to where he'd entered the lot and started taking the stairs two at a time.

Chaffin was standing on top of the far wall as Keenan ran into the open air. Across a service alleyway was the main roof of the Union. His weapon had been abandoned, and now he just looked like a kid, his T-shirt whipped around by the wind.

Keenan aimed his gun and barked, "Get down on the ground, Michael! We just want to talk with you."

Chaffin didn't even turn to look at him, instead jumping across the gap. Keenan heard cement slip against tennis shoes and a metal clang as Chaffin slammed into the far wall. Keenan ran to find him hanging on by the tips of his fingers. The force of the jump had probably cracked a couple of Chaffin's ribs, and his breath was raspy and thin. Keenan didn't even have a leg up on the wall to jump before Chaffin's fingers gave way. He knew without looking the outcome of that abrupt stop.

Keenan dropped to the pavement of the garage and leaned against the wall. He breathed in and out in huge gulps, partly to replenish his body from the exertion of running up the stairs, and partly to fight back nausea. His gun hung uselessly from his right hand. After a few seconds he tapped his radio.

"Caliente, our shooter's in the service way. No rush. He's not going anywhere."

. . .

It took the rest of the morning and most of the afternoon to clean up the scene. Fortunately, it looked like the only casualties were the shooter and Braxton, who'd been a bit grumpy about owing his life to a giant bronze nut, though shoulder wounds could bring out the cranky in anyone.

The emotional trauma for the students would take longer to heal, even with the activities board already booking extra shows. There was violence off campus to be sure; break-ins, assaults, the occasional stabbing, but never anything like this. And Keenan couldn't shake the feeling that this was all his fault somehow, that he should have seen Chaffin's actions coming. Caliente had assured him there was plenty of blame to go around, and that the deputy chief wouldn't be shy about assigning it.

Keenan had expected some awkward questions from Daily as well, about what had happened up on that roof, and why Chaffin had jumped. But surprisingly, there was nothing. Daily had found Keenan in the service way, starting a cursory examination of the body before the techs arrived. Daily had just quietly put a hand on Keenan's shoulder, and began assisting him with the work.

He wasn't sure why Chaffin had jumped. It could have been as simple as he was young and stupid, and he thought he could make that gap. Then again, with Jeannette gone, maybe the kid didn't have anything else to live for.

A small .38 caliber handgun and an assault rifle were found at various points along Chaffin's escape route through the garage, the rifle consistent with the damage Chaffin had inflicted at the benefit shooting. Even without the forensic analysis, however, Keenan could tell that neither weapon was the one that had shot Chaffin's girlfriend, Jeannette Beverly.

Chaffin had little on him, not even a cell phone—just a smaller micro SD card and adapter slipped into a plastic case inside the change pocket of his jeans. Apparently he'd still needed an access point to Surreality after his camera had been abandoned. Keenan told the techs to call him as soon as they found anything off the card.

Rather than walk back into the slaughter, Keenan decided to drop off home first for a clean shirt and something to eat. The Union had closed down after the shooting, and he hadn't been in the mood for visiting any of his old haunts along High Street after the events of the last few hours. The deputy chief would call him soon enough; he didn't need to volunteer.

Synthia was waiting for him when he got back to the apartment. He thought he'd turned off the computer before he left, but decided it must not have shut down properly. His avatar sat slumped in his chair, with Synthia poised on the edge as usual, Tux pacing back and forth in front of it.

"What took you so long? I've been waiting here nearly forty-five minutes with this 'secretary' of yours. I almost reprogrammed her."

Keenan laughed as Synthia threw her compact and hit Tux squarely in the nose, which in retrospect wasn't that easy of a target to miss. Synthia pulled another compact out of her desk and turned to Keenan. "I told him he could leave his information here, but he insists on being part of the planning."

"Planning for what?" Keenan said.

"For finding Ms. Klein, of course," Tux replied. "That second card you pulled from Chaffin was helpful in narrowing down the possibilities."

The second card Tux was referring to was something Keenan had handed to the techs barely an hour ago.

"Tux, if you're going to hack into the department computers, you could at least act like it was difficult."

"I'll keep that in mind in the future," Tux replied. "Shame somebody like Chaffin chose to rely so heavily on his physical skills. That trick with the traffic cameras really wasn't that bad."

"Can we get on with it?" Synthia grumbled.

In reply, Tuxedo threw a large set of blueprints onto the desk and began rolling them out, causing Synthia to jump up from her perch. Since the desk was higher than his body, his wings had to strain to roll out the whole page, and Keenan had to help him get it the rest of the way.

"Where were you carrying these, anyway?" Keenan asked.

"Very funny."

Tux tapped the corner of the blueprint, which activated a three-dimensional projection of a building. Tux pulled a laser pointer out of wherever he'd hidden the blueprints, and pointed it at the entrance of the building.

"This is one of several gathering places for Polos that operate in Surreality. There are several different hacker cabals that operate under the Polo main operation, and it was a little difficult tracking down which one Chaffin was a part of until I had a more complete access history."

"How does this help us find Klein? Even though Jeannette and Diane grabbed her avatar, what does breaking into some virtual warehouse get us?" Keenan asked.

"Someone with a character profile as complex as Ms. Klein's can't be stored in one place. Holding the person hostage only gets them the operator. The real secret to Ms. Klein's success is in her programming skill, including some of the subprograms she passes on to her employees. The Polos can't just replace her, even if they think she's a liability, without first finding out how to operate her special skills."

"You'd think Klein's programs wouldn't have to be that complex to do the job," Keenan remarked.

Tux shook his head. "That's where you're wrong, Detective. Klein's work is subtle, very attuned to muscle movements, minute gestures. Things the conscious mind doesn't pick up, but that turn on the subconscious. It's really a very complex science when you get down to it."

"So the Polos need to turn her avatar on to find out what they need to know."

"So to speak," Tux grinned. "And that gives us something we can trace, provided we can get in. Getting into this little safe haven is difficult. There are several barrier worlds with blind alleys and other traps, but I think I can figure out how to get us through the maze."

The image rotated to a top-down display. "Once we're in, the layout is a fairly conventional warehouse design. There are several layers of smaller storage rooms surrounding a two-story main loading bay. Catwalks line the outside wall and cross over the floor below."

"So in other words, there are plenty of places for Polos to hide themselves," Keenan observed.

"I certainly wouldn't recommend a direct approach. If we're lucky, Klein is being held in one of the outer rooms, though it will still take time to search them all."

"Isn't there some way you can track her once we're inside?"

"I'm afraid not. We're not talking about a typical Surreality structure. The building is hosted on dozens of different servers that communicate through an onion router administered by at least three hierarchical computers."

"In a nutshell, Tux?" Synthia asked.

Tux sighed. "It means that any kind of conventional hack I try will be bounced down so many rabbit holes I could spend a lifetime before I found the right path. As I said, if we're lucky, Klein is in one of the outer rooms, but I doubt the Polos will keep her there once they figure out we're inside."

Keenan sat up from where he was leaning back, both in the real world, and in the virtual world. "What do you mean, once they figure out we're in?"

"Here's the problem. Because of the setup of the servers, I won't be able to block out all of their scanners. That's why I suggest we try a different approach."

The building returned to an isometric view and panned to below the main floor. "There is one more way into the compound."

"A back door?"

"Exactly. It was probably built as a dependable exit data stream in case someone ever tried to take out the building. The tunnel resides on a single server, so it should be easier to block. We still won't be able to block everything once we're in the warehouse, but we'll be able to get a lot closer before we trip the alarm."

Synthia rolled back part of the blueprint to regain her seat on the desk, which caused the image to flicker. She leaned toward Keenan and said, "So what's the plan exactly? Even if the two of you manage to get in, once you're in the middle of that loading bay you'll be surrounded by Polos with no way to get out. I know you've been doing a lot of training, Hayes, but even you won't be able to pop that many balloons."

"We won't have to," Tux answered. "The disadvantage to the setup the Polos have created is that the whole thing falls apart if the main routing servers are taken out. Even with the redundancy of using three, it's likely they will all fail in the event of an attack from the inside."

"Sort of like setting off a bomb."

"Exactly. By collapsing the main servers, the building would collapse and erase the character data of any forces inside."

"Any forces inside?"

"Yes."

"Including us? As a rule, I like to be as far away from bombs as possible. What's the point of freeing Ms. Klein if we erase her and us too?"

"We'll have a lifeline keeping us safe from any effects of the collapse. We'll infiltrate the building with our own protected server; that way, our code will never directly interact with their world, acting instead through a barrier. There is a downside, however: a delay in movement commands depending on the complexity of the room we're in. I'm caching as much data as possible ahead of time to reduce this, but we may still encounter performance difficulties at unpredictable intervals."

"I only understood about a third of that, so I guess I have to trust you, though I think you made up that onion router thing earlier. Just try not to have any delays when we're retrieving Ms. Klein. I assume we'll have to bring her onto our server before we can implement your plan."

"See, you're catching on. Hopefully the part the Polos are running isn't too large, or we may have to leave a couple of her customizations behind."

"I'm sure she'll be able to manage for a while without her full repertoire. We need to find out what she can tell us about her relationship with Haines and why the Polos took her in the first place." Keenan looked toward Synthia. "How's that sound to you, Synth?"

Synthia was just standing, arms crossed, looking like a statue. At first he thought she was calculating a response, but her expression was blank, as if her program had locked up. Keenan looked at Tux, but the penguin seemed confused.

Keenan stood up and rounded the desk to look Synthia in the eyes. Instead of showing their usual spark, they appeared flat and dull, as if she were in a coma.

"Synthia, you in there?"

He'd gotten used to the variability of Synthia's responses, her sarcasm, her drawings, her gentle prodding, and even her unique sense of humor. He knew she was a program, but she never gave him an overt reason to think of her as one. Nothing he'd heard before, however, could have prepared him for her response this time.

"No."

CHAPTER SIXTEEN

Keenan narrowly dodged the gun as it swung up toward him. Tux's reflexes were not as well-honed and he took one straight in the white part of his gut, sending him flying into the far wall. Keenan raised his own gun and pointed it straight at Synthia, but did not fire. She faced him and returned his threat in kind.

Synthia spoke in a monotone. "Go ahead and shoot. You'll just kill your secretary and prevent us from having a chance to talk."

"I take it this isn't part of your programming, Synth."

"I told you, she's not here right now, and if you shoot, you'll never get her back."

"Who are you?"

"You know exactly who I am," Synthia replied coldly.

"Why haven't you shot me?"

"Because unlike your little mercenary, you'll just come back and keep chasing me. I just came here to talk."

"What exactly do you expect talking to accomplish?"

"Nothing." Synthia smiled a mechanical smile. "I want to make sure we understand each other. Haines has had two chances to get the message about Arcadia. He won't get a third."

It was rare that Keenan found himself facing a murderer with a gun pointed at his head. Rarely were things that clean and tidy. Most killers would just try to shoot you, then get shot themselves, without a chance to explain, threaten, or cajole. This murderer already had a flair for the dramatic in the way they strangled Haines, and now was enjoying the rare pleasure of taunting the man trying to find them.

"You'll never get near him."

Synthia laughed, a dead sound without any variation in her voice. "You may be right, but Mrs. Haines is a much easier target. Did you enjoy the opera?"

The lifeless form of his secretary shifted, twisting itself until it wore the face of Mrs. Haines. Keenan's face burned, his blood began boiling, and he had to restrain himself from firing. "You touch her and I'll—"

"Easy, Detective, nothing has to happen to her. The choice is entirely yours."

Katherine/Synthia's head flew back, her mouth open as if in shock, her body collapsing a few seconds later. Keenan ran to catch her and laid her out on the floor. Her face shifted again, back to his secretary's. She looked as lifeless as a piece of furniture. He knelt down and—not knowing what else to do—touched the side of her cheek. Nothing happened.

He turned away to look at Tux. A small pool of blood had formed around the penguin, and his head was collapsed into his chest. Keenan stood and angrily shoved all of the blueprints off his desk. He'd been tempted to do something similar in the real world, but managed to restrain himself. Suddenly Tux's eyes opened.

"Tuxedo, you all right?"

Tux surveyed the damage to his chest and nodded. "Nothing a few patches can't fix."

Keenan filled him in on the last few minutes, since he had apparently been knocked offline for the duration. "That was some world-class hacker to be able to get through my defenses. I actually couldn't control my character for a few minutes. This is very exciting!"

Keenan was not amused. "Exciting! Someone just threatened to kill Katherine Haines and nearly did the same to Synthia!"

Tux walked over to Synthia and lifted her head with his small wings. "She's not dead, just shut down. I should be able to reboot her, though I'll need to isolate whatever program took her over before I do. Otherwise we could have a repeat of what just happened."

"Do you think you can do it?"

"Maybe, though Synthia's a fairly complex program. Whoever did this was good enough to get past my defenses, so they probably hid their little infiltration program well. If the intent was to hamper your investigation, taking out Synthia and me was a good move, especially if they thought you wouldn't take their advice."

Keenan smiled ruefully. "How do you know I won't?"

"The same way you know I'm still on this case. I can't have another hacker acting in here unchallenged. It would hurt my reputation. Besides, neither of us responds well to threats." He stepped back from Synthia and moved his wings over her chest. She began to lift up from the ground until she was around Tux's eye level.

"I'm going to need to take her back to my part of Surreality to extract the program. I'll bring her back here when I'm finished. What do you want me to do if I'm not successful?"

"I don't know, just don't screw up, okay?"

Tux nodded and disappeared, leaving Keenan alone in the office. He stepped out the door into the transit tunnels a moment later, his gun sitting in the middle of the desk where he'd left it next to Synthia's open compact.

• • •

Keenan walked through Surreal-City's empty streets. The night was eerily quiet, something that was normal for Columbus this time of night, but was strangely disturbing here. Everywhere he'd been in Surreality had been full of life and sound, often more than he could process. Trees swayed in the distance, moved by wind he could not hear. He reached up to check the volume on his headphones, but felt only hair beneath his palm. The light pressure he usually felt on his ears was gone, and he realized he had moved without touching the keyboard.

He felt a breeze against his cheek. The wind had reached him, not a warm comforting wind, but one that sent a chill down his neck. He looked up to see clouds forming. Every environment he'd encountered in Surreality, at least those not in the dark net, had a perfectly manicured sky, with just the right number of puffy clouds. Now Keenan was glad his character wore a trench coat.

He felt a weight in his right pocket and pulled out his gun. It was loaded, and as he opened it, he could feel the cold steel of one of the bullets in his hand. The bullet felt tangible, its surface curved instead of angular. The street still had a textured quality, like wallpaper he could tear up to reveal bare drywall, but the gun was real.

The sky was darker now, and he felt moisture against his cheek. He put his hand up against it and felt another raindrop on the back of his palm. Dozens of drops turned to hundreds, and then to thousands, until it was almost impossible to discern the buildings. He knelt in the street as puddles formed, watching the intricate splashes of water as each drop hit the surface, exploding into thousands of tiny droplets. He wondered how his old machine was handling this. He remembered the fractal rendering Synthia had told him about and wondered if this was another example. It was too real.

The silence was broken by a woman's scream, followed by a loud clap of thunder. At first he thought it was a gunshot, but the whole sky ignited, nearly blinding him. The flash disoriented him, and he could not tell where the scream was coming from. He heard it again, far in the distance, but clearly in front of him, down one of the alleys of the virtual city. Keenan pushed the last bullet back into the gun and slammed it shut.

Water splashed around him as he ran, shooting as high as his waist. The rain fell in a torrent and threatened to knock him off balance, but somehow he pushed forward. He tucked the loaded gun into his jacket and gripped it tightly. The scream was getting louder. It would cut off for a few seconds, then resume with terrible urgency. Keenan's mind reeled and he pumped his legs harder. His mouth tasted metallic from the adrenaline.

Keenan rounded a final corner and was standing in a blind alley. He nearly stumbled but managed to raise his gun as he leaned against a nearby wall, catching his breath in gasps. The woman was clearly dead. Her face was unrecognizable through all the blood. A man in dark shabby clothing stood over her, kicking her even as Keenan stood with gun raised. From behind, Keenan recognized him as Sinclair, the man who just wouldn't stay dead. That maniacal laugh entered his mind as if from nowhere. Keenan's face flushed white hot and he fired, catching the man in the shoulder.

The force of the bullet spun his target around. The face that stared back was his own.

"Who are you?" Keenan growled through clenched teeth.

The jackal's laugh was the only response, this time colored with the sound of Keenan's own voice. Blood flowed from a wound in the man's shoulder, but he paid it no mind. The rain poured even harder now, and washed the blood away from the woman's face. Katherine Haines's lifeless eyes stared at nothing, a smile forever frozen on her lips, the same smile she'd given him when they first met, and right before she'd kissed him at the opera.

The sight of her brought the whole scene into focus. He was not looking at a computer screen, but standing on a real street, the same one he'd been dreading to see as he rounded every corner. The same street he'd stumbled down as he fell into the alley behind the Athenaeum. He could smell the garbage, see the steam rising from the sewers, and feel the friction of the brick wall against his hands as he steadied himself. It was no longer smooth but gritty like sandpaper.

The man continued to laugh and Keenan fired again. The gun sent waves of energy up his arm, but he kept it aimed straight at the man's chest, firing five more shots in barely an instant. The thunder roared from his gun and the skies above. Infuriatingly, the man just kept on laughing, his voice growing higher and more hysterical. It no longer sounded like Keenan's voice, and when he looked again, his face had been replaced by that of Franklin Haines.

Haines pointed at Keenan, and he could feel hot liquid on his chest. The rain struck cold against his cheek, and blood flowed from five neat little holes in his shirt. The trench coat was still smoking, and the powder burns had turned its tan to ash. He could smell his own burnt skin, feel the blood flowing out of him.

He collapsed onto his knees and vomited. He retched for several seconds, then pulled himself up onto his elbows and tried to reload the gun. He couldn't reason out how five bullets could have ricocheted into him. He turned to look at Katherine Haines, but she was gone, replaced first with the face of Jeannette Beverly, then Diane, then Caliente, and finally Synthia.

His hands shook as he tried to reload, rain filling the chamber of the gun. Haines laughed and put a hand to his face before pulling it off like a mask. It hung from his hand, a mass of hair and latex, his true face revealed.

SURREALITY

Tom Daily spoke. "Why'd you do it, Dan? Why'd you kill them? We know it was you. Don't try to cover it up by dying on me now. You murdered them all."

Keenan put the final bullet in the chamber and pulled back the hammer. He raised the gun toward Tom, his arm and upper body shaking as he tried to support himself on the other arm, his whole life draining out onto the pavement.

"You gonna kill me too, Dan? Go ahead, I won't stop you."

Keenan yelled and squeezed his hand to fire, but the gun had turned molten. His nerves screamed, the rain stopped, and the whole world fell apart.

• • •

Keenan woke to Garfunkel standing on his chest, nudging under his chin with his cold nose. Normally he would have scolded the dog for this, but the rawness of his throat told him he must have been screaming.

"I'm awake now, everything's okay."

The dog calmed down and curled up beside Keenan as he sat up. Keenan continued to pet him reassuringly, breathing slowly to calm his own nerves. His heart was pounding and his chest ached, though that was in large part due to the dog sitting on him.

"I'm sorry, boy. These last couple of months have been hard on you too, haven't they?"

In reply, the dog nuzzled up to his hand and licked it.

He stayed in bed for a couple more minutes, somewhat amazed that he had actually made it into his bedroom last night instead of sleeping on the couch. It wasn't a room he was used to seeing when he woke up in the morning. It felt like he was waking up in someone else's apartment.

He opened the door and stumbled into the kitchen. He called Caliente to check in on the protection detail he'd ordered for Mrs. Haines last night, then sat down in front of the computer. Garfunkel ran in front of his legs and jumped in his lap.

"I'll be all right, pooch."

Keenan logged in and walked out the door of his office as soon as he materialized. He'd expected its appearance to reset to defaults, but the office looked the same as it had after the attack, and he didn't want to linger. He jumped into the nexus of tunnels and moved toward the dark net, flying through the warnings and landing at the Source.

He smiled as he saw the same two guards blocking the entrance. Keenan waved, hoping this would be enough for them to recognize him, but was surprised to find himself stopped by beefy arms.

"I thought you guys were always open," he said, dusting off his coat as he stepped back.

"We've heard about what you've been doing," the guard on the left began.

"Yeah, we don't care much for cops around here. We have a habit of knocking them around." The guard on the right curled his hand into a fist and cracked his knuckles.

"I can't argue with the sentiment, but I have two questions. It was my understanding that you don't deal with cops much in these parts."

"What's your point?"

"Well, I'm just saying it's hard to call it a habit if you have no practical experience."

"We try to think of all the contingencies before they arise."

"Okay . . . but what's the threat in roughing up my avatar a bit?"

"Who said anything about roughing up your avatar?" the guard on the right replied.

Keenan assumed this was a bluff, but considering the crowd that hung out around the Source, maybe not.

"Look, we got off on the wrong foot," Keenan said. "So you don't like cops, but I'd also guess you're not friends of the Polos."

The guards stopped. "We run our own establishment. The Polos like to take a cut of everything they touch."

The other guard nodded. "We don't cater to thieves around here. It's bad for our reputation."

"I wholeheartedly agree. An enemy of the Polos should be a friend of yours, wouldn't you say?"

When the guards didn't say anything, Keenan continued, "I'm just here to meet someone for a quiet drink. I'm not here to cause trouble."

The guards looked at each other and must have decided he wasn't worth the trouble. They parted, and Keenan moved quickly down the staircase and over to one of the side tables. Tux had apparently been waiting for him to appear, and slid into the booth across from him before Keenan had even sat down.

"What took you so long?"

"I had to deal with the two statues outside. How's Synthia?"

Tux shook his head. "I think I've found the source of the hack, but it's going to be difficult to cut it out without damaging the main program. Turns out she wasn't speaking in a monotone just to sound menacing, but because someone was using part of her early development code to gain access. Apparently those old systems were kept as backups rather than being removed. The problem is: I don't know enough about how the main program works, so it'll be difficult to cut out the exploited areas. It'd probably help if I could get the original author involved."

"I'm not sure if we can track him down. Do you have a plan if we can't get him?"

"Synthia is millions of lines of code organized into thousands of subprograms. I'm actually kind of surprised her program is as mobile as it is. My best guess is that she's like the Polo warehouse facility; her base code resides on one server which keeps her appearance, base personality, and a cache of memory. The rest is spread over dozens of interconnected servers. I can tell they're out there, but I can't get beyond the base code. I just hope that's where the hacker tapped in or I'm at a loss."

Keenan was worried. He knew that a strong ego was part of any good computer hacker, and if Tux was admitting the problem was hard, there might be less hope than he'd realized. More than ever he wanted to talk to Synthia, to hear her yell at him for sulking so much, and to pull him out when he and Tux got into trouble on the crazy raid they were about to plan.

"What time are we going in tonight?" Keenan asked. "I'm not used to the whole Red Bull thing, so I might need notice for taking a nap or freebasing my coffee intake."

"Actually, I was thinking in a couple of hours. We may encounter more resistance at night since these guys are a mix of college students and the unemployed, both of whom keep late hours. That's when life in Surreality is at its peak. During the day, we may luck out and have fewer members logged in, though they may still have a few guard bots we'll have to deal with."

"That doesn't give me a lot of time, Tux," Keenan said. "I'll need Caliente to be able to move in with a team once we can give her a real-world location for Ms. Klein."

"I'm sure Ms. Caliente is always ready for action."

Keenan chuckled. "Try saying that to her in person."

Tux said nothing and took a sip of his drink.

Keenan continued. "These bots you're talking about, they're similar to the guards who attacked me at Klein's?"

"Right, but they shouldn't be hard to handle. I don't see what you have to worry about."

"You're right, first sign of trouble and I'll give them a nice bird to shoot at."

"Funny. Without me you wouldn't last ten feet inside that place. You haven't played any shooters since the 8-bit era except for that balloon ball thing your secretary calls training."

Keenan took a sip from the drink he hadn't realized he'd ordered. He didn't relish the thought of going on a raid with someone who could easily be an overweight man in his thirties living with his mother, or a snotty sixteen-year-old kid. Unfortunately he didn't have any other options.

"Just tell me one thing, you ever done anything like this before?"

Tux didn't skip a beat. "Nope, unless you count playing *Goldeneye* when I was a kid."

"That's encouraging."

"Relax, this is gonna be fun. By the time they know what hit them, we'll be long gone."

• • •

Tux told Keenan to meet him at another red zone island in a couple of hours to make the complicated trek to the hideout. The route involved several transfer points before they'd reach the final server, so they had to start early. Keenan thought about training before meeting with Tux, but didn't feel like facing his empty office. Instead he brewed coffee, which he left heated in the carafe, fed the dog, and took him for a short walk. He put his gun to the left of his keyboard. He doubted shooting his monitor would do him any good, but somehow it made him feel better.

Caliente had scared up a team of uniforms who were more afraid of her than anything the chief would have to say, and was waiting for Keenan's signal in a van a few blocks from the station. Daily was taking the morning off to visit Braxton in the hospital. If they were lucky, this might give them a few hours before the chief started wondering what the hell they were up to, in which time Tux assured him he should have Klein's location.

Garfunkel curled up on the couch as Keenan arrived at the first jumping-off point. Tuxedo was already waiting for him.

"You're late. This is going to take precision timing, and we'll have to wait another seven minutes to get back in sync."

"Relax, Tux, I'll pay you the overtime. I could use going over this again anyway."

Tux nodded. "These first couple jumps are gonna be tricky."

"Exactly how tricky are we talking?"

"Somehow I think explaining will do more harm than good at this point. Just be sure to do exactly as I do, exactly when I do it. Otherwise you'll fall down one of hundreds of rabbit holes the Polos set up, and we'll have to start over."

"I'll keep that in mind."

The two were standing in a clearing next to a small dirt road. On the other side was a single building, labeled simply "General Store." There was nothing for miles in either direction, not even traffic. They crossed the road and entered through swinging doors while two old men rocked in chairs on either side. Inside was a buzz of activity. Four attendants were serving dozens of customers, cooking up all sorts of crazy combinations from toys to candy to ice cream. One side had a set of stools, and Tux indicated they should sit down. As he checked his watch, which was pinned to his wing, a clerk came up and asked them for their order.

"Two peanut butter sandwiches with bologna and mayo, please," Tux said.

Keenan turned up his nose. "What kind of sandwich is that?"

"The kind that gets us in the first door. Besides, they're kind of good once you try one."

Keenan was thankful they were not served an actual example of the sandwich but instead were handed two tickets. Each had a stamp with a smiley face on it, and a seven-digit number.

Tux plunked a few surs down on the counter and thanked the clerk. They moved to what looked like a vending machine in the back of the store. Tux put the ticket into the dollar bill slot and punched out the seven-digit code. The vending machine opened to reveal a long dark hallway.

The penguin gestured for Keenan to follow and walked into the corridor. As Keenan was about to step through, the vending machine slammed shut, and he bounced off it onto the floor. Several kids at the counter turned to laugh, but Keenan was less amused. He punched in his own ticket and slipped through as fast as he could to find Tux waiting for him, stifling a laugh. Keenan grumbled as they began running down the corridor, the vending machine door clanging shut behind them.

"What gave you the idea for a peanut butter, bologna, and mayo sandwich anyway?"

"I was out of everything else in my fridge."

"That doesn't quite explain it. You could have made a peanut butter sandwich for lunch and a bologna sandwich for dinner."

"I'm a hacker. I don't have time, or bread for that matter, to eat two meals a day."

"So you eat a bologna sandwich and eat the peanut butter out of the jar."

"And get peanut butter all over my fingers? What do hackers do, Detective?"

"Well . . . they crack into things."

"Yeah, besides that."

"They type?"

"Yes, they type, and sticky fingers and keyboards do not mix. Now are we going to stand here all day and discuss sandwiches?"

Keenan shrugged. "Where to now?"

"At the end of this tunnel is a kind of subway. You'll need to remember your seven-digit number from the ticket."

Keenan searched his memory as they ran down the long hallway, colored lights growing brighter until they reached the main platform. A man in a red and white striped suit and a small cap stood by the turnstile. He held out a tray that was strapped to his shoulders, like a vendor at a baseball game.

"Greetings, gentlemen, I was wondering if either of you would like a snack after your long walk. We have some delicious chocolate cake, or, if you like, we also have fruit."

Tux answered before Keenan had a chance. "We'd both like fruit."

Keenan had been thinking about the chocolate cake but readily agreed when the man asked if the fruit was what he wanted. The man handed them each a banana, and they walked through the turnstile.

"What was that about?"

"When someone's trying to memorize a seven-digit number they'll usually go for the cake."

"So why didn't you tell me that?"

"I wanted to see if you'd follow my lead. Failure at this point isn't so bad. We'd still get the chance to try again in a few hours. From here on in it gets a little more difficult. Come on, we've got to move quickly. If we don't hit this next point we're going to be stuck here a while, and these bananas spoil."

They hurried down to the platform, but instead of a train waiting for them, all Keenan could see, or—more accurately—hear, was the sound of a rushing river. Tux moved toward the edge of the platform, and Keenan's screen flickered as he started to peer over, the scene lagging as it loaded. When the picture rendered correctly, Keenan looked at Tux.

"You gotta be kidding me."

Below them were what looked like thousands of floating sheets of paper, though Keenan hoped they were a little more substantial than that. They barely looked wide enough to hold one person, let alone two. There were at least nine distinguishable lanes, though they seemed to weave in and out further down the corridor. The lanes moved at different rates, though all in the same direction.

"Relax, this is a simple case of follow-the-leader. As you may have guessed, there is no direct route to our destination, but rather a finely timed sequence of jumps from each of these lanes. I've observed the sequence several times and believe we can gain entry as long as you do everything I do. Unless they've already changed the sequence."

"Changed it?"

"Well, you never know how paranoid a group like this is, but I think it's very unlikely. After all, they'd have to inform all their members, and it probably isn't easy to recode. Anyway, we'll be fine if you follow me precisely and as quickly as you can. Some of these passages will take you miles away in a matter of seconds, so you don't want to lose me. Just remember, my body mass is much lower, so try not to knock me off with a clumsy jump."

"All right, all right. Let's just get on with it."

"Whatever you say. Oh, by the way, if you miss the jump, your flight controls won't work," Tux said, looking at his watch.

"What?!" Keenan shouted.

"Okay . . . jump!"

The two leapt from the platform onto the fourth lane. Keenan missed but quickly corrected. Fortunately most of the lanes were going the same speed at this point. He didn't look down for fear of losing Tux, and because he had a feeling he wasn't going to like anything he saw.

The platform was gone and small overhead lamps provided the only illumination. Keenan could barely see the pad in front of him, let alone any of the other lanes.

Tux placed a wing on his leg. "Careful, Detective, we've got another one coming up. Two lanes to the right."

Moments later Tux jumped, much farther than a penguin could normally jump, but now was not the time for Keenan to criticize reality. He breathed in and leapt, landing on the edge of the pad. He waved his arms around to regain his balance, and Tux pulled him toward the middle, causing him to drop to a knee.

"It only gets harder from here. We've got to make two quick jumps in succession on this next one. The second jump's less than a second after the first. You didn't happen to play a lot of Nintendo when you were a kid?"

"Not really, that was more my friend Dan's obsession. Why?" Keenan asked.

"Oh, no reason." Tux shrugged. Suddenly the world dropped out from under them. The lighting improved slightly and Keenan could discern the bricks in the walls all around him, looking more like a sewer pipe than a subway. The camera shifted 90 degrees, and Keenan suddenly realized he was being carried over a waterfall into an impossible abyss.

As they continued to fall, Keenan could see interweaving lanes of white blurs stretching in all directions. From his current view they looked like strands in a tapestry, but as he got closer he could tell there was actually a significant elevation change between adjacent layers. The noise was increasing as well, like being in the middle of a tornado.

Tux pointed to one of the lanes on the left. "It's gonna be left, then down to the right. Follow me closely."

Tux put his wings together and shot like a bullet from the platform. He fell as if governed by the laws of gravity again, and arced his body as much as he could to the left. Keenan did his best to follow and could see the lane a few feet ahead. As they got nearer, Tux flipped 180 degrees, bounced off a pad, then leapt downward into another sea of panels. A second later Keenan flipped, losing sight of the bird.

Hitting the pad, he jumped on instinct and was gratified to see Tux a second later, still falling toward one of the lanes. Keenan's jump had put him a few dozen meters higher than Tux, who landed and began searching for Keenan. Finding him, the penguin began flapping his wings frantically before being carried out of sight. Desperately, Keenan searched for a little black dot in a sea of white.

Somehow he caught Tux out of the corner of his eye. A panel came up quickly on his left, and Keenan pushed off it with his arm, shoving his body in Tux's direction. Tux was now standing on a subway platform like the one they'd started on. Keenan ducked his head below opposing lanes, crashing into the platform a few seconds later. He flung his arms out to grab for something to stop himself and slowed a few dozen feet later.

"Maybe you should have sent your friend along instead," Tux said as he pulled Keenan up.

"Come on, Tux, this is just starting to get fun. Now tell me we don't have any more jumps like that one to look forward to."

"There's always a jumping puzzle. Fortunately the Polos' entrance requirements have gotten lax over the years."

The platform was dark and littered with trash. Keenan could see a tunnel at the back of the station, running about a hundred meters. At the end was a set of stairs with a bright light shining down. Keenan heard rushing water again and looked behind him, but the river of panels was gone.

"We can't go back that way. Those trains only come every couple of hours. It's all in now."

CHAPTER SEVENTEEN

Keenan and Tux walked down the tunnel and to the top of the stairs, crouching down to get the lay of the land. They were on another island surrounded by water. Just beneath the surface of the waves, Keenan could see the subway tunnel, which tilted upward until it was obscured by the shore. Hundreds of yards of green grass separated them and a tall cliff, on top of which was the Polos' hideout. At the top of the cliff was a plateau, several miles in circumference, with the warehouse located squarely in the center. The facility looked abandoned, though without the typical gang tags or graffiti Keenan would have expected to see.

"I thought this was supposed to be the back way in," Keenan said.

"Of course it is," Tux said. "See that entrance carved into the side of the cliff face there? We've got seven whole seconds before a sniper spots us to cross this grass. Then all we have to do is get to the cliff face and stick to it like glue. Then it's maybe a quarter of a mile around the cliff till we reach the entrance, which will probably be guarded. It'll be a cakewalk."

"Oh, sure. Anything else I should know?"

"Well . . . if you use your gun, the sound is probably going to alert every Polo on this island and send them swarming to our location," Tux answered.

"Good safety tip. So how are we supposed to take out the guard?"

"With these." Tux held up a couple of small potatoes.

"Come again?"

"They're silencers. I found them at the general store."

"You can't be serious," Keenan said. "You've been watching too many cop shows."

"And so have the people who designed this place. Don't worry, I know how to clean the gun out afterward."

Keenan shook his head and pocketed the potatoes. "On three, okay?"

"Whatever you say."

The grass came up to Keenan's ankles and slowed him down as he ran. Tux, on the other hand, was nearly half-concealed, and his running was even more sluggish than Keenan's. Keenan circled back and grabbed the sputtering penguin, hoisting him under one arm as he struggled to cover the rest of the distance. They reached the rock face a few seconds later, and Keenan pressed his body firmly against it in a move that normally would have knocked the breath out of him.

His screen shook from side to side, and he remembered Tuxedo, who was flailing wildly. Apparently he hadn't taken too kindly to his head being slammed against a rock. Keenan dropped him at his side. Tux dusted himself off and glared at Keenan. "You nearly got us killed!" he whispered angrily. "I would have made it fine without your help."

"You're welcome." Keenan pulled out his gun and stuffed the potato on the end before beginning to inch around the cliff. The ground was strewn with small branches that cracked under their feet and rocks that moved when touched. Tuxedo nodded in approval. "They must have finally made those upgrades to the physics engine."

Keenan did not share Tux's admiration, as the rocks and twigs were more things his awkward feet would have to avoid. After what seemed an eternity, he saw the edge of the cave. He raised an arm to stop Tuxedo and moved the last couple of feet on his own, crouching low as he leaned around the corner of the outcropping.

The entrance arced out on both sides with a hard transition from dirt to metal a few feet inside. Beyond was total darkness. At the entrance to the cave stood a single guard holding a gun that looked better suited to a tank. Keenan's potato-silenced gun looked laughable by comparison.

Breathing deeply, he stood and whirled around the corner, squeezing the trigger as he turned. The bullet must have stopped somewhere midway through the potato, because instead of coming out the other side, the whole potato shot off the gun and into the guard's chest. The starchy projectile inflicted about as much damage as one would expect from a complex carbohydrate. All the blow managed to do was startle and then amuse the guard. Keenan took advantage of the pause to close the distance between them, and to strike the guard with the butt of his gun. The guard disappeared a few seconds later, along with the pummeled potato.

"Tuxedo!"

Tux poked his head around the corner and was quickly knocked backward as Keenan pelted him with another potato. "Get up," Keenan growled a second later. "We haven't got a lot of time."

Tuxedo grumbled and kicked the errant vegetable aside. Keenan moved through the entrance of the cave, his feet making a low metal clanking as he walked. The light grew worse with every step and was cut off altogether when a pair of metal doors closed behind them. Keenan turned to look for Tux, but the low light was making him difficult to spot.

"This just keeps getting better and better," Keenan sighed.

• • •

Keenan inched forward in the dark, wondering if he was actually moving at all, since the scene gave him no frame of reference. He could hear himself walking, and Tux assured him that it would sound different if they were hitting a wall, but this did little to comfort him. So far they weren't being met by hordes of armed Polos, but Keenan had the feeling that was because the Polos wanted to draw them in so they could cut off all means of escape.

Tuxedo was holding a small tablet between his wings, which gave off just enough light to illuminate the bottom of his beak. "Listen, the model for this building can't be a single map. The game engine for Surreality isn't set up to handle areas of this size. We should be switching to a new map soon, and when we do, I should be able to track the load."

"What does that do for us?"

"If I tap the data as it's loading, I should be able to get a map of the area in front of us. That way we'll be able to see in the dark."

"I thought you already had a schematic of this place," Keenan said.

Tux nodded, or at least Keenan thought he did, since the only way he could tell was that more of the penguin's beak became visible for a moment. "I was able to construct a rough blueprint from cached data, but the Polos probably change this place around all the time. If I can get the map on a load, then we'll have the latest intel."

Keenan continued to walk forward, his hands stretched out in front of him. After a few seconds he saw his arm begin to bend, indicating he'd run into something. He veered to the left to avoid the obstacle. Tux remained focused on the tablet, and thus did not detect the object until he'd slammed his beak into it. Keenan smiled at the organic thump as the penguin fell on his back.

"Thanks for the warning," Tux said as he picked himself up.

"Oh, yeah, there's a wall there. There seems to be a staircase just to the left."

Tux grumbled and collected his tablet. Faint light shone down from high above them. The staircase Keenan had found stretched for what looked like hundreds of stories, circling around the outside of a square shaft. As Keenan rounded his second complete loop, the screen froze for a second, and he suddenly found himself only two flights from the top. Keenan spun around to look for Tux, but the penguin was nowhere to be found. He drew his gun and whispered Tux's name.

No answer.

He scanned again, but still nothing. He climbed down several of the steps and continued to call out. Behind him a light flashed and something hit him across the chest. Keenan fell backward down the rest of the flight of steps, his gun clanging loudly beside him. The gun slid dangerously close to the edge, but Keenan somehow managed to block it with his arm and bring it up in the direction of his attacker.

"You all right, Detective?" Tux said, barely able to suppress a laugh.

"Where the hell were you?" Keenan growled as he pushed himself back on his feet.

"Right behind you, and there's no need to shout. We are trying to infiltrate a secret Polo base at the moment. If you had listened to me, you would have known we were transferring between two maps. Evidently whoever designed this complex didn't want people to have to climb all those stairs."

Keenan whispered a brief blessing for whichever Polo had come up with that idea. The thought of his screen going round and round for untold minutes was making him dizzy.

They finished the rest of the climb in silence. Overhead lights provided some visibility, but much of the stairwell was still dark, making for slow going. At the top of the stairs was a solid- looking metal door, presumably leading to the warehouse.

"Here goes nothing." Keenan put his hand on the knob and cracked the door open a few inches. Seeing nothing but an empty hallway, he gave the thumbs-up and they both stepped through. The hallway stretched about twenty meters to his left, and seventy to his right. Circles of light spaced by dark gray cement floor provided the only illumination. Doors lined either side of the hallway at irregular intervals. Small slits provided the only clue as to what was in each room. Most were either locked or empty.

The rooms around the corner on the left were more interesting. Several contained tables with cards strewn across them, a large TV blaring static in the corner. There was even a laundry room, whose function in a virtual world Keenan could only guess at. All of the rooms were empty, and showed no signs of recent use. Something about this wasn't feeling right; it was too easy. So far they'd only encountered one Polo, and he hadn't put up much of a fight against Keenan's potato gun. Even at slow times of the day this place shouldn't be so empty.

Tux was still huddled over his tablet, though now he was scanning for any part of Klein's program. After a few minutes he cursed and tapped the device hard with his wing.

"No luck?" Keenan asked.

Tux shook his head. "The scanner's useless. I'm not even detecting objects that are right in front of us."

"Meaning we'll just have to use our eyes," Keenan offered.

Tux shrugged.

The screen lagged as it loaded the second part of the hallway. They passed a room full of free weights, and the kitchen. "All the comforts of home," Keenan said.

Midway down the hall Keenan noticed a small set of stairs which led to the main loading dock of the warehouse. Most of the lights had been shattered, but the remaining dull streams showed a woman tied to a chair in the center of the room.

"Tuxedo," Keenan whispered, "I believe we found Ms. Klein."

Klein was naked save for thick ropes tied thoroughly around her. Her head hung limply by her shoulder, probably meaning she was logged out. Tux said he'd be able to make the trace either way, but with her logged out it would take longer. Keenan didn't exactly like the idea of walking into an open dark room with untold dangers above them, but Klein was his only lead at the moment, and her life could still be in danger.

"So how do we do this?" Keenan asked.

"It's easy," Tuxedo explained as he handed Keenan two small police badges. "Slap one of these on her and one on yourself. That'll transfer both your characters' data to my server and will start the trace on Klein. Once my program gets a location it'll transmit that data to your lovely Detective Caliente. In the meantime I'll be learning all I can from the Polo main servers before I take them down."

Keenan patted the penguin on the back. "Be careful, I still need you to fix Synthia."

"I'm overwhelmed by your concern."

"Don't mention it," Keenan smiled. "Let's go!"

Keenan jumped down the stairs and began running toward Klein. As soon as his feet left the stairs, Klein seemed to fall beneath him, and his forward momentum dropped. He looked down to see he was more than six feet off the ground.

"Tuxedo!" he shouted. Keenan tried to engage his flight controls, but they were locked out. Tux was nowhere to be seen. Gravity resumed functioning normally and he dropped to the ground, striking the side of his head. Blood began to trickle down his face, blocking his visibility. He looked around for Klein and found her hanging from the catwalks tied only by her wrists.

She was not alone.

. . .

Tuxedo hid behind a set of crates just inside the entrance. He'd seen Keenan go flying and had dived for the closest cover available. He'd thought of answering Keenan's calls but knew there was little he could do to help, and he didn't want to give away his position. When gravity was restored, Tux slid on his belly along the floor, trying to move closer to one of the server taps hidden inside the large backup generators. Keenan was sure to find a way to get to Klein, and Tux needed to be ready for that moment.

. . .

Standing on all sides of the upper catwalk were at least twenty Polos, all with guns pointed straight at Keenan. One of the Polos—presumably their leader—pointed at Keenan, and six men jumped down, surrounding Keenan on all sides.

"Well, that's much better," Keenan said. "Turns out I have a bullet for each of you."

The Polos just smiled, reaching behind their backs to pull out masks. When pulled down over their faces, the masks blended in with their skin until it was impossible to see a seam. Keenan's blood froze as he saw the face, a face he knew all too well.

"Looks like you've done your homework."

Smiling back at him from all sides was Sinclair. The screen blurred and swayed. The Sinclair directly in front of him opened his mouth like a hand puppet, and laughter spilled out into the warehouse. The sound was artificial, synthesized, like it was being played through bad speakers, but it was that same laugh: high-pitched, hysterical, like a wild animal.

Keenan shot the first Sinclair in the forehead. Blood was flying everywhere, and Keenan's vision grew red as the blood from his own wound started to cloud his vision again. He whirled around, and in seconds two more Polos were on the ground, while the men from behind charged in to tackle him.

That's when the door to Keenan's real apartment shuddered, splintered, and burst open.

. . .

Tux watched the six Polos jump down and walk steadily toward Keenan, while the detective's avatar stood motionless. A second later one of the Polos hit Keenan and sent his gun sliding across the floor in Tux's direction. Tux jumped for it and fired three shots in rapid succession, taking out the three Polos in front. One of the Polos behind Keenan tackled him and shoved him several feet across the floor, hitting the crates above Tux's head. Tux cursed as he slid to the side, narrowly avoiding being crushed.

Tux slid over to Keenan's limp body and tried to push him up, but there was no response from the avatar. Keenan was still logged in, but he was not at the controls.

"Hell of a time to grab a sandwich, Detective!" Tux shouted as he ran for cover.

CHAPTER EIGHTEEN

Tux barely had time to slap one of the badges on Keenan's avatar before he was forced to run for cover. A soft oval of blue electric light began to shimmer around the detective's inactive avatar. Two Polos went after Tux, while a third moved toward Keenan's motionless body. Tux smiled as the first Polo was thrown twenty yards across the room seconds after touching the field. Keenan would no longer be able to interact with the environment, but he was also safe from tampering.

This, however, did little to solve Tux's current dilemma, as he was now without a partner to get to Ms. Klein. He could simply log out and try again at a more opportune moment, but by then the Polos would likely have changed their security procedures and squirreled away the real-life Ms. Klein to somewhere she could never be found. If he was going to do something he had to do it now.

Tux pocketed Keenan's gun and pulled out his own. The two Polos in pursuit closed the distance between them in seconds, in part due to the hacker's choice of a short flightless waterfowl as his avatar. As they closed in, Tux turned and jumped onto his back, slipping between the legs of one of his pursuers. He fired twice, hitting both Polos squarely in the back and freezing them in place like statues. The two had been removed from the warehouse much like Keenan, but their destination was not as pleasant. Tux had devised a separate world within Surreality, a game within a game, which would permanently integrate itself within their characters. Every time they tried to log on they'd be shown horrors and creatures of Tux's own devising.

Despite Tux's swift removal of three more Polos, their numbers were far from dwindling. There were at least half a dozen between him and Klein, and an equal number coming up from either side. Tux briefly contemplated trying to throw the badge in Klein's general direction, but his throwing arm wasn't a whole lot better than his top running speed as a penguin. Looking into his inventory, he smiled as he saw one of the potatoes.

Sticking the potato on the end of his gun, Tux slapped the badge on the other end and fired. The potato and badge struck Klein in the midriff, the badge activating as it made contact with her character. A moment later she was illuminated in the same blue glow as Keenan, which made quick work of her bonds and lowered her body gently to the ground.

Tux took a brief moment to appreciate his handiwork before he was buried underneath six Polos.

• • •

Caliente's phone lit up with the text a few seconds later. She handed coffee cup number three to the uniform on her right and tapped hard on the metal between her and the driver.

"1024 North High, the old Fireproof Warehouse building," she shouted.

Food wrappers and playing cards flew around in the backseat as the driver peeled out of the space. One of the other detectives cursed. "I almost had gin."

• • •

Tux slammed against the far wall, his gun flying uselessly out of his hand. The Polos who had buried him had fallen into the background after tossing him aside. A moment later he crashed to the ground, apparently shattering his avatar's leg, as he found it difficult to regain his balance. Typically Surreality didn't operate with such realistic damage. Apparently something in the coding of this environment turned the physics engine to its most realistic.

He pulled Keenan's gun out of his inventory and fired, the shots bouncing uselessly off the floor. The generator was a little to his right, but his body was held in place by some unseen weight. A new Polo stepped out of the crowd and walked toward Tux casually before raising his arms and shooting the penguin with lightning from his fingertips. Evidently this Polo had a deep and abiding love for *Return of the Jedi*.

"So you're Tuxedo," the Polo said with equal dramatic flair in his low voice. "Somehow I thought you'd be taller."

"I'm a penguin, what exactly were you expecting?" Tux replied, trying to stand again before being slammed back by another onslaught of lightning.

The Polo laughed as he fired again and again, picking Tux up by the wings and smashing him along the outside wall. The cement cracked and crumbled from the impact, leaving a deep carved channel until the hacker dropped Tux on top of the generator. The move would normally have knocked the wind out of him, but instead it gave Tux a critical second with which he could access his inventory. He flipped over on his side and tossed the proxy badge he'd intended for himself at the Polo as he closed in for the kill. It bounced a couple of times on the ground before attaching itself to the Polo's leg.

"That the best you can do, Tuxedo? Throwing rocks?"

Tux only smiled. The badge lit up, and instantly the Polo was bathed in harsh red light. His avatar began dissolving from his feet on up. He tried to fire the lightning, but it bounced around inside the shell as he slowly disappeared.

"It's nice to know someone knows my name, though I doubt anyone knows yours. In case you're interested I've transferred you to my personal server, which deletes all unauthorized files automatically, though not until my scanners have made a thorough meal of you."

The Polo cursed and then was gone.

• • •

The Fireproof Warehouse building was a five-story warehouse with a storefront right in the Short North, not far from Keenan's apartment. It had been abandoned for years, though some developers had been working on a plan for developing some low-cost housing and storefronts in the space. A long black sign hung facing the sidewalk, elongated at the base with letters in faded white paint from decades past.

Behind a chain-link fence Caliente could see the crumbling red brick of the side of the building, underneath which were thicker gray cement blocks from the days when this building had been a fallout shelter. From the High Street side you could see a thick vault with what looked like a ship's wheel on the door, all painted in fading seafoam green. With a building that size it would be difficult for the developer to account for every inch of it, even with cameras and motion sensors, and a team like the one Keenan described to her shouldn't have a problem carving out a piece of that building for themselves.

"How much longer, Walchek?"

The tech had been the only one Caliente hadn't had to playfully cajole into coming. Evidently the prospect of some field work was incentive enough for people who spent most of their time behind a screen, even though that's exactly what he was still doing now, just crouched low inside a van with four other cops.

"I'm running a passive Aircrack scan, seeing what clients I can pick up in the area. A few more seconds of packet sniffing and I should be able to tell you where those cameras are."

"Walchek, it's okay to just say 'It'll be a few more seconds.'"

"Right," Walchek said, looking back at his screen. "Got it. Looks like they piggybacked onto the developer's existing camera system rather than setting up one of their own. I've got one camera facing High Street from the first floor, another pointing down at the lot behind the chain-link from the roof, and another inside, though I'm not sure which floor."

Caliente nodded. "All right, Stelso and Ramirez, take the rear. Try to get up to the roof if you can and work your way down. Connor and I will take the front door. Hopefully they'll focus their attention on us, giving you a chance to slip in behind. Walchek, take out the cameras after they've had a chance to see Connor and me."

"That'll be tricky," Walchek said nervously. "Those are transmission-only cameras, not designed to receive any external commands. I can't just remote in and turn them off."

Caliente smiled and clapped him on the shoulder. "I'm sure you'll think of something. Let's go."

. . .

Keenan breathed heavily, his back leaned against the cheap cabinets of his kitchen. The actual counters would offer little protection, but hopefully some of the Revere Ware his grandmother had given him before she passed away would fare a little better. He couldn't hear how many of them there were, just hard footsteps on his floor. Garfunkel was probably crouched underneath the couch ready to strike, should anyone's shins make themselves readily available. He hoped for the dog's sake that he had the sense to just stay under the couch.

Keenan wished one of the Polos would say something, would try to intimidate him or draw him out. How could a bunch of college-age hackers be so disciplined? They were just slowly sweeping the room, already more than certain of the only place he could be hiding. He heard his bedroom door open and figured it was as good a time as any to spend his six shots.

Keenan pivoted on his hip, leaned up, and fired.

• • •

Caliente took point, with Connor never more than a couple of steps away. They passed by the vault with no incident and were now working their way along the outside wall to a crumbling stairwell. The floor was littered with old newspapers, cigarettes, and food wrappers, the walls tagged with every symbol imaginable. Caliente wondered if these Polos had a tag of their own or if it was the kind of thing they just left digitally.

The second floor was another open space. A family of rats had taken some of the detritus from downstairs and built a surprisingly large nest in one corner of the floor. Caliente discovered this fact when they scattered in about six different directions when she stepped too close. A look was all it took to tell Connor that whatever sound he thought he might have heard, it was neither girlish, nor a scream.

The third floor was subdivided into several dozen smaller rooms, defined by thin retaining walls that went up about two-thirds of the way toward the ceiling. Long metal bars hung at intervals from the ceiling with the remains of ceiling fans clinging on by a couple of rusty screws. The prospect of two cops clearing this labyrinth was unappealing, given the untold places their perps could be hiding.

Caliente's approach was less than orthodox.

Raising her gun, she aimed at the closet pair of ceiling fans and fired. The metal flared and creaked in a shower of sparks, then came crashing down to the floor a few seconds later. The noise bounced off the back wall, but before it had traveled back to Caliente's ears she fired again.

The muttered curse was low, but clearly audible. Connor grinned as they took opposite sides and practically ran to their suddenly revealed Polo. As it turned out, there was little need for the haste, since part of the ceiling fan blade had caught the unfortunate youth in the calf. He was armed with a small knife, but was in too much pain to care about using it.

As Caliente cuffed him she took another look at the wound. "Barely a graze," she said, clicking her teeth, "though you might want to get a tetanus shot later."

Their perp, a young blond man in his early twenties, just glared at them.

"I thought situations like this called for stealth," Connor said, glancing around the perimeter.

Caliente shook her head. "That's what the other guys are for. We're shock and awe, attention grabbers."

"What about Detective Keenan's hostage?"

"They won't hurt her, at least not until they've had a chance to threaten us with her. Isn't that right, buddy?"

She gave the kid a friendly slap on the other leg. The boy twitched, expecting far worse and feeling it either way. Caliente held up a finger and smiled. "Care to tell me how many of your friends are up there?"

. . .

Keenan's first six shots had been wild, but a muted cry indicated that at least one of them had been a hit. He rolled back in less than a second and reached in his pockets for the reload. His hands were shaking as he tried to put bullets into the chamber.

He'd only managed to slam in the second round before the room exploded with noise.

・ ・ ・

Caliente wasn't inclined to believe her new friend's estimate of only two more compatriots, though given his reaction to even minor injury, he didn't seem particularly predisposed to lie, either. With the reputation the Polos had apparently gained for themselves in the virtual world, she would have expected at least half a dozen men armed with better than a pocket knife. Still, it didn't take that many people to guard a prisoner, especially if you had no reason to expect anyone would find out your location.

The ruckus they'd created on the second floor wasn't attracting the sort of attention she'd been hoping for. Usually that kind of big noise would draw out at least one more baddie to try and take them on. No sound either meant the Polos had a really good place to hide, or they were smart and staying near their prisoner so they'd actually have some bargaining chips.

Connor crouched down beside her on the stairs leading to the fourth floor, their prisoner safely handcuffed in one of the decaying bathrooms. With enough strength he might have been able to pull himself away from the piping around the sink, but considering part of the concrete floor directly behind him had fallen away, he was in for a little more bodily harm should he attempt it.

"Stelso, where are you guys?" Caliente whispered into her radio.

"Still on the roof. The door up here's been welded shut. Ramirez is contemplating rappelling over the side using a fire hose, but I think he's seen *Die Hard* too many times."

"There's no such thing as too many times with that movie," Caliente said, "but that's not quite the stealth plan I was hoping you boys could come up with. I have a feeling our guys are staying near the target, and if you swing in guns blazing it'll only put her life in jeopardy."

"Or more likely, Ramirez will fall sixty feet into the alley," Connor added.

"I'll have you know I taught knot-tying classes in the Boy Scouts," cut in Ramirez.

"That's a story we're gonna have to cover another time," Caliente replied. "Get back down to the ground and try the rear stairwell. You've got two minutes before we start clearing out these other floors."

Caliente turned to Connor. "I want you to stay a couple of paces behind me when we go up. Stay in my line of sight but keep out of theirs."

"What are you going to do?" Connor asked.

"Hope these guys are in more of a talking mood," Caliente replied.

"After you started shooting up the place?" Connor observed.

"I'm hoping that hotness will compensate for a little hotheadedness," Caliente answered. "Come on."

• • •

SURREALITY

Walchek had disabled two of the three cameras with ease, but was having a little difficulty with the third when he noticed Caliente entering the viewing window.

He'd gained enough control of the camera to be able to pivot it slightly on its axis, and he panned it slowly to the left as Caliente turned to the right. At first the glint of metal looked like lens flare, but upon closer examination he could see it was a figure concealed by a number of crates directly behind Caliente.

Walchek watched helplessly as the figure stepped out from behind the crates and dove toward Caliente.

• • •

Out of the corner of her eye, Caliente saw Connor's flying tackle and heard an organic thump a second later, followed by a few grunts and a small metallic clinking sound.

Connor, who was breathing heavily and sitting on top of the suspect, shot a grin at Caliente.

She just shook her head. "I knew he was there."

"Of course you did," Connor replied.

A second later the crates behind them exploded in a shower of splinters.

Connor fell to the ground, rolling off the suspect and landing hard on his back. He groaned slightly and tried to regain his feet. Caliente hissed at him to stay down.

• • •

The bullet tore through the skin on Keenan's forearm. The truth about grazes, any graze, was that they hurt like hell. It was like a paper cut, only considerably worse, since actual layers of your skin were torn off, flesh was burned, and pain was sent searing up into your brain. Keenan had only been shot once in all the years he'd been working as a detective. It hadn't even been Sinclair, just some punk kid trying to get a few bucks out of the carryout three years into Keenan's career.

As he felt blood drip from his arm, he tried to remember that kid's name. But his brain wasn't coming up with much since it was too busy trying to coordinate loading a gun with his one remaining useful hand.

David? Or was it Steve?

It was interesting the things you thought about before you were going to die.

• • •

Caliente was stuck. She couldn't fire blind for fear she'd hit the hostage, but at the moment she was pinned with little room to maneuver. Stelso and Ramirez were hopefully making their way up behind, assuming the stairwell on the other side of the building was even sound. She could see Connor across the way, where he'd managed to drag the other Polo into cover and cuffs.

The shots were too far apart to be an automatic, maybe a handgun with an extended magazine. Had it been thirteen or fourteen shots? Reloading would take a couple of critical seconds that might at least give Caliente an idea of the tactical situation. The pause between shots seemed long enough that she could risk it. She breathed deeply and turned to lean around the corner when she heard wood splintering and loud cursing, followed by something metallic sliding across the floor.

She whipped around with her gun drawn and had to suppress a laugh. Their Polo, another kid in his twenties, was tangled on the floor underneath the remnants of the chair they'd apparently used to restrain Ms. Klein. Evidently the shooter hadn't kept enough distance between himself and his prisoner, an athletic woman who looked to be in her early thirties, and she was able to execute a successful leg sweep, throwing her weight and the weight of the chair into the maneuver.

"Get her off me!" the Polo shouted.

Caliente holstered her weapon. "From what I'm led to believe, most men would pay extremely well to be in your position. You're not being very grateful," she scolded.

Connor, who was back on his feet and currently shoving his own prisoner against a wall, chuckled.

"Stelso! Ramirez! You can come out of hiding anytime now," Caliente shouted.

Stelso was the first to appear. "Sorry, boss. I had a shot but Ms. Klein here beat me to it."

"Not likely," Ramirez said. "From your angle all you would have hit was Connor."

"Thanks, buddy," Connor replied, tapping Stelso on the shoulder.

Caliente raised a hand. "Easy, boys. Just do something useful and untangle these guys."

The two men grumbled while Caliente pulled out her radio. "Walchek. You can tell Dan we've got his witness in custody."

"I think you better get down here," came Walchek's concerned voice a few seconds later. "We've gotten multiple reports of shots fired near Detective Keenan's apartment."

Caliente's heart went cold. These thugs might have been just a distraction, something to keep them busy while the rest of the crew took out the real threat.

"Stelso, call this in." Caliente gestured to the two Polos in cuffs and the still-tangled form of Ms. Klein. "You and Ramirez clean up here. Connor, get your ass in gear. If you're not down to the van before I get there, I'm leaving you behind."

CHAPTER NINETEEN

The street in front of Keenan's apartment was quiet, almost peaceful. Caliente's driver had nearly turned the van on its side speeding around the last curve, but from the looks of things they were too late. If it had been a hit, Keenan wouldn't have had much time to react, and even a cop didn't expect a gun battle in his own home.

Caliente jumped out of the back of the van, Connor behind her a second later. She should have assessed the tactical situation. She should have called for backup, done all the things she had calmly done dozens of times before. But something in her told her she couldn't wait, that she had to go in now. She'd leave it to Walchek or Connor to have the cool head.

She leaned next to the door, which—strangely—was still tightly closed. She would have expected it to be kicked in, swinging wide open. It looked as if Keenan had let his attacker in and then closed the door neatly behind them. She gestured for Connor to stay a couple of steps back, then turned and kicked in the door.

The shot missed her thigh by barely an inch. It had come up at an angle from somewhere on the floor of the kitchen. Instinctively she dove for cover behind the couch and was surprised to see Garfunkel cowering underneath. The dog and she exchanged a look before two more shots tore into the wall behind her.

"Get out of my home!"

There was no mistaking that voice.

"Dan! It's Sonya, they're gone!"

She had poked her head up over the edge of the couch to verify her claim, then ducked down again as another bullet sailed over her head.

"You'll pay for what you did to her!" Keenan shouted.

Caliente could see Connor just outside the door and gestured for him to get back.

"Dan! Listen to me," she tried again, "there's no one here, it's just me."

She could hear him breathing heavily, unevenly. A quick survey of the apartment showed bullet holes embedded in the brick above his futon, and above the doorjamb. There was no trace of anyone else having been there.

"Don't come any closer!" Keenan fired two more shots, one finding the television and shattering the glass in a shower of sparks, the other tearing the cushion to her left. The dog whimpered and buried his head in his paws. She was lucky Keenan's shots were going wild. Even a few months out of practice, Keenan had always outscored her on the firing range. If he'd really been trying or able to shoot her, she'd be dead.

She heard metal clinking on the tile floor. Six shots. Keenan's anachronistic choice of weapon meant he only had six shots, and if his aim was any indication, his hands were shaking too much to be able to reload with any efficiency. She rolled to the right and kicked forward, crawling and sliding until she was in the kitchen.

Keenan was breathing heavily and sweating, the gun hanging limply in his right hand. He made some effort to point it in her direction, but she just put her hand on his. She palmed the gun a second later and slid it toward the living room. Keenan didn't react; he stared blankly and mumbled to himself.

"How could you do that to her? How could you do that?"

Caliente put a hand on his cheek. "Dan, it's me. It's all right."

He looked at her but didn't see her. She'd caught a glimpse of this look outside the Athenaeum but had dismissed it as stress. She could hear the door swing open again as Connor moved in, sensing that the situation was under control but wanting to be sure.

"Connor," she said calmly. "Go back to the car. I've got everything here."

The young officer seemed about to protest, but Caliente's tone left no room for objections. Connor was a good kid, and if she had a talk with him he'd probably keep his mouth shut about what he saw, or thought he saw. For all they knew, a suspect had been in Keenan's apartment and he was just defending his home. There was no reason for an official record to say otherwise.

"Sonya?" The word was quiet, like Keenan was waking up from a dream. "What am I . . . why are you . . . ?"

Keenan sat up slowly, his eyes seeming more focused as he stared at the counter behind him.

"Who shot my coffee pot?"

Caliente chuckled softly as she turned and noticed for the first time the brown stains of liquid dripping down the counter, and the glass that had draped itself over the legs of Keenan's jeans.

"You've been needing a new one for ages, Dan," Caliente replied, rubbing his shoulder as she talked. "I thought I'd put it out of its misery."

"Oh," Keenan said, his tone flat again.

"I think your TV might have bit the dust too," Caliente added gently.

"Damn." Keenan shook his head. "Better get a new one for the game Saturday."

"You could just come over to my place," Caliente offered.

Keenan shook his head again. "And drink your fruity beer? No thanks."

They both chuckled softly, neither wanting to acknowledge what had really just happened. Keenan was avoiding the shrink because if he talked to one, then he'd have a diagnosis. She'd seen plenty of cops in this situation, and she understood. You expected to be the kind of person who could deal with stress, who could deal with the necessities and the hard choices of your job. But life wasn't that cut-and-dried, and no matter how good a mind, or how good a heart you might have, sometimes an experience could just seep into you and not let go. Sinclair was the first man Keenan had ever killed. He'd had to brandish his weapon a dozen other times, but a kill was different, no matter how long you'd been a cop.

What was it about that man Sinclair? She wanted to shake Keenan until he told her, and she wanted to just hold him, to tell him everything would be all right.

"Sonya," Keenan began again in that weak voice, "I'm sorry."

"*De nada,*" she replied. "It's nothing."

• • •

The drive to the hospital and the doctor's examination all fell below Keenan's notice. His mind was still trying to get a handle on what exactly had happened. One moment he'd been at his computer, about to fight a group of Polos who'd jumped down to attack, and the next he was sitting on his kitchen floor, shattered glass and coffee all over him and a gun in his hand. And Sonya sitting there beside him, telling him everything was going to be all right.

Keenan rubbed his arm where he'd felt the bullet tear into it. The skin was unbroken, but he could still feel a dull ache. He guessed he must have hit his arm on one of the kitchen cabinets, but he wasn't sure.

He heard a familiar bark from down the hall and limped his way off the hospital bed and into the lobby. Caliente had had Walchek circle back for Garfunkel once they dropped Keenan off. Garfunkel, for his part, rather than seeming scared or resentful of Keenan for suddenly shooting up the apartment, pulled Walchek off his feet and bounded toward his master, tail threatening to wag itself off.

Keenan leaned down and scratched behind the dog's ears. "It's good to see you too, buddy. Sorry about all this."

Keenan spent a good thirty seconds giving his dog the rubdown before he noticed Walchek. "It's okay, Chris. He'll pull your arm off if you let him, but I can take him from here."

The young man smiled and handed the leash gratefully over to Keenan. Caliente walked up to the three of them and slipped a five into Walchek's palm. "Get a coffee, Chris, on me. I need to talk to my partner."

The tech nodded and headed off in search of vending machines.

"You okay, Dan?" Caliente asked.

"Truthfully? Probably not. But I feel better now."

"Good, 'cause I wanna know what happened back there."

Keenan shook his head. "I don't remember. One minute I was at my desk, the next I was on the floor in my kitchen. Reminds me of my college days, really."

"This isn't the first time this has happened," Caliente pressed.

"I don't know what you're talking about." Keenan stood, the dog moving behind his legs.

"After the benefit shooting. You want to tell me what really happened?"

Keenan's face grew ashen. "I saw Sinclair."

"I know," Caliente said. "And you saw him again at the apartment?"

Keenan shook his head again. "I don't know. I think so."

Caliente put a reassuring arm on his shoulder. "I talked to Connor and Walchek and they've both agreed to go along with whatever I write in my report. You're going to need to make a statement too, but I think I can push the deputy chief off for a day or two. He's in a better mood now that we've got some of Chaffin's associates in custody, and rescued Ms. Klein."

"How is she?" Keenan asked.

"Fine, but a little uncooperative. She didn't have any ID on her, and she's refusing to give her real name. We're holding her for questioning and for her own protection, but she'll probably be out by the end of the day."

"I need to talk to her," Keenan said.

"That's our next stop after the doctor gives you a clean bill of health."

"I'm fine, really," Keenan protested.

"I know you are, I just want to make sure the doctor feels the same way," Caliente said. "One more thing, you're staying at my place tonight. No arguments. Your dog too."

For this at least Keenan was grateful. The truth was, he wasn't sure if he could face the damage they'd done—that he'd done—to the apartment. He needed to get a better handle on what was going on around him before he could go back.

"Thanks," he said. Garfunkel pawed at his leg and he remembered something. "The dog has this Nylabone he likes to chew on before dinner."

"I'll send Walchek for it," Caliente smiled.

• • •

Keenan's phone buzzed on the way to the station. Looking closer he could see that he'd already had ten missed calls. Whoever was trying to get ahold of him wasn't about to give up after eleven.

"What the hell happened to you?" Tux shouted over the phone.

"Got tied up for a bit."

"At OSU Medical Center?"

"Never mind. How are things coming at your end?"

He could hear an agitated grumble on the other end of the line, but evidently Tux's news was too interesting to let frustration keep him from sharing it. "I've been looking over some of the code the Polos used to manipulate Ms. Klein. It looks pretty similar to the algorithm used to infiltrate Synthia. I should be able to isolate the malicious virus in Synthia using Klein as a guide."

"How long?" Keenan asked.

"Several more hours at least. The purge takes time."

Keenan felt an unexpected surge of relief, like hearing that a friend who's been in the hospital for weeks will get to go home soon. Not that he could tell her that. After all, getting emotional about a program was just silly.

"That's good news," he said. "I'm on my way to have a talk with the real Ms. Klein. Got anything you want me to pass along?"

"Just ask her about any connection with Dr. Glassner," Tux replied.

"Why do you think she'd know anything about him?"

He could hear Tux's smirk over the line. "Just a hunch. Meet me back in Surreality when you're finished."

"Oh?" Keenan said, but Tux had already hung up the phone. If he didn't know better, he'd think that Tux was taking charge of this investigation.

The CMPD interview rooms were dark cement holes. There'd been some talk about trying to at least brighten up the paint, which at the moment was seafoam green and chipping, but some of the older lieutenants had blocked it. They said that a cold dark place made people more inclined to answer questions. Keenan's experience had taught him it was better to make people comfortable, though even a new coat of bright baby blue or off-white eggshell was unlikely to brighten the mood in that room.

He wasn't quite sure what he'd been expecting from the real Ms. Klein. Most people he'd met in Surreality used their avatar to explore their fantasies, or to present the way they really saw themselves. The woman sitting in front of him looked about his age, curly black hair close cropped around her head, nothing like her image in Surreality. Was that Ms. Klein just a playful fancy, or her ideal self?

"Sorry to keep you waiting," Keenan said, sitting down across from her. "Can I get you anything? Water?"

"No thanks," Klein replied. Her voice was measured, controlled.

"All right. I don't want to keep you here any longer than we have to. I know the last few days must have been difficult. I just have a couple of questions."

Klein nodded without saying anything. Keenan continued. "Do you have any idea why those men were holding you?"

Klein shook her head. "I'm afraid not. I'm just grateful somebody found me."

"Had you seen any of them before?"

"Not in real life," Klein replied.

"What about Surreality, then?"

She shook her head. "Most people I see in Surreality are very . . . exclusive."

"What happened exactly? We've been looking through missing persons reports trying to find someone matching your description, but no one seems to have noticed you were gone."

Klein smiled ruefully. "My work in Surreality provides me with everything I require. I'm afraid I live a very solitary life in the real world."

"No family?" Keenan asked.

"Not anymore." Klein lowered her head.

"You were last seen in Surreality at the Arcadia premiere," Keenan continued.

Klein nodded. "That's when those men found me. They slipped something into my avatar that gave them complete control over it. They were in my home about ten minutes later."

"Did they say anything to you about what they were after? A ransom?"

She shook her head. "There might be a few of my clients who'd be willing to pay it, but I never heard anything."

"Would Franklin Haines be one of those clients?"

Klein leaned back in her chair. "That's the question everyone wants to know. But surely you can see I can't divulge the names of any of my clients. Bad for business."

"So why were you at the Arcadia premiere?"

Klein smiled. "The opening of the Arcadia Casino was one of the biggest things to happen in Surreality since it was created. How could I miss it?"

"So you and your girls weren't hired as . . . entertainment?"

"Not hired, but very entertaining."

"The girls you took with you were new, right?"

Klein nodded. "We got six new girls a few weeks ago; I brought five."

"What about the other girl?"

"This business is not for everyone. She quit shortly after she was hired."

"And the others?"

"Very promising. Already some of my highest earners, though my loyal customers always like to try out new merchandise. Everyone finds their level eventually."

Keenan wasn't used to someone in Klein's line of work talking about her business so brazenly, but nothing of what she described was illegal in Surreality. "What was their job at the Arcadia premiere?"

"Nothing much, just to meet a few of the more important faces, make a good impression. Premieres like this one are one of the ways we ease new girls in. People tend to be a little more civilized in public. In private, men think they can say or do anything they like because it isn't real. What was that passage in the Bible, committing adultery in your heart is the same as committing it in real life, or something?"

"So you're a philosopher too?"

"After a fashion. It comes with seeing the best and the worst men can be. Already the idea of the Internet being separate from real life is fading away. Actions, even ones initiated with a keystroke, have consequences."

Keenan opened a folder and slid photos of Jeannette and Diane's avatars across the table. "Are these the girls who set you up to be taken by the Polos?"

Klein leaned forward and examined the prints closely. "These two were some of the most promising. They had that quality I demand of all my girls, the ability to make a man feel like he's the only one she cares about, like he's the only man in the whole world. Apparently they did a good job of making me feel that way as well. Is there anything else, Detective?"

Keenan nodded. "Just one more thing. You wouldn't happen to know a Dr. Glassner, by chance?"

"I know what everyone else knows, that he and Franklin Haines built Surreality together before they split over how it was to be used. But I don't know him personally. Does he have something to do with the men who kidnapped me?"

Keenan shook his head. "I don't think so. Just curious."

He stood up and held open the door. "If you'll follow Detective Caliente, I'm sure she can get you all checked out."

Klein rose and nodded. "Thank you."

When the two had gone, Keenan walked back into the interview room and closed the door. He fell into the chair and put his head in his hands, breathing slowly in and out.

CHAPTER TWENTY

Keenan couldn't actually remember the last time he'd been in Caliente's home. Her husband hadn't liked it when she brought her friends from work over, meaning they usually hung out at Keenan's place or one of the bars nearby. Like a lot of the homes in this area, it was older, probably from around the 1920s or '30s. In the basement, the old-growth tree roots were pushing into the cement, a small crack forming from one end of the room to the other. If you knelt at just the right angle, you could see daylight. Eventually the wall would collapse, or Caliente would have to pay out the nose to have it fixed, which was unlikely on CMPD salary.

"You can take Gabri's room," Caliente said, dropping her bag on the kitchen counter. "She's nearly ten, so her bed is probably the closest fit."

For a ten-year-old girl, the decor was surprisingly understated: pastel bedspread and walls, and a few forlorn stuffed animals tucked up high on the dresser.

"Do you have a laptop?" Keenan asked.

"You sure, Dan? You've had a long day. We all have, actually."

Keenan smiled. "I just need to talk to Tuxedo."

Caliente frowned, then walked back to the kitchen and pulled something small and rectangular out of her bag.

"Daily gave me this for you. Said it was his cousin's, but she can't seem to own anything older than two years. It'll be miles better than your heap anyway."

Keenan looked hesitant. Caliente frowned again. "What? I know it's small. Tom called it a netbook or something, but it's supposed to be as good as regular laptop."

"It's pink," Keenan finally said.

Caliente held it up in front of her face and turned it over from one side to the other. "You know what, I think it is. Yep, it's definitely pink."

"That'll be just fine, thanks," Keenan said, accepting the little laptop and heading back to his room. The laptop was very light, less than three pounds. Despite having a ten-inch screen the keyboard felt fairly comfortable. He picked it up and looked along the side and noticed it lacked a CD drive. Fortunately Tom had already installed Surreality and his login credentials on the desktop.

Tux was waiting for him in his office when he logged in.

"Where've you been?" Tux asked. "Your interview ended hours ago."

"Sonya suggested I buy her dinner at Moretti's since I shot at her this morning."

"Imagine where you'd have had to take her if you actually hit her," Tux mused. "Doesn't Moretti's have that homemade garlic butter with the bread, and Italian sausage they make themselves?"

"Yeah, and something called 'Four Fathers' with Maker's and four other kinds of liquor."

"That rough, eh?"

Keenan slumped down in the chair behind his desk. "Wouldn't know, but Sonya seemed to like it. She might just be tired of me making fun of her choice of beers. Do you want to hear about Klein or not? I really need some sack time."

"Actually, I've got a few things to tell you. You'll never guess who dropped by while you were gone."

Tux pulled a transparent page out from somewhere in his feathers and tossed it onto the desk. The paper activated, projecting an image of two people engaged in an enjoyable activity. One was clearly identifiable as Ms. Klein, displaying her natural talents, and the other was Franklin Haines.

"Son of a bitch! Where the hell did you get this, Tux?"

"Dr. Glassner stopped by a little while ago looking for you. Seems one of Klein's girls sold this to him as a way to embarrass Haines."

"You could've mentioned this earlier. Is that why you wanted me to ask about Glassner?"

Tux nodded. "I think it's better if we don't tip our hand or give her a chance to denounce the video as a fake. I've reviewed it thoroughly and confirmed its authenticity."

Keenan rubbed his eyes. "But that doesn't make any sense. If the Polos were trying to blackmail Haines, or hold him up for ransom, why would they sell the blackmail information to his rival? And for that matter, why would Glassner just sit on it and only give it to us now?"

Tux shrugged. "Maybe he wanted to save his stepsister the embarrassment. He told me he only gave it to us because he thought it would help our investigation."

Keenan thought for a moment, then something clicked in his mind. "Wait a minute. How did Glassner know about this office, or you for that matter? Synthia's always been with me when we visited Alexandria. Why would he trust some penguin he's never met with something so sensitive?"

Tux chuckled and threw up his hands. "I was wondering when you'd work it out, Detective. Glassner's the one who hired me to look into Haines."

It hadn't occurred to Keenan until that moment how much of his trust he'd placed in someone he didn't even know face-to-face.

"You got a good reason why I shouldn't throw you out of my office?"

Tux raised a wing. "Easy, there's no need to overreact."

"Glassner is a material witness and a victim in this investigation." Keenan stopped cold for a second. "The attack on Glassner's office, you staged that, didn't you?"

"Why would I do that?" Tux asked.

"To keep my investigation away from Glassner, make me think that he's just another victim like Haines."

"Relax. I'm as much in the dark about the attack as you are. Dr. Glassner had reason to believe Haines was in with some disreputable people, and he wanted me to find out who. You'll have to agree he had a point."

"Maybe, but we still can't prove a direct connection between Haines and the Polos, other than the fact that one of them tried to kill him."

"I'm sorry I kept this from you, but I would never do anything to hamper this investigation. A woman is alive and free today because of our actions. I meant what I said when we first met: information is all I'm really interested in, the puzzle, same as you."

Keenan looked warily past the brim of his fedora. "All right, but I don't want another word getting back to Glassner about this. You work for me now, exclusively, until this case is over."

Tux extended a wing. "Agreed."

"So, why would Glassner choose now to be helpful? If you're right and Glassner has had the footage for some time, what's the point of giving it to us at this moment? What's changed?"

Tux shrugged. "It all depends on who sold him the tape in the first place. If it was Klein, then maybe Glassner would rather tell us about it himself, rather than have her out him. If it was someone else working for Klein, then I'm not so sure."

"Klein never denied having sessions with Haines, but I suspect she knows more about the men who abducted her than she's telling," Keenan mused. "Klein said some of the new girls worked with her in private sessions. Were any of them on that tape?"

"As a matter of fact . . ." Tux started the tape again, and the view panned to show Jeannette and Diane, the two women who'd handed Klein over to the Polos. The camera stayed behind Jeannette's avatar throughout the whole video. A couple of times both Diane and Ms. Klein came into the frame, and Haines's avatar clearly seemed to be enjoying himself.

"So how would you shoot this kind of footage anyway?" Keenan asked. "I'm assuming you don't set up a tripod and start rolling."

"Not exactly," Tux answered. "The 'camera' in this case is the viewing perspective of one of the women in the room. As you've probably already noticed, you can view your character from the first- and third-person perspectives in Surreality. In either view you can record your actions to a video file, upload it directly to YouTube, Vine, or Vimeo, or save it to your computer for later use."

"So that means this video was either shot by Jeannette . . ."

"Or someone standing right behind her."

• • •

Gabri's bed had not been kind to Keenan. His shoulder throbbed, and one of his feet had fallen asleep from dangling over the metal footboard. He gingerly swung it over onto the floor and waited for the feeling to return, shaking his foot as the tingling sensation signaled the return of blood flow.

Caliente had already left for the station. A note lying on the kitchen counter suggested they get coffee later in the morning and offered the last bagel in the fridge as Keenan's breakfast. There was no cream cheese or butter, but Keenan did find a jar of chunky peanut butter in the cupboards. Keenan licked his lips as bits of peanut butter got stuck, and he rubbed his shoulder.

He examined the bottle of pills the doctor had given him, trying to decide if he was actually going to take them. Holding one in his hand, he could hardly believe it was going to have any effect; it was little bigger than a grain of rice. Keenan wasn't much for taking things just because a doctor told him to, and he didn't like the idea of something changing the way he thought, no matter how troubled that thinking had been lately. He tipped his hand, and the pill fell back into the bottle. He tucked the bottle of pills in his jacket and called the safe house where they'd moved Diane.

He didn't think there was much she could tell him that she hadn't already, but the video had raised some questions, and hopefully she'd at least tell him enough to get his thought processes going.

Caliente had one of those K-Cup machines with a revolving rack of pods next to it. Keenan selected the darkest thing he could find and set the cup size to the smallest setting. He'd used one of these machines before when he'd been waiting for an oil change and hadn't been particularly impressed. They were convenient, sure, and offered a lot of variety, but they tasted little better than instant.

Keenan debated briefly whether he wanted to take the laptop with him, or whether he'd be better off just going back to his apartment. Grumbling, he put the bright pink case in his bag and walked out the door, surprised to see his car sitting in the drive. Apparently Caliente had thought of everything, though Keenan did have a brief moment of sympathy for whichever uniform she'd tasked with trying to drive his old jalopy.

The coffee shop where Caliente asked him to meet her was just around the corner on High Street. The parking lot was slanted, both the spaces and the pavement, and Keenan had a devil of a time fighting his failing power steering into a space. The shop itself was a little below ground, stepping down about two feet in among the assortment of chairs, couches, and tables.

Often this place was filled with students, but it was still a little early in the morning for them to make the trek from campus. Right then it was just Keenan and the man behind the counter, a teenager with gauged ears and disheveled brown hair. Plain black breakfast blend was not on the menu, so Keenan settled for the closest thing, an Irish Grog whose flavor Keenan had a hard time placing.

At first he sat in front of one of the little tables, but it was considerably lower to the ground than the chair, forcing him to lean forward as he tried to type. He leaned back and put the netbook on his lap, putting his feet up on the table. His arms felt a bit cramped trying to move the mouse with the touch pad, and he found himself swerving occasionally from side to side. A seasoned player might have thought his character was drunk or malfunctioning, but after a few minutes' practice, Keenan managed to walk well enough to get where he needed to go.

He'd arranged to meet Diane in the park again. He spent a couple of minutes uncomfortably attempting to arrange his character on a bench, the trench coat crumpling awkwardly underneath him, until he saw the girl approaching. She'd changed her avatar considerably, and was dressed more modestly than their first encounter. She was wearing a simple button-up shirt and slacks, her hair pulled back in a tight ponytail instead of being teased up.

"I like the new look," Keenan said, gesturing to the seat next to him. "It suits you."

"Thanks. I think it's good for me to look as I really am for a while."

She crossed her legs comfortably and looked out straight ahead at Surreal-City in the distance. "Your officers told me you found Ms. Klein. I'm glad to hear she's okay."

"That's actually what I wanted to talk to you about," Keenan said. "I'm still trying to fill in the details on Klein's kidnapping. We have her captors in custody, but they've been a little less than cooperative."

"I'm not sure I can be of much help, but if I can I will."

"That's okay," Keenan said gently. "Sometimes it's just helpful to have a sounding board for these things. The Polos seemed to be connected to both Klein and Haines. From what we've been able to figure out, they had a stake in the Arcadia Casino, a stake that disappeared with the rest of the money Haines had invested in the project. What I can't figure out is the timing. Did the Polos take Klein to extort more money out of Haines, or to ensure he would get their money back after it was stolen? The Polos recruited you to take Klein before the Arcadia attack, so did they know the theft was coming and were just trying to get Haines from both sides, or is the timing just a coincidence?"

"I told you before, Jeannette was the one who did most of the planning, along with Michael."

Keenan scratched his chin. "And that's the other thing I can't figure, why did your friend Michael attack the benefit? Was it just to provide an additional incentive to Haines to get the Polos' money, or something else?"

Even without the visual cue of Diane's expression, Keenan could tell he'd struck a nerve. "I don't know why Michael did what he did. He was never like this before he met her. The Michael I knew wouldn't have hurt anybody."

"I'm sorry. You must have cared about him a lot," Keenan said.

Diane shook her head. "It's all right. He's gone now, they both are. It doesn't really matter anymore."

"Did Jeannette and you ever do any private sessions with Ms. Klein, maybe for a particularly important client?"

"Ms. Klein only lets the more trained and experienced people into her sessions. There's a lot of money at stake, and she only trusts the best. Jeannette and I had only been working there for a few weeks."

"Is that a fact?" Keenan pulled a photograph out of his coat and handed it to Diane. The picture clearly showed both her and Jeannette in frame with Klein and Haines.

Diane pulled away. "Where did you get that?"

"Someone sold a tape of your activities to Haines's former business partner, Dr. Glassner. We're not sure who would try to blackmail Haines after he was already being extorted by the Polos, but it's a pretty good guess to assume it's one of the people in this photograph."

"There's a tape?" Diane asked quietly. Her voice seemed small, like someone lost in a storm. "I didn't know that anyone taped the sessions. It's bad enough doing that work, even as a way to make a few extra bucks online. It's not the kind of thing you want to remember in detail."

"I understand. You don't have to look at the tape if you don't want to. I just need to know if anyone else could have taken this film. Did anyone else join these sessions with the two of you?"

She shook her head. "I don't think so. We didn't get many clients who wanted more than two or three of us, and Ms. Klein provides price disincentives for one customer taking her girls away from other potential business."

Diane's avatar swayed from side to side as it entered idle mode, a few minutes of silence that threatened to stretch into hours. Keenan wondered if she had abruptly logged off, and tried to think of something to get her to talk to him again, when she turned and held out a hand. "It's all right. I'd rather know what was on the tape than have to keep imagining."

Keenan handed her another tablet he had tucked in his jacket, and turned slightly away while she watched the video next to him. When the tape stopped she tapped him on the shoulder and asked, "Is this all of it?"

"Yes." Keenan said, taking back the tablet. "As far as we can tell. Why do you ask?"

"Well." She paused for a moment, then continued. "Ms. Klein demanded a level of 'personal involvement' in the work. The services we offered to these kinds of clients are not pre-programmed. We . . . improvise, depending on the situation. This allows the clients to request whatever they like. The tape cuts off at a moment where it would have been difficult to disengage the video while providing those services."

Keenan nodded. "So if whoever recorded this was in the middle of having sex with your client, she wouldn't have been able to turn off the recorder."

"Well, it's not impossible, but it doesn't make a lot of sense. If you were making a tape like this to blackmail somebody like Haines, why wouldn't you just record the whole session?"

Keenan hadn't really thought about it, but what she said made sense. What they had on tape would be enough to embarrass Haines, but why settle for that? And if Jeannette or Ms. Klein were the one recording, how were they able to switch off the tape without Haines noticing?

"You're sure no one else was in the session?" Keenan asked.

Diane thought for a moment, then shook her head. "I didn't see anybody."

But as the Arcadia premiere had proved, just because you couldn't see someone, didn't mean they weren't there.

Keenan smiled. "Thank you, you've been a great help."

The girl nodded and stood up to go before logging off, leaving Keenan alone in the park. Caliente still hadn't showed, so he started walking in the general direction of the Arcadia rebuild. In the distance he could see the work crews turning rooms on and off. It looked like each room was being inspected individually, illuminated floating cubes sometimes hundreds of feet off the ground. Some rooms were clean, while others still had bits of dust and debris, malicious code that still needed to be cleared.

This case was beginning to feel how Arcadia looked. Some pieces seemed to fit together, but only if you ignored other pieces. If the Polos were behind everything, they didn't provide a uniform front. Michael and Jeannette seemed to have been running their own plan, as well as whoever sold the tape to Glassner. Something was missing, without which the whole case was hanging on nothing.

As Keenan was thinking, the screen went blank. A moment later a message popped up. "We're sorry, but your time has expired. During our peak hours, use of the Wi-Fi is limited to 30 minutes." The coffee shop was still empty save for him and the kid behind the counter. Keenan cursed softly and slammed the lid closed, tempted to toss the laptop on the table, but forcing himself to put it down gently. He finished off the rest of his coffee, grimacing as he realized it had turned cold.

"Tough morning?" Caliente spoke from behind the chair.

Keenan nearly spit out his remaining coffee. "Jeez! How long have you been there, Caliente?"

"Not long, just long enough to see your little tantrum against borrowed hardware. Any particular reason for the morning rage against the machine?"

"I got logged off. It's the busy time."

Caliente looked around and shrugged.

Keenan continued, "I'm getting a refill. Care for an Irish Grog? Or perhaps something in the hazelnut family?"

"See, a good night's sleep did you a world of good, though you could have used my shower if you wanted."

"Somehow apricot shampoo doesn't really say *me*." Keenan set two more cups of coffee down on the table.

"Hmm . . . you're right about that. Perhaps some oatmeal vanilla . . ."

It had been a bit chilly that morning, and Caliente warmed her hands with the hot liquid as she held the cup a few inches above her lap.

"Caliente, I . . ." Keenan began.

"Don't," she said, holding up a hand. "When you get home you'll find a new twelve-cup cone filter coffee maker. I even got you a thermos carafe so you won't cook it all down to sludge."

Keenan looked down into his cup. "Thanks. And I am sorry."

"Don't mention it," Caliente smiled. "You would've done the same for me."

She leaned forward to pick up her drink and brushed the bottom of her cup with a look of disgust. "Is it too much to ask that they dust the tables every now and then?"

Caliente ran her hand along the table, then held up in evidence a thin layer of gray dust clinging to her hand, outlining the shape of her palm. Keenan stared for a moment, and smiled.

"What?" Caliente asked, wiping off her hand on her pants leg.

"Nothing," Keenan said, shaking his head. "You're right. They should definitely clean the place more." Rising from his chair, he said, "Hey, listen, I just remembered something I need to check on. All right if I take a rain check?"

Caliente smiled. "Okay. But you better tell me all about it."

Keenan nodded, already in go mode, grabbing the laptop and downing the rest of the coffee, then pounding his chest as he realized it was still pretty hot. Caliente laughed as he ran out of the coffee shop toward the nearest Wi-Fi signal.

CHAPTER TWENTY-ONE

Fifteen minutes later, Keenan burst into his virtual office, immediately turning to run into the closet where the mock-up of the crime scene should still be running. He nearly had the door open when something caught the corner of his eye. He turned around slowly, not sure what to expect. To his surprise and relief he found himself looking at Synthia, perched on the edge of her desk, redoing the line of her lipstick and looking in her hand mirror. Tux was sitting behind her with his webbed feet propped up on the desk.

"'Bout time you got back," Synthia said, tossing the compact behind her.

Keenan walked over to the desk and kissed her on the cheek. "I missed you, angel." He attempted a hug, but he couldn't get the avatar's elbows looking right.

Synthia returned the hug a little more expertly and planted a friendly kiss of her own on his cheek. "Good to see you too, Hayes."

"What? No kiss for the penguin?" Tux kicked his feet off the desk.

"Maybe later, if you're nice to me," Keenan replied.

Tux chuckled. "Well, I'll leave you two to catch up. I've still got some patching to do."

Tux waddled to the door and jumped out into the transit tunnels. The door closed noiselessly behind him.

"Any side effects from Tux's handiwork?" Keenan asked.

"Only a tattoo on my bum saying 'Tux rules.' He needed it at that level so he could see it on his short stubby legs."

"That son of a—"

Synthia laughed. "Relax, Hayes. I was just kidding. My tattoo isn't on my butt, and it's a good deal more tasteful."

Keenan's shoulders eased. "I'm just glad you're all right."

"Me too," Synthia replied. "Heard you had it a bit rough yourself."

"Shot my coffee maker, but Caliente bought me a new one," Keenan said.

"Wanna talk about it?"

"Maybe later. Right now I've got something to show you."

Keenan rubbed the sleeve of his jacket along his desk lamp. Holding the dust up to Synthia, he said, "Place has gotten filthy since you left."

He walked toward the closet door, Synthia following a moment later. The cool breeze of Arcadia Island began to buffet them. As the two of them walked, the scene moved forward in time, the Arcadia Casino forming around them. The crowd gathered, and there was Haines, standing behind his podium, mere seconds before his untimely demise. The light from the chandeliers bounced off every surface, much brighter than usual. Keenan tilted his head level with one of the rays of candlelight and watched its diagonal fall to the floor.

"I hadn't noticed before, but there is an incredible amount of detail in this world, not just the people and buildings, but everything around them."

Synthia stood above him, next to Haines again. "It's all part of the physics engine. Each world can have a few of its own rules, but they all run on top of the hundreds of subroutines that dictate the movement of every object."

"But it's more than just movement, it's every exact detail, from raindrops, to micro wind currents . . ." He gestured toward the light. "To dust."

His eyes focused, and he could see dust particles, lit brightly by the candlelight for a moment, then disappearing out of sight. "My old computer couldn't handle this, but the scene models hundreds of tiny specks of dust."

"Surreality aims to be as much like the real and the fantasy world as it can. The more real it is, even in the smaller details, the more time people will spend here. Your mind is given fewer inconsistencies that reveal the unreality, and is therefore more at ease. That was the theory of the original designers, anyway," Synthia said.

"Where is the code that controls this dust?"

"It's actually several dozen random walks, governed by a couple of discrete algorithms in the base code. The algorithms are constantly tweaked to provide a more realistic effect and to keep the system as truly random as possible. Even if someone completely masked their avatar, they'd still interact with this code."

"And they'd be covered in little bits of dust," Keenan said, looking up again at the ray of light.

Synthia smiled. "I think you're starting to get the hang of this place." She waved a hand, and a set of controls appeared in front of her. "So we need to take this up to the moment when Haines was attacked."

The scene slowly lurched forward, playing back in slow motion. "We'll need to make the dust a little bigger," Synthia said. "At this resolution they'd only be a pixel or two wide at most."

Small dots the size of quarters began to appear all around them, some shining brightly in the light like little fireflies.

"These things don't have much of a half-life, since the program keeps a limited number of them active at any one time. Otherwise the computer would be so busy calculating the position of every bit of dust that the people wouldn't be able to move. Once one lands, it's deleted a fraction of a second later. Fortunately, I can compile the data for a number of consecutive time steps so I can give you a better picture."

Keenan was finding it difficult to see with all of the particles around. "Delete the dust outside a three-foot radius of Haines."

The spheres dropped out of sight, and Keenan was left staring at a figure about six inches shorter than Haines, though still without discernible features. The shape was floating on the other side of the railing, hands reaching up around Haines's throat.

"That's almost got it," Synthia said. "Let's play a little connect-the-dots."

Yellow lines began dancing between the dots, switching connections almost as if they were etching out an image with a laser. Gradually the lines solidified into more human-looking shapes. Curved surfaces began to appear as the lines got closer together, and before long Keenan was presented with a wire frame of a person. From the beginnings of facial features, he could tell that the person was definitely a woman, or at least chose to be one here.

"That would be our killer," Keenan said.

"And Klein's new girl who quit before the Arcadia launch," Synthia said. "She did a nice job masking herself. All the data Tux collected from the crowd didn't show a trace of her."

"How would a person do that?" Keenan asked.

"Well, the appearance part is easy," Synthia said, putting her head on her arm. "Hiding her complete physical presence would have been a lot harder. She probably had to hide inside someone else's avatar while it was brought in, then break off into her own with no one around."

"Sounds a little bit like what she did to you."

"More than I'd care to admit. She would have had complete control over whoever she was inside, though voluntarily or involuntarily is harder to guess at."

"But why kill Haines here?" Keenan asked. "Why not wait until you could get him alone? If she was Klein's employee, she must have had opportunities."

"Maybe, but Arcadia is probably the place where Haines is the least secure. Sure his company built the casino, but it's still connected to public code, and the casino is designed for user modification and input. Any security would have to be updated constantly to be any protection."

Keenan nodded. "And Klein's is more centrally controlled, so less outside server access."

Synthia raised an eyebrow. "I think you and Tux spent a little too much time together while I was gone."

"Just trying to pick up the lingo. Can you show me where she came in?"

"I can extrapolate the trajectory using the particles as a reference, though the projection will get less accurate the farther I go back."

The image lowered its arms as the scene played in reverse. It floated silently down to the floor, stopping an inch or two above the ground.

"That's one way to erase your digital footprint," Synthia observed.

She removed all of the crowd except for those in the immediate vicinity of the blur. The figure stood motionless for quite some time, below the spot where Haines had first appeared. Keenan wondered how long this person had just stood there, watching Haines, taking in the scene, waiting for an opportunity to strike. Invisibility gave the killer the luxury to savor, and to pick the optimal moment.

The figure finally began to move backward, inching her way through the shifting crowd, which appeared and disappeared with her. Keenan smiled as he saw Tux being pushed aside, and gesturing rudely at no one in particular.

As he watched, Ms. Klein came into view, as well as the girls who were leading her to her impending fate. The figure seemed to slip around the girls blithely, as if she knew exactly where they were going, inching ever closer to Klein as they approached the entrance. The image finally superimposed on Klein and changed shape as the dust particles conformed to Klein's appearance.

"She rode in on Klein!" Synthia said. "Makes sense since she was working for her, but Klein is an experienced user. It took two girls just to extract her real-life location and nudge her character in the right direction. For someone to take complete control like that, Ms. Klein would have had to have known."

"Maybe." Keenan scratched his chin. "You know, Synthia, I think it's high time we celebrate your return to the land of the living. How do you feel about a night on the town?"

"Why, Hayes, I thought you'd never ask."

• • •

Klein's place was in full swing. The villa had been reconfigured into her jazz club. It seemed she was in the mood to sing after her long confinement. The hostess smiled and leaned over her podium. "We all heard about what you did for Ms. Klein."

The lithe young woman breezed off her stool and pressed her hips against Keenan. "I'd be happy to give you any kind of private service you like. Fancy a 'His Girl Friday'?"

"No thanks," Keenan said, politely pushing her away. He put his arm around Synthia. "I have my own date tonight."

The hostess turned to Synthia. "You must feel lucky to have a man like that."

"And here I thought he was lucky to have me," Synthia said.

The hostess ushered them both to a table, shooting a last look at Keenan before returning to her stool. Synthia had cleaned up nicely, wearing a strapless red dress and thin pearl necklace. Her blond hair was short, cropped in a style more appropriate to the period of the club. She wrapped her arm around his as they walked in, and Keenan had to admit they actually did make a good pairing.

Klein was moving from table to table, chatting with everyone, laughing and putting her hand on everybody's arms. Her replacement had not done this, and Keenan wondered if this was the way she usually acted before a performance. Business at the club didn't seem to have suffered. In fact, the room looked more packed than ever, but Klein seemed to be taking that extra step to thank everybody for coming back.

Before long Klein was standing at their table. She took a seat across from the two of them. Keenan offered her a drink, which Klein accepted before speaking. "How nice to see you again, Detective. Lovely date you've brought with you."

"I sure am," Synthia chimed in.

"This is my partner, Synthia," Keenan replied.

"Pleased to meet you," Klein said, extending a hand.

"Aren't you going to introduce me?" a voice called out from underneath the table. A moment later, the hacker fowl pulled up the tablecloth and sat down next to Klein, slipping a wing onto her arm in a single smooth motion.

"It was getting hot under there. I thought you guys were never going to stop talking."

"How did you . . . ?" Klein gasped, smacking the pernicious penguin's flapper away.

"Easy," Tux said, straightening a ridiculous-looking bow tie he wore with a white collar around his neck. "Rode with this one," he said, gesturing to Keenan. "I would have rather worked with Synthia, but she's a little funny about having someone inside her programming lately."

Klein smiled. "I really don't have time for this right now. I'm on in two minutes."

"Don't worry," Keenan said. "We've taken care of everything."

Klein turned to the stage to see a perfect replica of herself take the microphone and begin to sing. Everyone in the audience fixed their attention on her facsimile, failing to notice the real Klein sitting only a few feet away.

Keenan nodded in the direction of Tux. "Sorry if my friend was a little forward before. He just needed to transfer you back to his home server."

Klein looked down at her arm to see a small silver bracelet hanging from her wrist.

"Now we can talk," he said, lighting a cigarette, "about that other girl you employed."

CHAPTER TWENTY-TWO

The island was teeming with life. The soft sigh of the cool breeze was overpowered by countless voices raised in anticipation. The sky was dark, save for the moon hanging high, gray clouds illuminated at its edges. The tranquil seas and grasslands were lit up by the moonlight and hundreds of spotlights trained on the crowd. A man stood at a podium, ready to speak, and somewhere in the crowd were a detective, a hooker, a hacker, and a synthetic intelligence algorithm.

Arcadia stood tall in the night sky with only its base clearly visible. The grand lobby had been restored, the ballrooms and gambling floor redecorated, and all of the staff were in place and smartly dressed. It had been a few days since they'd talked to Klein, and Haines was finally ready to premiere his masterpiece for all of Surreality to see. The crowd looked twice as large as the first one. Keenan could only guess at the motives of those people in the crowd, whether they were attracted by the premiere or the prospect of another murder.

For his part, Haines was putting on a show of force. Several guards stood directly next to him, as well as countless others mixed in with the crowd. The area around the podium was protected by a barrier that kept any unauthorized avatar from getting anywhere near him. Keenan doubted this would offer any protection against the real killer, since their prowess at hacking had been proven on multiple occasions, but it was part of the conditions Haines had laid out before he would try Keenan's plan.

Even with the evidence Keenan had been able to gather, he had to catch the killer in the act. So much of what happened in this world was ethereal. But if he could catch the person, have Tux track them back to their home server, or talk to them face to face, he'd have his answer. Haines had been tough to convince, though he had acquiesced when he realized that delaying any longer would hurt his chances of capitalizing on the hype of the murder. The deputy chief had been another matter entirely, especially when Keenan told him who he planned to arrest.

Keenan scanned the crowd, his gaze falling briefly to Glassner and a group of his students. Tux was nowhere to be seen, but would make himself known when the time was right. Synthia stood next to Keenan in the front row. She gave his hand a little squeeze, which Keenan almost believed he felt. She was wearing the same red dress she'd worn to Klein's, and Keenan had put on his best suit under the trench coat, complete with fedora. He stood out in this crowd of ordinary people and fantasy characters, but it didn't matter. He knew his presence wouldn't stop this killer. It might even egg them on a little, to be able to pull off another murder right under the watchful eyes of the person who pursued them.

In real life, Keenan sat in a coffee shop not far from his suspect. Caliente, Walchek, and company were stationed in a van just outside, ready to go at his signal. Walchek had rigged something to Keenan's computer so that his player activity could be streamed to the van. Keenan wanted to go with them, to face Haines's killer in person, but part of him knew that the only way he'd get the answers he needed was to face the killer here.

With a sound like turning on a searchlight, Haines was engulfed in a stream of light emanating from the base of his podium. The effect made his avatar look even taller than its already imaginative proportions. The crowd grew suddenly quiet as Haines began to speak.

"Welcome! Tonight you will see the fulfillment of a dream, a dream that some have tried and failed to crush. We stand in a world built from dreams, from fantasies made manifest. No force, no matter how determined, can stop our dreaming. There are some who would call my work decadent, maybe even obscene."

Keenan looked over at Glassner, who stood watching Haines's speech without expression.

"They say this place should be about the advancement of knowledge, of human potential, and I agree! For what better way is there to enrich humanity than to widen the variety of his experiences? What man, when he has seen what it is like to fly not in a machine, but alone amongst the clouds, would not want to try it for real? Surreality isn't meant to take people away from reality, but to make people want to turn the real world into fantasy. That's why I'm glad you are all here for this historic day. This isn't just a great day for Surreality, but for reality as well. I give you . . . Arcadia!"

The lights inside each of the rooms began to shimmer, surging up and down like waves on the sea, revealing Arcadia's many wonders. The crowd applauded in earnest, any previous uneasiness cast away. Keenan scanned, searching for what he knew had to be there, but which he still could not see. Haines was smiling benevolently, almost laughing with delight. He was getting a better premiere than he could have ever dreamed of, and each moment he laughed, Keenan felt his chance of catching the killer slipping away.

But as quickly as the grin spread across his face, Haines's smile disappeared. In seconds, Haines was solid red, and stumbling into the podium. The crowd backed away as one, leaving Keenan and company standing in a clearing around Haines. As the ground rumbled, Keenan hoped the reinforcements Tux had incorporated into Arcadia would hold.

Slowly he walked toward the still-choking Haines. The killer saw him; this much he knew for certain. They were probably wondering if Keenan could see them, assuring themselves that he could not. Haines looked at Keenan, his mouth gasping for air like a fish stranded on shore. The amount of control the killer had on Haines was amazing; there was nothing he could do to fight back.

Another loud rumble roared across the sky, and all eyes rose toward the building, all eyes except Keenan's. Synthia jumped up beside him and Tux waddled his way behind them. The color was returning to Haines's face. The killer was hesitating. The skies opened up, and thousands of drops of rain fell from the simulated sky.

It was a downpour. The first drops struck the air next to Haines and stopped in a gentle curve. As more drops fell, the curve expanded downward, forming ears, a nose and mouth, shoulders, arms, and finally a full form, the same form that had stood in front of Haines in the crime scene reproduction. Her hands were still wrapped around Haines's throat, but quickly dropped as she realized she was visible. While her identity could not be easily ascertained from the thin outline of moisture, Keenan already knew his guess was correct.

He did not have much time to study her, however, for as soon as she dropped her hands she was running, faster than any person should have been able to. She was obviously trying to lose herself in the city. Keenan followed half a second later, his steps tracing the path of hers, moving with a speed he had not yet mastered.

They dashed through the city, half gliding over water as the sky poured buckets all around them. They reached the park in seconds. A few seconds more and they were running through the empty subway. His companions, who were doing their best to keep up, were still hundreds of meters behind. Some of the crowd had broken away and were also giving chase.

Bending around one corner after another, the woman finally slowed her run to a walk, and Keenan did the same. They came to a stop at the entrance to an alley. She stood only a few feet away. She knew about this alley, what being there would do to him. But he had always known it would end here.

"I think it's time we drop our masks, wouldn't you agree, Mrs. Haines?" Keenan said.

She dropped her defenses slowly, pulling the veil away little by little, in much the same way the rain had first outlined her. It was as if the rain was washing away the invisible cloak she wore, slowly revealing the person underneath. She was wearing the green dress, the one she'd worn in the park, and in the Surreality transit tunnels. Her long flowing hair and the face he had seen in the low light of the theater now faced him again.

She smiled softly at him, seeming to understand the moment, but not knowing what she should do next. Finally she asked, "How did you know?"

"It wasn't easy," Keenan began. "Not all of the pieces fit together. There was the attack on your husband, and the theft here in Surreality, followed by the very real attack at the benefit. Dr. Glassner, your husband's former business partner and your stepbrother, is also killed in Surreality, his project assets stolen. And a madam is captured, both virtually and physically, at the same time your husband is killed. A young woman is murdered, our benefit shooter goes on another spree before falling five stories off a parking structure, and Dr. Glassner receives incriminating footage of your husband with the kidnapped madam, the girl who was killed, and her accomplice.

"Your husband in particular is very unlucky. He's robbed and threatened, then shot protecting you, then almost blackmailed. It seems like too much for one man to endure."

"I was at the benefit at the head table. The shooter nearly killed me and my husband. I couldn't have been your killer then."

"No, but your accomplice could."

A gasp betrayed Katherine's surprise even as her avatar remained stoic.

"Of course he wasn't working for you at the time. In fact he was just trying to clean up loose ends," Keenan said. "See, the robbery and the blackmail both serve to try and ruin Haines's reputation and take away his assets. By robbing your husband, our thief also robs the Polos, making it difficult for Haines to operate or continue his plans. Even defunding Dr. Glassner takes some of the sport out of the work, since he can no longer beat his old rival at his own game.

"But the benefit shooting and Ms. Klein's kidnapping do nothing to further that goal. So obviously, they had to be orchestrated by someone else."

"Then you don't think I'm responsible for the murders," Katherine said.

"Oh, you're responsible all right, even if you didn't plan them. Jeannette knew how Polo money was getting into your husband's accounts, which gave her the best ability to drain them and scatter the assets without it being traced back to you. Ms. Klein gives you a lift to attack your husband, and her girls turn on her, take the money, and hand Ms. Klein over to the Polos.

"Jeannette and her boyfriend knew that if the theft of the money was traced back to them, the Polos would kill them. So they tried to eliminate the only other people who knew how the money was taken, yourself and the other girl, Diane. Killing your husband might even have been a bonus, since he was the best chance the Polos had to get the money back, and probably the only thing keeping Ms. Klein alive, since she was just collateral to keep Haines motivated. Klein was the only person our lovers couldn't get to, but I think she had her own reasons for keeping quiet."

"Ms. Klein is a remarkable woman," Katherine said. "I can see what my husband saw in her. She was so compassionate when I explained my situation to her. She's the one who came up with the Polos holding her hostage, as a ruse, of course. The Polos' money was supposed to be shifted back to their accounts immediately after the theft. Keeping Ms. Klein was just to make the Polos' threats seem more credible, until they needed her as a real incentive."

"You took that film of your husband, didn't you? You were Klein's sixth girl."

"Yes. I followed Franklin in one night and found out what he was really doing with some of those late nights. It wasn't jealousy. I didn't lose him to his mistress; I lost him to this place. Surreality was supposed to be a way to build his business, to give Franklin the capital to do some real good. He has a brilliant mind, there's no telling the good he could do for the world.

"But this," she said as she punched the brick of the alley, "this is all nothing. What good is building a life here when you are not living the first one? He began spending more and more time locked in his office, withdrawing himself from life . . . from me. I need reality, Dan." It was strange to hear her use his name.

"I spend so much time inside computers that I need the outside world to remind me why I do it. You know how many days I worked where I never knew if it was sunny or raining? My husband didn't even seem to know if it was day or night anymore. I want to be with him in my world, not just as some character in his."

"Is that how you saw Synthia, another nothing?" Keenan asked, his voice growing colder.

"She's a machine, a thing. She isn't real, none of this is."

"But it is real, Katherine." He gestured all around them. "Four people are dead because of what you did here."

"None of that was supposed to happen!" Katherine Haines cried. The avatar stood still, the emotion not changing on its face, but Keenan watched the falling rain stand in for her tears. "I just wanted . . ."

Keenan nodded. "I know, but you had to know who you were dealing with. These were practically kids, Katherine, faced with an opportunity to steal more money than they'd ever see in a lifetime. You opened that door for them."

"Franklin had already made his first million by that age," she sighed. "We were so in love then. How did it get like this?"

"I don't know," Keenan said. In the distance Keenan could hear the crowd finally catching up to them. In a few minutes they wouldn't be alone. He thought about Katherine sitting in her apartment, probably not far from her husband, waiting for the end.

"I know what it's like to lose someone," he said finally. "I know what it can make you do. How it can make you feel. Your husband was a fool for choosing a game instead of you, but you still walked down this road."

"And you had to chase me."

Katherine Haines would likely not see her husband for a very long time. The actual charges would be light, most of the crimes being committed by the dead. But they both knew her husband would not be waiting for her when she got out. Synthia, Tux, and the rest were only a few hundred feet away. Because of the alley, they couldn't see behind him, couldn't see the killer, but as soon as they did, the Net would be ablaze with the story. Her arrest in the real world would probably bring the same attention, but as he looked at her, he didn't want her to share the same fate in the world she so despised.

Without a word he raised his gun, and fired. Katherine smiled as her body slowly faded away. Her eyes were the last thing that caught him. They seemed very lonely, even for a simulation. By the time Synthia and the rest had caught up behind him, she was gone.

Tux broke his thoughts. "Did you lose her? That tracking virus I planted on her should have mirrored your movements precisely."

Keenan put his hand on the bird's shoulder. "We got her." He nodded to Synthia, who nodded back and shuffled the small bird out of the crowd.

Everyone was bunching in, trying to see if they could see some trace, some scrap of fabric of Haines's killer, but finding nothing. Franklin Haines was nowhere to be seen, but he was most likely facing the real killer at this very moment.

Finally one of the people in the front of the crowd asked, "What was it all about, anyway? Why did they do it?"

Keenan thought for a moment and said, "Because that," he pointed toward Arcadia, "is not the stuff that dreams are made of."

CHAPTER TWENTY-THREE

"What're you doing here, Hayes?"

Keenan's office was dark, the only light coming from the single green banker's lamp on the desk and the tip of a cigarette in Synthia's mouth.

"Shouldn't you be home getting some rest?" she asked, leaning forward as he quietly sat in the chair across from her.

"I shot up my home, remember?"

"Well, yeah. But Caliente is letting you stay with her, right?"

Keenan nodded. "I told her I'd be back in an hour, that I hadn't had a bite to eat all day, which I guess I haven't."

"So why'd you come here?" Synthia asked with what sounded like genuine concern.

"You got another cigarette?"

"Yeah, but it's not going to do you much good." She opened a metal case and slid it across the desk.

"Oh, I don't know," Keenan said, lighting a match, "so much in life is just about the ritual."

"What's going on?" Synthia said, snapping the case shut and putting it back in her handbag.

Keenan took a drag. "I need to tell you something, something I haven't told Daily or Caliente or anyone else at the CMPD."

"This isn't a come-on, is it?" Synthia said. "Not only am I a synthetic intelligence algorithm swimming in a sea of servers and computer code, I'm also your partner."

"I'm telling you this because you're my partner. Now just listen, okay?"

Keenan flicked ash onto the green blotter. "Three months ago I met a woman. Her name was Amanda Parker, though I didn't know her last name until I saw her file."

"Her file? Were you doing a background check on her?"

"No. Well, yes, but not for the reason you're thinking. See, I had a feeling about her from the moment I saw her across the coffee shop, and as it turns out, she did too. We had three dates in eight days. But on the ninth day . . ."

"What?" Synthia asked.

"She was murdered. A man named Sinclair grabbed her on the way back to her apartment. He smashed her head against a brick wall, and when he'd caved her face in, he dropped her to the ground and started kicking in her chest. It took days to identify her from what he left of her, days when I wondered why she wasn't returning my calls."

"Sinclair? Isn't that . . . ?"

"Yes. He didn't take anything from her. He didn't rape her. He just beat her until he was tired, then tossed her in a dumpster."

"Oh my God," Synthia whispered.

"I don't know if he had a motive. We were never able to find one. He was just . . . an animal. I don't know why I didn't tell them about Amanda. At the time, I thought it didn't matter. We hadn't even been seeing each other for that long; I may have kissed her once. It might have gone somewhere, and it might not, but Sinclair took away any chance of my finding out.

"He was so easy to find, it was almost as if he wanted me to come after him. He gave me a little chase from outside his apartment to the alley where he'd . . . taken . . . Amanda. He looked at me and he just laughed. You've never heard anything like that laugh, Synthia. He just tilted his head high into the sky and belted. I had to make it stop.

"After I... put him down, it was just easier to leave the lie intact. The knife he was carrying was enough for self-defense, and anyone who'd seen the pictures of what he'd done didn't want to ask too many questions. It would have ended there if the press hadn't sensationalized it. This city doesn't trust its cops. They saw it as brutality, not justice. Even after someone leaked pictures of Amanda to the press... well, you know the rest."

Synthia was quiet for a long time. The tip of her cigarette quietly burned to ash until it fell from the weight of it onto the desk. Keenan wasn't sure what she was doing, if this was something that was just taking her time to process, or whether she was turning him in. Finally she spoke.

"Why tell me? Shouldn't you be telling Caliente or your best friends about this?"

"If I told Caliente, I'd just be getting her into trouble if anyone else found out. And Tom... well, I don't know what he'd do. He might turn me in, or he might help me, and I'm not sure which one would be worse."

"But they can help you in ways I can't. I'm just a bad-tempered collection of computer code that looks great in a red dress."

Keenan smiled. "You do at that. But I don't want you to help me. I want you to keep being my partner."

"But the case is over. I'd have thought you'd never want to set foot in Surreality again."

Keenan leaned back. "I'm taking a leave of absence from the CMPD, effective tomorrow. I'm going to have a lot of time on my hands and I could use a diversion, maybe even an escape. Plus, solving cases with you will keep me sharp enough to get back to pounding real pavement someday."

Synthia was quiet again, then leaned forward until she was looking him directly in the eyes. "Did you know you were going to kill him when you walked into that alley?"

It wasn't until she said it that Keenan realized he'd been living this question for the last few months. He'd thought about it every waking moment, and every restless night, and in all that time he should have had an answer for her.

"I don't know. I think so. And I don't know what that makes me."

Synthia leaned back and extinguished the cigarette. "Go home, Hayes."

Keenan put out his own cigarette and walked to the door. As he opened it, Synthia called out behind him, "I'll see you in the morning."

He smiled and touched the brim of his fedora.

• • •

Keenan leaned back in his chair several days later, surveying the wreck of his apartment. The cleaners had managed to remove most of the broken glass and bits of drywall. There were numerous holes that needed patching if he wanted to keep in any heat during the winter. The computer had been toasted, a stray bullet frying the power source and barbecuing it from the inside. The plastic from the still-unopened graphics card had melted and fused into the fans and processors, rendering it even more useless than when it was just sitting on top of his computer. Daily had been gracious enough to let him keep the pink netbook, though Keenan was still on a mad search for decals or skins or even markers to cover up the color.

Tom Daily stood behind him, taking the same survey of the room. "I'm surprised your landlord didn't kick you out."

"He was a little more agreeable when I said I'd keep his beer cooler filled for a year, plus covering the cost of any repairs."

"That's no small offer. I've seen how much that man can drink."

Daily ran a hand along the wall behind the computer. "You gonna patch these too?"

Keenan shook his head. "I thought I'd keep them as a reminder, y'know, of why I'm doing this."

"Are you sure about this, Dan?"

"It's just a leave of absence. I'll be back before you know it. You can wrap up the Haines case from here."

Franklin Haines hadn't said a word when the police walked his wife out of their building. Keenan wasn't sure if he had wanted him to defend her or condemn her, but Haines had done neither. Arcadia's re-launch, despite a rough beginning, had been a success. From what Synthia had told him, it was even more profitable than Haines could have hoped for. In all likelihood, he owed his success to his wife. After all, nothing sold like a good scandal.

Caliente had handled Katherine Haines's brief interrogation. She confessed to everything. Keenan hadn't seen Katherine since that rainy night in the alley. He wasn't sure if he wanted to. Her trial would begin quietly in a couple of months, but Daily and Caliente could handle any of the post-processing.

"I was right, you know," Keenan said. "This was the case where they showed me the door. Only difference is, I walked out it myself."

"Maybe, but the deputy chief told me to tell you your job is yours if you want it back."

"We'll see," Keenan replied.

Garfunkel sauntered over, demanding attention from both of them, though settling on Daily for the variety. Keenan had been sure to spoil the dog with as much people-food as he could get his hands on, plus a brand-new doggie bed and one of those bacon treat dispensers where you can catapult the treat across the room.

As they played with the dog, Keenan's phone rang. He groaned, not even needing to speak before he heard his partner's voice on the other end of the line.

"We're not gonna get any customers if the detective isn't around. I don't need this, you know. I could get a job with just about any of the research firms setting up shop here. It's not my best option sticking around with a gumshoe like you."

"I like her," Tom said.

"Shut up," Keenan said. "Still, I suppose it's time to go to work."

Keenan pulled out a fedora he'd bought down at the thrift shop, causing Tom to burst out laughing. Ignoring him, Keenan stepped through the door to his new office. The model had been updated with pictures from the case, including one of Keenan's favorites, of Glassner flat as a pancake. The door which had led to the training grounds now opened onto a proper flight of stairs, with led down to a real San Francisco street, straight out of film noir. In the distance, cars could be heard, as well as paper boys shouting out the latest news of the 1940s. Synthia wore a smart dress in blue with her desk pushed across from Keenan's instead of farther down the room. She was moving papers around, though this activity was probably as unnecessary as the makeup.

Keenan tossed his imaginary trench coat and hat onto the rack behind his desk, sat in his chair, and listened to the wood creak as he leaned back. He looked at his partner, who smiled, put down the papers, and leaned back in her own chair.

"Know a good place to get a Reuben around here?"

ABOUT THE AUTHOR

Ben Trube lives in Columbus, OH with his wife, Hannah, and their three four-legged furry companions, Riley, Murphy and Dax. By day Ben works as a full-time programmer, which sometimes leads to writing books about fractals (two so far). During the week Ben blogs about technology, writing, and comic books over at [BTW] Ben Trube, Writer.

Made in the USA
Charleston, SC
23 April 2016